W9-BDX-421

Nominated for a 2014 RT Reviewers' Choice Award for Best First Historical Romance

"A charming romp. The witty repartee and naughty innuendos set the perfect pitch for the entertaining romance. Though there are serious themes and carefully researched historical details, it's the banter and sensuality that are sure to enchant readers."

—*RT Book Reviews*, 4 Stars

"A witty, seductive historical romance that is sure to gain this new author many fans… Misguided influences, colorful characters, naughty innuendos, humor, passion, romance, and true love are only part of what makes this second-chance love story so delightful."

—*Long and Short Reviews*

"A quirky but steamy historical romance…very entertaining with marvelously spirited interactions."

—*Tome Tender*

"A lovely romance…a very lighthearted romantic tale."

—*Kwips and Kritiques*

"A hoot. It is a laugh a minute."

—*Romance Junkies*

"A sweet, well-paced romance between two intelligent adults…most definitely a good read."

—*All About Romance*

To CATCH a Rake

SALLY ORR

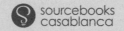

sourcebooks
casablanca

Published by Sourcebooks Casablanca, an imprint of Sourcebooks, Inc.
P.O. Box 4410, Naperville, Illinois 60567-4410
(630) 961-3900
Fax: (630) 961-2168
www.sourcebooks.com

Printed and bound in Canada
MBP 10 9 8 7 6 5 4 3 2 1

*This book is dedicated to the wonderful
author Wendy Kitchen.
Thank you.*

One

London, 1825

WHAT MANNER OF LADIES WOULD HE FIND ON HIS doorstep today? Wilting Flowers or Happy Goers? Previous experience taught George Drexel that any lady who managed to discover his place of residence must be displeased with her perceived category in his book, *The Rake's Handbook: Including Field Guide.*

Four years ago, George had agreed to write the field guide on a drunken wager. A friend challenged his reputed successes with the fairer sex, so he wrote the book to prove his greater knowledge of females—and their bedroom behaviors—than the average gentleman's. In his field guide, he created fictional initials to describe each lady's best features and intimate habits. He then grouped these ladies into six representative categories. Of course, he'd never dare use the initials of *real* names, or he could find himself facing some husband seeking satisfaction.

At the time, the book proved his expertise and turned out to be a monetary success. The extra funds were welcome to a young man-about-town. Then last week the field guide's publisher announced that he planned to print a second edition in three months' time. Upon this news, many of London's older females—widows and married women—started to appear on his doorstep. The ladies called to plead for initials similar to their real names to be included in the next edition.

Sitting at his large desk by the window, he tucked his black hair behind his ears and examined the women on his doorstep. Since the day was a warm one, the ladies wore light muslin walking dresses, so he could easily admire the details of their figures.

The older, gray-haired lady, busy directing the younger one where to stand on his doorstep, likely possessed more experience in bedroom behaviors. She probably paid him a call today to ask him to move her presumptive initials into the higher category of lady termed "Happy Goers," a very popular category in the field guide. The other, possibly younger lady avoided her companion's direct gaze and appeared hesitant in her manners. From previous interviews, she likely suffered from an unhappy marriage. Still, he was able to discern that she possessed a very fine figure, indeed. This aging beauty might have assumed her initials appeared under the category of Wilting Flowers, a great injustice, so she had joined her companion today to complain to the author directly and request an elevated category too.

Much to George's surprise, these female visitors never complained about the impropriety of his book. Instead, every lady requested her position to be elevated to a more notorious category in the next edition. Whether the presumed advantage of a higher category resulted in practical gains, such as additional lovers, or greater bragging rights during card parties, he had no way to determine. But now after numerous interviews, he suspected these older ladies derived their greatest enjoyment from the excitement of believing themselves to be naughty.

Regardless of the ladies' aspirations, George resented this upcoming distraction, since he had an important business deadline to meet. He had been given a month to diagram a new drain for the Thames Tunnel, and with a little over a week remaining, only half of the plans had been completed. Picking up his pencil, he resumed work on his drainage plans.

A predictable thirty seconds after the ladies arrival, his ever-efficient housekeeper, Mrs. Morris, entered the cluttered parlor. "The first of the female callers has arrived today, sir. Shall I show them in?"

"Can I refuse?" George ground his teeth and kept his eyes focused on the detailed drawing in front of him.

Mrs. Morris did not reply. A distant cousin of his mother, she had successfully run the household staff with apparent ease and privately treated him like her own son.

Once aware of her unusual silence, George looked up and noticed her watery gaze. He dropped his pencil on the desk, moved close, and gave her a brief hug.

Her lower lip trembled. "Oh, sir, I *am* sorry. You worked so hard on that bridge. In my opinion, it's a crime to ask an engineer to work diligently, give him hope, and then crush him by refusing to fund it. All because of some stuff and nonsense about that silly field guide. A book I'd bet not a single one of those Bristol townsfolk would even admit they read." She sniffed. "If there is any justice in the world, those Bristol scoundrels should be arrested and jailed." She pulled out a white handkerchief from her apron pocket and wiped her eyes. "Your iron suspension bridge is beautiful, sir. I know someday another city will be fortunate to have it."

Mrs. Morris's vigorous defense of his latest failure brought him out of his doldrums and fortified his resolve. He'd never give up his dreams and ambitions. Perhaps someday his unique chain bridge would be built elsewhere. He desperately hoped so. Every gentleman knew that the future would be built using iron and steam, and he wanted his chance to contribute. He dreamed of building a grand structure to serve the people of England for centuries. Then, like the Pantheon in Rome, he'd credit himself as the builder by marking his creation front and center: George Drexel Fecit. "Thank you, Mrs. Morris, for your unbiased belief in my abilities." He winked. "But we don't want to keep the ladies waiting. I suggest you remain in the hallway, since this interview will last exactly five minutes."

"You sound like you plan to eat them."

"Right, a happy thought. I'll enter the hallway and growl at them. My brown bear impression should frighten them enough that they will flee the house immediately. Then I can return to my work."

"I doubt that will prove effective." She shook her head, making the gray curls peeking out from under her lace cap bounce. "While in person you appear quite dark and scornful, your habit of spontaneous drollery usually endears you to the more clever ladies within minutes."

"I'll have you know my drollery is excessively planned." He took a deep breath. "Well then, if my growl is insufficient, I'll throw in a snarl or two."

"Any lady in her right mind will realize you pose no threat. These ladies may even like bears."

Mrs. Morris had been the housekeeper since his parents' marriage, so he could rarely fool her with any sort of gammon.

"Besides," she said, "these ladies are always very determined. They would have to be, wouldn't they? They must have a vulgar nature, indeed, to ask for the favors they seek. I would have expected them to be offended and take you to task for penning such a foolish book, but this forward behavior"—she shook her head—"well, that beats everything."

"I'm thankfully ignorant about the subject of ladies' jumbled motivations and wish to remain so. We'll just ask them to leave as soon as possible. Then I can finish my drainage plans on time." He'd rather instantly march them out of the door, but he must try to behave like a gentleman.

Just a month earlier, the youthful mistake of writing his shocking field guide had mostly been forgotten by society. But the news of a possible second edition revived all sorts of tittle-tattle. Today he needed a gentleman's spotless reputation to earn building contracts from local officials. The publication of a second edition might revive the scandal and damage his reputation. His new career as an engineer of public works would be finished before it even had a chance to start.

He chucked Mrs. Morris under the chin. "I also take exception to your evaluation that I pose no threat—I certainly feel like a dark beast. Let's get this interview over with, so I can return to work."

Mrs. Morris headed back to the ladies waiting in the hall, while he took a position in front of the fire with his fists resting on his hips and legs set in a wide stance.

The two ladies stepped into the parlor and froze. Their eyes widened as they glanced around the cluttered room.

George remained silent, waiting for the women to criticize him for the disorder created by the many wooden models of bridges, tunnels, and steam engines covering most of the tables and floor. If a lady smiled after viewing the untidy room, he would show his gratitude by making the interview quick but courteous. However, if the many tossed books, bits of iron, and wooden human models elicited the universally recognized frown of feminine disapproval, then he'd resort to the angry bear to hasten their departure.

The older woman frowned and shook her head. "Oh dear."

A wide-eyed, fixed stare graced the other lady's features. "So deplorable."

Right, time to open the cage door.

"Ladies, please take a seat." He motioned to a pair of ivory tub chairs directly in front of him. "I'm honored you've called upon me today. However, it is an inopportune moment. So speak up."

Both ladies stiffened. The older lady, perhaps fifty, held her lace handkerchief to her mouth and cleared her throat. "Well, I…I don't know how to begin." She continued to glance around the disordered room. "We…we heard a rumor that a second edition… Such horrid conditions," said the older lady. "You obviously lack a wife."

The prettier lady, not much younger, slouched in her chair.

He flashed his most wicked grin. "Are you applying for the position? As head of the household the position of wife is, of course, under me."

"Well, I never—" The older woman balled a fist.

"I doubt…" He paused and mentally kicked himself in the arse. For the sake of what remained of his gentlemanly reputation, he should at least try to adhere to his resolution not to offend them. "Let me be of assistance. Even though you fully understand my book is fiction…you ladies *do* understand the field guide is satire?"

The other lady quickly glanced at her companion.

Her friend patted her knee and gave him an affirmative nod.

Regardless of the lady's nod, most of them rarely believed that.

"But, sir, all of our friends gather so much pleasure from the assumption that you just altered real names," the older lady said.

The prettier lady turned to her friend. "Yes, trying to match his initials with real people is a very amusing game. But do you know, I'm not sure what satire is. Is it—?"

"I know my friend Mrs. Wittle—Mrs. Smith—is confused, but even though you say the names are fictional, surely they must be based on real females. Correct, Mr. Drexel?"

"Loosely based, madam, more exaggeration than fact." For some reason—he attributed it to the mysterious, unfathomable female mind—most women chose to believe that the initials in the field guide represented *real* people. Thankfully, none of the ladies sought satisfaction or felt ill-used, although one widow had brazenly volunteered to be "tested" for the next edition.

Time to deliver his well-practiced speech to quicken their departure. "At this moment, you're unsatisfied with the placement of your perceived initials in the book *The Rake's Handbook: Including Field Guide*. With some effort, you have learned that I penned the field guide. With my address in hand, you *tracked me down* like a hound on the scent. So you are here to request a favor—for reasons you wish to remain private." He gave them both a respectful, deep bow.

They tittered.

"Right. Your presence here is to request that your initials be moved to the heading describing a higher, or rather, more notorious category of lady. It goes without saying that you realize this cannot be done immediately. However, you would be deeply appreciative if I make the change before the next edition is printed." He inhaled deeply and wistfully glanced at his drainage plans resting on the enormous desk by the bay window. "As a result of my granting your request, I will enjoy your utmost gratitude for years and years to come."

This time both ladies giggled loudly.

"I see you have been solicited before," said the older female wearing an indelicate, inappropriate grin rarely seen on a lady of quality. "Just how many ladies have made a similar request?"

"Including you, twenty-two."

"Oh." The other lady widened her eyes before dropping her gaze to the fine mesh reticule resting on her lap.

With a great deal of effort, he stifled a growl. "Now, ladies, if you will excuse me, I have work to finish." He grabbed two paper cards from a stack on the mantel. "Please write your initials on these cards—your privacy will be assured—and the appropriate heading you desire in the next edition of the field guide." He handed each lady a white card and pencil.

The two women exchanged glances, and the older lady nodded several times. They wrote their initials as instructed and handed him the cards.

"Thank you." He read their requests. "Wise choice."

Both ladies beamed.

"Now leave."

"But, sir," the older one said, wearing an indelicate leer. "Can you tell us the details? Will our initials be included in the next edition?"

The other lady whispered to her friend. "Do you really think we can trust someone like him to do our bidding?"

Her companion nodded. "Granted he is a"—she moved to whisper in her friend's ear—"scoundrel." Her voice returned to normal. "But even they must have a code of justice."

He ground his teeth. Misjudged in his own parlor; it was time to release the bear. He strode directly up to them and growled, "My housekeeper will show you out."

As if on cue, his housekeeper opened the parlor door, and both ladies fled the room.

"Ah, Mrs. Morris, please show these ladies to the door," he said with regained gallantry. Without waiting for a reply, he spun and returned to his drawing on his desk.

Seconds later he heard the front door close.

Mrs. Morris came into the room to retrieve the cards thrown haphazardly on the desk. "Oh, sir, I hate to give expectations that another edition will be published. It seems such a deception. Can't you rule it out forever?"

He gazed out of the large window at the ladies scurrying down the street. "You're a female, Mrs. Morris. Why do you think these women risk scandal to appear on my doorstep?"

She sighed. "When we get older, attention from gentlemen can be a lovely experience." Following a pause, she added, "Regardless of age, every female harbors a secret wish to find love."

"Love? What's the use?" He gathered up the wooden figurines. "But to answer your question, the decision to publish again is not mine. My friend Lord Parker's brother owns the rights. He controls whether or not a second edition will be printed. He even hinted he might add new names, so we owe these ladies' company to that piece of promotional gossip, the scoundrel." George had requested Lord Parker to plead with his brother to stop the publication. All he could do now was wait for an answer. If his friend proved successful, then this regrettable example of his youthful transgressions would be entirely forgotten.

"I've been keeping these ladies' initials, just in case they are needed." She headed for the door and paused. "You might let these interviews last awhile longer."

He failed to reply.

She ignored his reticence. "If you spend more time in conversation with these ladies, you might discover a suitable wife. After all, most of these woman are likely available. A respectable marriage would go a long way to lessen any tittle-tattle arising from that book."

"Mrs. Morris"—he looked up—"I'm shocked. You have never suggested a leg shackle for me before." He waved his hand. "I thought you believed in romantic love and all of that faradiddle."

She blushed. "Of course I do, but I know you better. Others have had their hearts broken at sixteen, and they all recover. I've seen many ladies in your life, yet you have never fallen in love. So I realize you're a hopeless case when it comes to romantic love. It's just that when you are as old as your parents, I don't want you to find yourself alone in life without a partner to share it with."

George glanced upward. In the bedroom above him, his father was reading a book to his mother or, more likely, just holding her hand. After her stroke, Michael Drexel had refused to spend any significant time away from his wife's side.

As a result, George had taken on the responsibilities of completing many of his father's contracts. On certain projects, when he had been overwhelmed by problems or needed his questions answered, he had asked his father for assistance or to join him at a construction site. But Michael refused to leave his wife's side. The reason always consisted of some incoherent mumble about feelings. Not spousal duty, or his mother's request, or any other reason that might rightly keep his father at home, but a reason George failed to understand—love.

What is the use of love, if it leaves you with nothing more than holding hands?

He had tendered a simple request for a father to assist his son. Was that too much to ask?

Mrs. Morris must have read his mind, because she narrowed her eyes. "Mr. Drexel would not want to be anywhere else in the world, except beside the woman he loves. Perhaps someday you will understand that."

"I'll protect their rights and privacy to my last breath. Nor have I ever even hinted my need for Father's assistance in front of Mother. But I refuse to engage in unseemly, emotional balderdash." He lifted his chin. "I'm an Englishman, after all. For the sake of our family's future, I only ask for his presence and advice now and then. Otherwise, if my new drainage system is unsuccessful, I may not be promoted to resident engineer. Then I'd lose my best opportunity for advancement and chance to escape the notoriety generated from the publication of that damnable field guide." He sighed and dropped the wooden figures. "Please add these ladies to your list. I recommend the younger one"—he moved close to read the card—"the Mrs. A** W*****"—he smiled—"boot dear Ann up to the category of lady she desires. As for the other lady"—he chuckled and shook his head—"let's be generous and give her the category she desires too: Ruling Goddess. Ambitious that."

❧

"Please open the door, dear," Meta Russell said, evaluating the two ways to break into her sister's room. She could knock the door down or climb in through the window. Her sister, Lily, must need her, so something had to be done.

Last evening, Lily had escaped to her room in a fit of tears. At the time, Meta had questioned Lily's fiancé, James Codlington, about the reason behind her sister's distress. James simply announced the end of Lily and his betrothal, before he hurriedly exited the Broadshams' town house on Swallow Street.

"Lily, please." Determined to render assistance, Meta knocked harder than she had yesterday evening. "You cannot spend your life in your room. Please let me in. You obviously need my help." She placed her ear on the cool wooden door and listened. No sound from the room reached her ears, only the soft breaths of her brother, Fitzhenry, standing directly behind her. "I'll ask Fitzy to break the door down with a hammer if you do not open it this instant. Please, dearest, let me help you out of this muddle."

Her sixteen-year-old brother tapped Meta on the back. "Please move aside. Only a bang-up, out-and-out cove can properly handle this situation."

Meta stepped back. "I don't see how you can have better luck changing her mind."

A broad grin crossed his handsome, youthful face shadowed by slight whisker growth at least a year away from needing a regular shave. "I say, Lily, no use glumping. Meta is once again determined to render assistance. If you do not open the door, she'll make me use a hammer to knock it down. You know what that means. There is every chance my hands will be permanently damaged and it will be all your fault."

Meta shook her head. "You know I only want what's best for you and would never knowingly let you damage your hands. Box your ears, maybe." She reached out in a mock gesture to do so, but he leaned back out of her reach. "So why did you say such an unjust thing?"

"Because last week you asked me to shovel coals. A large lump of coal or the shovel could have fallen upon my hands and ended my artistic career before it even started."

"That was a temporary necessity, you must admit. You received nothing more than a little coal soot on your hands, and I doubt dirty hands would stop you from becoming a successful artist." She grinned. "It might even be a necessity for that profession."

Lily's muffled voice came from inside the bedroom. "I can hear both of you." The door swung wide, and the twenty-two-year-old Miss Lily Broadsham stood in the doorway. She wore an old muslin gown covered with embroidered purple diamonds that matched her eyes, which appeared violet in bright light. Considered the prettiest of the three Broadsham sisters, Lily could not claim that title at the moment. Standing erect, her swollen eyes, long black hair in a haphazard plait, and trembling figure indicated she had spent a sleepless night. "If you ruin your hands, Fitzy, that will be the last straw, and I'll just have to kill myself. There is nothing you can do, any of you. I apologize, Meta, but Polite Society might hear I've been jilted and will consider us all to be tainted. Susanna and I will never find a husband who will love and support us." She sniffed and struggled to hold back tears. "Fitzy will be unable to keep himself on the earnings from his art, so he'll have to beg a woman with a significant dowry to marry him." A tear started to fall. "And because of me, you will never find another gentleman to love you again." She buried her face in her hands.

Meta rushed forward to grab both her sister's hands. "Nonsense. Even if that happens, society's gossip is short-lived. As soon as the next bit of news arrives, your broken engagement will be forgotten. Please dearest, all of you will have the future you desire. I promise. And as far as my welfare is concerned, widows are on the shelf, even at twenty-four." As the eldest sibling, Meta had assumed the responsibility of shepherding her siblings into successful marriages and professions. Besides, once her siblings were settled, she'd be in her dotage. So even though she held dear secret dreams of falling in love and another marriage, her chances of achieving them seemed unlikely. Instead, a life sacrificed for those she loved suited her temperament, and serving her family's needs constituted the greatest goal of a successful life. She turned to her brother. "Fitzy, you can leave us now. I appreciate your help, but Lily and I are going to engage in female conversation. That means we'll indulge in talk of romance and most likely cry lots of tears."

"Eww. Right then." Wearing a guilty smile, the young man backed down the hall.

Meta leaned back out of the doorway to address Fitzy. "From what I've heard lately, it's all the crack for out-and-out coves and bang-up artists to study their mathematics."

"Mathematics could never be all the crack. What a hum. Human feelings"—he sighed and tilted his head—"are the medium of the artist, not equations."

"Then I suggest you study your Renaissance artists again. They used mathematics to mark out the proper perspectives."

"No, surely not?" he said, his eyes widening.

"Determine for yourself. I left a book on the schoolroom table open to the very chapter you need to read."

Without a word, he spun and ran down the stairs.

Meta smiled, closed the door, and led Lily to a comfortable window seat almost covered in soft, peach-colored damask pillows. The two sat, and Meta reached for her sister's hand. "With all this rain, this seat is colder than it usually is. Shall we move closer to the fire?"

"Does it matter?" Lily's eyes focused on her lap for a full minute. "I've changed my mind. I wish to remain on this seat forever, the place where I write my stories. You see, I will never marry now. Instead, I'll publish novels about jilted heroines suffering cruel fates at the hands of fickle men."

"But it is chilly, and I don't want you to become ill." Meta had returned to the Broadsham family home after the accidental death of her husband. Despite rushing over two hundred miles to be by his side, she did not make it in time.

He died alone.

For as long as she drew breath, she would never forgive herself for not providing comforting words when her husband needed them the most. Since her father had become senile and rarely left his rooms, she had assumed the duties of meeting the needs of her family. This endeavor suited her to perfection and provided much needed relief from the remorse of not being with her husband after his accident.

Lily started to drag the cane chair next to her bed close to the fire. "Oh well, if we must move… But I am not in the least chilly." She took her seat, blew her nose into her handkerchief, and then stared listlessly into the glowing red coals.

Meta grabbed the dark oak chair in front of the vanity table and placed it next to Lily's chair by the fire. She reached for her sister's hand again. "James told me of your broken understanding, but he did not elaborate. So please, tell me what happened. I am absolutely confident we can set the situation to rights and get him to reconsider."

Lily shook her head. "No, he will never change his mind. He said his judicial career would be at risk if he resumes his engagement to me. He might remain a common lawyer for years and never ascend to serjeant-at-law. If society discovers my initials in the field guide, he says it will have serious repercussions. Serious enough for his mother to claim that if we wed, she will cut off his funds to save the family's connections and reputation. Then what will he do?"

"Field guide? I don't understand. How can marriage to a sweet girl like you risk his career in the court?"

Lily rose and fetched a small book from her vanity. Handing it to Meta, she sighed and took her seat. "James claims the entry on page one hundred and sixty-one is me. It isn't, of course, but he will not change his mind. Our families have been acquainted for ages, and I was eighteen when this book was published. How could he even consider the possibility that the entry was me?" She blew her nose again.

"That is something I intend to find out."

"It's no use; he's too frightened. Any hint of scandal, much less having your fiancée's initials appear in *The Rake's Handbook: Including Field Guide*, would be an end to his professional aspirations. He would become the lawyer with the scandalous wife and everyone knows that once society has spread tittle-tattle—even if false—it is impossible to change their opinions. Turn the pages and see for yourself. You must admit the initials are unusual and similar to mine."

Meta examined the small tome. Covered in plain paperboards, the palm-sized book contained just over two hundred pages. Turning to the indicated page, she saw the entry: *"L****** B*******: This blue-eyed beauty enjoys the sport and is known for joining in the festivities with a lot more than just her heart. She is famous for her plush lacteal hillocks of passion."* Meta shook her head. "Oh my, oh my, how vulgar." She snapped the book shut. "Enough! Except for the loose similarity to your initials, how can this entry be tied to you?"

Lily shook her head and shrugged her shoulders. "I told James the book must be about—well you know—*those* females. But he disagreed and said the book is about proper ladies and their—well, you know—bedroom habits." She sighed, then gave a dainty sniff. "He told me that down at his club the common name for the book is *The Field Guide*. I guess gentlemen are supposed to carry it so they can readily spot these women on the streets. He even told me that over a thousand of these horrid books were published and sold to men around Covent Garden."

Meta considered James Codlington to be an honorable, intelligent young man. Although he was still young and gangly in appearance, she had complete confidence in his good character. He would follow his father and be a successful justice in the Court of Common Pleas one day, an honored position held at various times by several members of his family. "How did James come by it?"

Lily glanced up, wide-eyed. "You know, I forgot to ask him. That is somewhat suspicious, don't you think? Maybe he is the sort of gentleman that purchases books like this one. Perhaps I should not wish to wed James after all. Maybe he is one of those men that keep secrets from their wives and cannot be trusted?"

"Nonsense." Meta had known James and his family for years. He did not have a secretive personality—far from it. "Lily, a more honest gentleman never lived; you know that. Besides, the two of you acknowledged your love a year ago and recently announced your engagement to your family. You even assured me it was true love, remember?"

Lily's almost violet eyes began to shimmer with unshed tears. "I-I certainly thought it was, I truly believed it was mutual, until yesterday. Oh, Meta." She covered her face with both hands. "Why has he insulted me in this way?"

Meta examined the small book again. The text was divided into two sections, with the first section titled: *The Rake's Handbook*. The second section, consisting of about fifty pages, bore the title: *The Field Guide*. Each page of the field guide described a lady's best features and amorous personality. It also provided tips upon how to recognize her in person, for example, a penchant for a favorite type of bonnet or colored spencer. "How could someone be so heartless as to write a book like this?"

Lily did not reply, resuming her vacant stare in the direction of the hot coals.

Meta flipped through every page in the book, then returned to the page in question. "How can James say it's your name on this page when the spelling is off? There are too many spaces for the word Lily and too few spaces to spell Broadsham properly. Therefore, this female cannot possibly be you. Did you point that fact out to him?"

"Yes, but it made no mark upon him whatsoever. He thought the extra letters in the first name were only because it meant Lillian. You know, while we all call you Meta, your full name is Margaret and would have eight spaces. James said the lack of a letter in the last name was merely a printing error."

"I wonder if his mother had anything to do with that excuse, since it does not sound like James at all."

Lily ignored her. "Most of all, he seemed consumed by the fact that my initials appeared under the category of Happy Goer—a subject he could not leave alone, although I had no idea what he was going on about." She looked up at her sister. "Oh, Meta, why didn't he believe me? Why didn't he know in his heart it was not me in that book?"

Meta glared at the small tome. "That is something I plan to discover. Indeed, I have numerous questions for James. But first, I don't see the words 'Happy Goer' under the entry that he presumably thinks is you."

Lily blew her nose somewhat indelicately. "It's a term in the index, at the front of the field guide."

Meta flipped the pages and found the index, which consisted of six different categories of lady. She read the title of each category aloud: "Widow Makers Tied Up, Goddesses Who Rule the Roost, Happy Goers, Eager Out of the Gate, Wilting Flowers, and Rabbits. Oh my, I've truly never seen anything so vulgar."

"So vulgar," Lily repeated. "I don't really understand it. How could a lady be considered a rabbit? Cute and fluffy? Her breeding abilities?"

Unlike Lily, Meta had been married for almost two years, so she had heard enough of private masculine conversations to understand the section titles likely referred to the lady's amorous behavior in bed. "No, dearest, by using the word 'rabbit,' I doubt the author meant the lady's number of children, or cute and fluffy, or even jumping."

Lily widened her eyes. "Jumping? Oh, what does that mean?"

Actually, Meta did not know the precise definition of each term, but she believed Lily would probably be listed under "Rabbits," speculating that the author meant "scared as a rabbit" as a metaphor for the ladies' lack of courage. "What sort of coarse and indecent man wrote this odious book?" She examined the title page and found the names Ross Thornbury and George Drexel. Mr. Thornbury's name was attached to the handbook section, and Mr. Drexel's name was listed on the title page of the field guide.

"Do you know the identity of any of these gentlemen?" Lily asked. "I suppose I cannot call them that, can I?"

"This Mr. Drexel is certainly not a gentleman. He's some vile creature that haunts the streets of Covent Garden, a heartless and jaded rake, no doubt. He might be dangerous, so I will try and talk to James first. Perhaps after a day of private contemplation, he now realizes the injustice of his accusation." She patted Lily's knee. "I don't want to elevate your hopes prematurely, but we might resolve this situation with only a little fuss. James might even be eager to make amends. I'll go have a word with him."

For the first time that morning Lily smiled—not a happy smile, more of a resigned one. "Thank you. But on this matter I do not need your help. James and I have already had a long conversation about this field guide. I pointed out the differences in initials, and he summarily dismissed me. Truly, all is lost. Please do not argue the point with James on my behalf. I have come to accept the fact that I will never marry, and you must too." She reached over to grab her sister's hand.

Meta had no intention of causing Lily additional distress by talking to James against her wishes. But she would do anything to ensure that Lily married the man she loved. "Then we must find this Mr. Drexel person. He wrote this filth, so we'll ask him to convince James that it's not your name in his cursed field guide. I'm sure when the scoundrel realizes he has hurt an honorable woman, he will do whatever it takes to right the wrong he created. I don't know how this can be accomplished, but he has no other choice, does he?" She turned to the front page and discovered the address of the publishing house. "The three of us will pay a call on his publisher and inquire about the whereabouts of this Mr. Drexel. Then we'll pay a morning call—if the man has a decent home to receive callers—and ask him to enlighten James about the real name of the woman mentioned on that page."

"But, Meta, you've seen his field guide. This Mr. Drexel is obviously a scoundrel of the worst sort. He is probably the sort of man who abuses his servants. The sort of man who spits in public. It's far too dangerous to ask Fitzy to join us, because Mr. Drexel may even be the sort of man who *eats children*."

Two

"HE EATS CHILDREN! I TOLD YOU SO, META. YOU thought my comment was in jest," Lily said, following Meta into the front parlor of the Drexel house. Before them they found a tall, dark man with a wooden figurine of a small boy in his mouth.

While the torso protruding from the man's mouth might be considered an alarming sight, his hands held several larger human figurines, so his mouth was probably the only place left to hold the wooden boy. In front of him, the large oak desk almost disappeared under piles of paper and small models of buildings. Directly under his scrutiny sat a model of a round structure, like a theater, with stairs descending on the inside.

Meta expected that a gentleman interrupted by two women and a young man unknown to him would have immediately given them his attention.

He did not.

He blithely ignored all of them as he carefully balanced a small piece of wood along the final step at the bottom of the model's stairs. Once the wood remained in place, he gingerly set a wooden figure of a soldier on the step. The soldier toddled on the slim piece of wood, causing the man to drop the other figurines on the pile of papers in order to steady the crimson-coated figurine with both hands. "Damnation," he said from the side of his mouth.

"Let me assist you," Meta said, stepping forward to gather the figurines and pulling the boy from his mouth. She watched the man's large hands deftly handle the wooden model and marveled at the combination of strength and dexterity in his active fingers. The gentleman before her must be an engineer, architect, or builder, not a scandalous man who could pen a field guide. So, before she could request him to change James's mind, she had to devise a way to confirm his authorship, without insulting a busy, innocent man.

He continued to have difficulties balancing the soldier on the piece of wood. "His legs are too wide. Set the boy in the exact position instead."

She held the boy inches over the bottom of the stairs. "Do you want him placed here?"

"Yes, against the inner wall."

Once she finished her task, she gathered up the remaining figurines. "I'll just hold these for you. Let me know when you need one." She then examined the model to discover the other positions where a wooden figure might be placed.

"Who in the blazes are you?"

She looked up and found herself under his intense stare.

He narrowed his dark eyes and then looked past her to Lily standing in the doorway. "Mrs. Morris!"

Meta flinched at the shout just inches away from her ears. "Ah, allow me to give the proper introductions. My name is Mrs. Margaret Russell, the other lady is—"

"I don't care if she is the Queen come back to life." He caught sight of Fitzy, who had stepped out from behind Lily and stood there mesmerized by the books, models, and drawings draped over every horizontal surface. "And you brought your son—that's a first." He whipped the figurines out of Meta's hand. "I'll take those. Now is not the time for this. Damnation, where can she be? Mrs. Morris," he yelled again.

"Is that your housekeeper?" Meta asked. "She showed us in and pointed to the drawing room, then hurried to the kitchen. Perhaps something downstairs required her attention. Now please let me finish the introductions. My name you already know, the other lady is my sister, Lily Broadsham, and the young man is my brother, Fitzhenry Broadsham."

He gave each of them the briefest of bows. Then he put down a figurine and strode to the mantel. "Please write your initials on these cards—your privacy will be assured—and the appropriate heading you desire in the next edition of the field guide." He handed the two cards and pencils to Meta, since Lily stood by the door.

Meta stared at the cards. "I don't understand."

Fitzy had moved over to the table in the back of the room and now stood before a model of an unusual iron bridge.

Mr. Drexel's gaze followed him. "Don't touch anything. All of my models are very fragile."

"Oh, no, I would never do that. I plan to be an

artist, so I wish to admire these models and drawings for their artistic merit."

"Hmm." Mr. Drexel appeared satisfied that Fitzy would not harm his models, and Lily remained unmoving by the door, so he turned his focus back to Meta.

Focus was indeed the correct word. He glanced carefully at the top of her head before he examined her face.

She swallowed, a movement he noticed. Should she say something—anything—to break the awkward silence?

Without a word, he studied her in some detail, as an engineer might study the framework of some building or bridge, from the solid foundation of her half boots to the decorative style of her hair. His gaze seemed to linger around her neck, so instinctively she reached her hand upward to adjust her intricate gathered lace collar. This movement caught his eye, most notably when her arm brushed over her bosom.

She inhaled and attempted to stifle a blush, knowing full well her meager figure now came under his scrutiny. Unfortunately, her unsettled nerves necessitated an even deeper breath, which lifted her breasts upward.

He acknowledged her action by a small, knowing smile.

She froze. Mesmerized by his seductive perusal and significant physical allure, she felt the rapid warming of her cheeks. How could one glance from an unknown gentleman excite her the way this man did? Just gazing at him thrilled her with naughty, dangerous thoughts.

Horrified, she closed her eyes and tried to divert her mind by recalling her breakfast.

He stepped forward until he stood a mere foot or two away. "You have interrupted my concentration today. Let me guess. You wish to be considered a Happy Goer?"

She held her breath. His question was followed by the wickedest smile Meta had ever seen given by a gentleman. Wicked because it revealed an intimate knowledge of Happy Goers. Wicked because it contained a veiled challenge for her to retaliate in kind. And wicked because, regardless of her response, he possessed complete confidence in his ultimate victory. She no longer entertained any doubts that the man standing before her wrote the field guide.

"No words? Well, madam, you can beg"—his eyelids lowered slightly—"but since you have interrupted my work, I do not feel generous at the moment." He stepped even closer.

Her heartbeat thumped erratically. For every person she met, she tried to determine what they needed and if she might be able to help. For this man, she readily answered her own question. Whatever he needed, it wasn't her assistance. Clearly his potent charm could easily obtain anything.

"Meta, I really do believe he plans to eat you." Lily's voice trembled.

He looked at her sister and made a low growl. "I see that lady learns fast." His stare returned to Meta.

She regained her composure and met his gaze. "Why are you pretending to be a rabid dog?"

He lifted his chin, which was marked by a deep

cleft in the center. "I'll have you know, madam, my bear impersonation is much admired."

"Ah." She shook her head. "Yes, I can see that now. Silly me. I should have thought of a bear first, but I was too lost in admiration of your baritone growl. Very exciting indeed." Actually, she spoke the truth. The deep tone of his voice stimulated her and elicited wondrous memories, the low erotic grumble of a man fresh from sleep desiring a morning romp. The sensual nature of this response shocked and thrilled her in equal measure. This sudden attraction left her without a doubt that this man must have extensive experience with females. Moreover, for the first time, she understood the reputed, potent allure of a bona fide rake—some men just proved to be irresistible.

"If you do not leave now, you will discover bears eat children." He lowered the tone of his voice even more. "And ladies. The taste of ladies reminds me of…" He glanced at Fitzy. "A rather good mutton stew, don't you agree?"

With her wits muddled by his impossibly deep voice, she babbled on. "Oh no, not at all. I would imagine ladies would be rather tasty. Mutton stew is too bland. It's not in the least my favorite."

Lily nodded. "That's because Cook always puts in too many carrots."

He glared at both of them, chuckled, and strolled around them to the door. "A decidedly salient and well-timed observation." He opened the door.

"I say, sir, this is rather splendid," Fitzy said, from the back of the room. He held up a large diagram of a tunnel, showing little men shoveling dirt deep inside, but a hundred feet directly above them flowed a broad river. A large schooner seemed suspended in watery air above the men in the tunnel toiling below.

Mr. Drexel ignored the ladies and moved to the back of the parlor to join Fitzy. "I'm pleased to hear someone say that. This drawing took sixteen days to finish. Do you know what it represents?"

"A tunnel or shaft of some nature. Are they digging for coal, sir?"

"Please," he said with excitement, "any man who admires the skills of an engineer is a friend and can call me Drexel." He pointed to a double row of tunnels, side by side, with vaulted roofs of elegant brickwork. "This is a diagram of the new Thames Tunnel."

Meta moved to admire the drawing too.

He held it up to catch the meager light of an overcast day coming from the bow window, so they both could view it properly. "The Thames Tunnel is expected to provide an inexpensive way to cross the river. Mr. Marc Brunel, Esq. is the main inventor and engineer, while I work as a junior engineer. I also have taken my father's seat on the tunnel's board. I cannot wait to see the tunnel completed; it will be the eighth wonder of the world. Many foreign newspapers already describe our endeavors in great detail. Imagine it, a great tunnel *under* a navigable river. Not merely a coal tunnel under a stream, but pedestrians and carriages traveling just feet under the massive ships floating on the Thames. It will be a first, of course, and proudly constructed by Englishmen in England's greatest city."

Watching him talk about his beloved tunnel, Meta marveled at the man standing next to her. His dark eyes lit with excitement and the barely veiled sarcasm and bad temper vanished. He transformed into an amiable, enthusiastic gentleman of some intellectual significance, a man to admire and respect.

Fitzy's fine blue eyes widened. "I have never heard of it. How far away from completion is the tunnel, sir?"

Meta spoke to her brother. "So newspapers do have some use."

Fitzy wrinkled his nose.

Mr. Drexel's excitement about the tunnel continued. "We have only just started the assembly of the shield, a scaffold that will allow the miners to dig the proposed tunnel. With the current difficulty of obtaining funds, due to many of our subscribers losing money in the recent incident of reckless speculation, we are proceeding at a slower pace than initially planned. But we hope to start the lateral digging under the Thames in a fortnight."

She tried to remember what she heard about a previous attempt to dig a tunnel, in order to ease the traffic on London's overcrowded bridges. "Wasn't a tunnel under the Thames attempted before that suffered numerous leaks until it closed? Surely this failure proved the futility of such an endeavor?"

"Yes, but that tunnel was poorly built; it was too small and collapsed due to engineering incompetence. We plan to shore up the walls with brickwork immediately after the men remove the dirt from in front of the frames."

Admiring his skills as a draftsman and speaker, Meta readily absorbed his enthusiasm. "What are the frames?"

"Mr. Brunel came up with the idea of frames when he watched a shipworm bore through English oak. After he examined the creature's head under a lens, he came up with the new idea of boring through dirt using a giant shield made of twelve frames. Each frame resembles a ladder with three men standing on it, one above the other. Think of the shield as the giant head of a mole tunneling through earth. The miners dig out four inches of dirt in front of them and then place a poling board against the dirt. When all of the dirt is removed from the face, they move their frame forward. Then brick walls are built behind them, using cement that sets within minutes to permanently keep out the Thames."

"What a marvel." Fitzy reverently placed the drawing on the table and turned to address their host. "I plan to be a sculptor, but Meta suggested I needed to practice all forms of art to be a success. Your drawings have convinced me that significant skill and art can be found in engineering drawings. Perhaps I should take up the study of drafting buildings, bridges, and tunnels, since this is all very exciting."

Mr. Drexel smiled and gave her brother an encouraging pat on the back.

Thankful for his welcome attentions to Fitzy, her opinion of his behavior softened. She realized all females would find this warm, charming side of him just as irresistible as the naughty side—irresistible enough to pave the way for his successes with the ladies. Knowledge he then used as the basis for his regrettable field guide.

Fitzy's newfound enthusiasm continued to grow.

"I mean, humans are merely complicated objects to master, you know, all feet and limbs. Toes are particularly hard to get right. I admire this drawing of the tunnel, since there is a useful purpose behind the beauty. This really is a bang-up plan—imagine traveling under water. Oh, Drexel, I must see this tunnel in person. Will you show it to me?"

"I'd be delighted, but not yet. We have dug the pit for the entrance and are in the middle of finishing the descending staircase, but the site is still dangerous. We expect the possibility of floods at any moment. That is why my drawing of a new drainage system is so important."

His warning about the dangers brought her mind back to the matter at hand. "Fitzy, we have paid a call on Mr. Drexel for a reason, and it does not include asking him to show you his tunnel."

Mr. Drexel faced her, his smile gone. "Let's get to it then."

She straightened. "It's about your field guide."

He frowned and nodded at the white piece of paper from the mantel still in her hands. "Please indicate your initials and the new position you desire on this card. Then hand it to my housekeeper. She will then see you out." He yelled again, "Mrs. Morris."

Meta failed to understand his direction. "I beg your pardon."

"Begging, Mrs. Russell? You can beg to your heart's desire, but it will not move you up." The wicked smile returned.

Lily, who had been watching the conversation with increasingly wide eyes, became alarmed by his change in mood. She moved closer to the door. "Meta, ask him to speak to James so we can leave immediately. This time I really do think he plans to eat you."

Mr. Drexel's gaze never left Meta's. "Your fate, madam?"

"Pardon?"

Before he could answer, an older gentleman with a full head of gray hair entered the room. He appeared slightly stooped, but otherwise many of his other features resembled those of the younger man. He introduced himself as Mr. Michael Drexel, then proved himself a gentleman of good manners by engaging in a pleasant conversation with each member of their party. Once he learned of Fitzy's ambition to be an artist, he invited their party upstairs to the small gallery on the landing to view his collection of paintings.

With great enthusiasm, Fitzy agreed.

Lily requested to join her brother, since she appeared relaxed in Michael Drexel's company, and without doubt, she seemed eager to escape the presence of the bear.

The older man addressed his son. "Mrs. Morris has gone to help her sister for an hour, so there is no use bellowing." He headed to the door, Fitzy and Lily following directly behind him. "You know, I once wanted to be a sculptor too," Michael Drexel said, "but I quickly changed to being an engineer and inventor, because those professions suited my taste in all things mechanical. When you have more experience, you will find great beauty can be found in the diagrams of machines."

Fitzy enthusiastically agreed, and the party of three left the room and shut the door.

"Please join them, madam," Mr. Drexel said, holding out an arm.

"No, thank you. I wish to have a private word."

The frown returned to his lips. "Delighted, I'm sure." He walked back to the desk by the bow window and picked up a figurine. Then he concentrated solely on the round model.

If he never spoke another word during her visit, it would not surprise her. She took a moment to thoroughly examine the room. She noticed the lack of a flower arrangement or needlepoint display and the stale stench of tobacco, indicating the lack of a woman's touch. Clearly this cluttered room was the realm of gentlemen only. Undaunted, she strode to stand by his desk. "We have paid a call today in order to request a favor."

He failed to look up. "Yes, well, as I explained before, take a card and write your initials and category of lady desired. If a second edition of the field guide is printed, I'll see that the initials you give me are included."

"Oh, so that's what the cards are for. No, that is not the reason for our visit."

He stilled, then straightened to face her. "I must say I'm shocked you do not wish to move to a higher category."

"I'm shocked you assumed my reasons to call upon you today."

His stare hardened. "Right. I'm busy. State your business."

Meta flashed him her cheeriest smile. "Yes, thank you." She stepped next to his desk.

In contrast to the disapproving frown on his face, he watched her move with a gleam in his eye.

"Mr. Drexel, my family and I have come to express our concerns in regard to your field guide. I understand from the publisher that you are the person who penned this…I beg your pardon, effrontery to all womankind."

"All womankind?" He moved a foot away. "My dear, dear, what is your name?"

"Mrs. Russell."

"Forgive me, Mrs. Russell, but you are obviously not acquainted with all of womankind. Most ladies are not affronted in the least."

"Do you mean to tell me that you have taken a survey of all of womankind about their feelings in regard to your field guide?"

The wicked smile beamed from his handsome, lean face. "Indeed, I have made some effort to…survey all of womankind."

"Ah…" She nodded, lost in the hazy allure of his shiny black hair and the seductive dimple in his chin.

He waited.

She swallowed. "Frankly, I do not believe you. Your categories, as you call them, are nothing more than male fantasies—goddesses ruling roosts. Ha."

Wearing a smirk, he countered. "And from whence have your obtained your knowledge of—shall we say—the *friendly behaviors* of all womankind?"

"Well…I am a female of some learning. Indeed, I am currently the acting secretary of the Learned Ladies Society. So…" The possible variations of friendly female behaviors described in the field guide ran through her mind and began to warm her cheeks. To mask her embarrassment, she moved to stand in front of the fire. She needed to stop his innuendo, which fanned the flames of her imagination, request he pay a call on James, and return home.

His low chuckle revealed he was not fooled by her attempted diversion or obvious lack of experience. "Due to our long acquaintance—"

"Pardon?" She wheeled around to face him.

"Madam, due to our long acquaintance, several minutes at least, I can readily discern that you're right. Your particular type of friendly behavior requires me to invent a new category of lady."

She widened her eyes. "Sir, I have come here to request your assistance in a delicate matter of some importance. The happiness of two people is at stake."

He paused; a single dark brow rose. "Continue."

"Due to your obvious appreciation of brevity, I will just say this…ah." A ready explanation escaped her.

He inhaled, and his broad chest expanded.

She had first been attracted to his tall, lean figure. But the comforting sight of the broad plane of his large chest beckoned her to lean in for an embrace. Naturally, her words became even more muddled. "Ah…yes, well, you see—"

"Madam, the earth just rotated a full degree."

Recognizing her inability to look away from his attractive person, she forced herself to finish at least one coherent sentence. "Recently, my sister became privately engaged to a fine young man by the name of James Codlington. Their engagement had been anticipated for years, and her family was delighted with the match. While Mr. Codlington sometimes suffers from the repression of his opinionated mother, Lady Abigail Codlington, he himself is a kind and self-effacing young man. It is because of these kind manners that I believe he will be a successful spouse for my beloved sister."

He tapped his fingers on the pile of papers.

Undaunted by his obvious indifference, she soldiered on. "Recently, Mr. Codlington called off his attentions to Lily. This, of course, has left her heartbroken—"

"Bears are not interested in conversations about feelings, madam."

"Mr. Codlington called it off because he claims that Lily's initials appear in your field guide."

He whipped his head around and glanced toward the staircase, in the direction Lily had taken.

Now she had his complete attention. "All I—we—request is that you pay a call on Mr. Codlington and apprise him of the situation. Tell him he is mistaken. The field guide is fiction, correct?"

He nodded.

"Then tell Mr. Codlington the field guide is fictional and the name is…oh, I don't know, make one up. Mrs. Lynette Buckleham, an old acquaintance of yours."

"Perhaps…Bearsham for the surname. Tell me, what do I receive in return?"

"Service to a lady should be enough for any true gentleman."

A small grin lifted a corner of his lips. "But you doubt I'm a true gentleman."

He was right of course, but she had no intention of revealing that fact. "Ah…all I ask is that you please consider my sister's feelings."

"I can honestly say that I've never met a man who considers the feelings of some unknown woman on a regular basis. You must do better, madam."

"How would you feel if an unknown woman put your name in a book, and not under complimentary circumstances? Then if your superiors at the tunnel heard of it, what would you do to fight the injustice?"

Sporting a magnificent scowl, he inhaled deeply. "You have a point. Of course I wish to right any perceived wrong arising from my field guide and counter any mark upon my family's good name. You probably don't believe me. But believe this, madam. I am the son of a respectable gentleman. I will, of course, do my best to straighten out the misconceptions of your sister's reluctant Romeo." He moved to the mantel and retrieved another small piece of paper. "However, at this time my attentions are needed elsewhere." Taking a seat in an ivory-colored chair, he penciled in a few lines. "This should do the trick." He handed her the paper.

She read aloud.

Dear Mr. Codlington,

I give you my word as a gentleman that Miss Lily Broadsham is not a female of my acquaintance, so her name is not in my field guide. You mistake her initials for Lady Lynette Bearsham.

Regards,
Geo Drexel

She bit her lower lip. "Ah, this is all very well, but surely it would be best to call upon Mr. Codlington yourself and provide any further explanations, if required."

"Mrs. Russell, you fail to understand the time constraint I am under at the moment. I have plans that must be finished by a deadline."

"Yes, I understand. Therefore, I will do anything in my power to assist you, if you perform this one task. So how may I be of help? What do you need?"

"Besides my good name…your departure."

"Ah, you are being droll. I am quite serious about providing some assistance."

"The only assistance I require is additional investors to fund the construction of the tunnel. That will go a long way to impress my superiors. But I fail to see how you could be of any assistance to me on that score."

"As I have mentioned, I belong to the Learned Ladies Society. Many of the members have wealthy and influential fathers and husbands. Perhaps I might ask them to solicit monies to fund the tunnel."

He rolled his eyes. "Learned ladies asking their husbands for favors. What could go wrong? Tell me, do you ladies sit around, read books of questionable taste, and learn languages?"

She lifted her chin. "And do good works for those whose situation in life is less fortunate than ours."

He nodded. "The only advantage for a lady to acquire multiple languages is the delight she obtains when she finds additional opportunities to scold her husband without his understanding. Your plan, madam, will not work. The weak link is the futility of a wife asking her husband for investment funds."

"All I ask is a brief call upon Mr. Codlington. Hand him your note. You needn't say a word, but your presence is necessary for sincerity and to answer any questions he may have. Your total stay need not exceed five minutes."

"Five minutes is too much. I could pay a call after a fortnight, perhaps. First though, I suggest you and your sister go home and then breathe deeply. It is very likely that by the end of your breathing exercises, your sister's suitor will have changed his mind. Now, I really must ask your party to leave." He headed for the parlor door and held it open.

"Sir, the matter is urgent—a lady's future is at stake. I don't pretend to understand your time constraints, but I know spoiling the hopes of a respectable couple may harm your reputation and cannot further your professional intentions."

"You're a widow?"

She nodded.

"Your ignorance of gentlemen tells me you were not married long. No gentleman in possession of a sane mind would visit a stranger to discuss the man's engagement. It's just not done. And no man would discuss another man's love match, because the wits of one person in the party has gone to the dogs. This letter will prove successful. Trust me, I'm right."

He was wrong, of course, the ridiculous man. "Your words 'trust me' were spoken in almost a growl. Very heartwarming," she mocked, "since I have become fond of the bear. Please pay Mr. Codlington a call."

He stepped directly in front of her, his gaze holding hers.

She froze, except for the small movements made by her rapid breaths.

He leaned close to her ear. "Grrr, be off with you."

She straightened. When a gentleman became particularly exasperating, her mother had advised her to stand tall, call him troublesome to his face, and wear a fetching bonnet. It was a truth universally acknowledged that no item of dress fortified a woman's courage more than fetching millinery. Except hers hung in the vestibule at the moment, so she must summon her courage without it. "We had a Staffordshire figurine of a dancing bear on our mantel for years. Then my youngest brother, Tom, broke it when he ran through the room."

He took a step forward, enough to touch her body with his, chest to chest. The soft, but quite menacing, growl returned in a whispered, "I have plans to finish, madam."

"Mr. Bear"—she bit her lower lip—"I'll wager *you* dance delightfully."

He said nothing for at least thirty seconds. Then the bear disappeared in a fit of whooping laughter. Without his usual scowl, he transformed into an uncommonly handsome young man. "Now who is being droll?" He swept up her hand, placed his broad palm on the center of her back, and led her into several quick turns of a waltz.

"Stop! Release me."

He stopped twirling. "There, you got your wish, a dancing bear. Now give me mine—your absence."

Glancing at his black fathomless eyes and the dark whiskers shading his skin, she experienced an overwhelming urge to stroke his cheek and maybe even outline his rosy lips with her finger, before placing her lips on his. Having never, ever, felt this strong physical attraction for a stranger, she concluded it would be best to leave as soon as he granted her request. She felt a blush expand across her cheeks. "Promise to call upon Mr. Codlington, and I will leave in the next second."

He sighed, carefully released his grip, and stepped back. "Present this billet first. Men understand men, take my word. The young buck will understand no slight was intended and the engagement will be resumed to everyone's satisfaction. If satisfaction could be found by becoming leg-shackled."

"But—"

"If you continue to argue, I will include your *real* name in the next printing of the field guide."

"Sir!" *He wouldn't—he couldn't—would he?*

She realized that the note was the best offer she would receive for the time being. If the letter failed to convince James, then she would have to make progress with the Learned Ladies Society in finding investors for Mr. Brunel's tunnel. "I will try your note first, as you suggest. And to thank you properly, I will add to your happiness by allowing you to put forth my name in the next edition of the field guide." She lifted her chin. "But I only glanced at your categories. I do not remember one labeled 'Kind Service to Family' in that…that tome of yours."

He winked. "And here I expected you to demand to be a Ruling Goddess." He approached her again and stood close—near enough that she felt his warm breath on her forehead. He chucked her under the chin. "You, madam, belong under the heading of Rabbits."

"Rabbits! I fail to comprehend your reasoning." She glared back at him. "No, please do not explain."

The wicked smile reappeared. "Rabbits because you are all pink and white, hop about a great deal, and stick your nose in where it is not wanted."

"Ah, very amusing, I'm sure. If I penned a field guide, I'd include you under the category of bear. Bear because you're big and black."

"And bite."

"Yes, I'm sure you bite."

He leaned close enough to whisper in her ear. "Bears do not bite ladies, madam, they nibble."

She had not blushed in years. Today in the presence of this man, she seemed to blush every two minutes. Her physical attraction to his large, dark form must be due to her lack of sleep caused by Lily's vexing situation. At least, she hoped that was the reason. With any luck, the letter would prove successful, and she would never have to see him again. "I am so excited, and quite flustered, as you no doubt observe. This must be an example of the wicked charm you rakes exert on females. As a widow, it doesn't have the same effect on me—"

"Of course," he said with feigned sincerity.

"But I understand how an unsuspecting lady might be led astray by your seductive rough-and-tumble wiles."

"I'll have you know that many ladies actually eagerly anticipate my seductive rough-and-tumble wiles."

"Of course they do." She pushed him backward several feet. "I assume they swoon onto the street upon your approach. If we ever meet again, I too promise to do so, since I'm pleased you wrote that letter to Mr. Codlington. After all, I do not wish to appear ungrateful for your efforts. I only hope you're correct and your note proves successful."

Three

"WELL, I'M NOT QUITE SURE WHAT TO MAKE OF THAT adventure," Meta said as she stepped over the threshold of the Broadsham town house.

Lily entered directly behind her. "I do. I became so angry by his forward manners, but they frightened me to the point where I couldn't say a word. I hope after Fitzy and I left the room, you gave him a proper set-down." Without waiting for an answer or taking off her gloves and bonnet, Lily ran upstairs.

Meta tried to follow her sister, eager to get her opinion on the letter's chances of success, but her father approached her from the direction of the library, his frail arm held up, pointing a finger.

Her father's once fine slim figure had stooped soon after the death of his wife. Now within the last year, his mind had aged to the point where it retreated into a realm his children could no longer recognize or comprehend. He rested his bony hand on Meta's shoulder. "Are you my wife?"

"No, Father." She took his cool palm and held it. "I'm Meta, your eldest."

Short silver wisps of once dark whiskers framed his smile. "Meta, you really must take care of our home. The ceiling is making noises, very odd noises. Something must be done."

Since she had never heard these noises, she attributed his concerns to a mind muddled by age. Nevertheless, she assured him that their butler would investigate the situation. "Thank you, dearest. I'll have Sampson take care of the matter. He'll likely send a boy up to the roof." She kissed his cheek. "I'm busy this afternoon helping Lily, so I am afraid I cannot read Scott to you, but I'll send Susanna up with your tea. Afterwards, she can start reading *The Talisman* where I left off. Remember? On a whim, the Queen stole Edith's ring right off her finger." She lowered her voice and spoke in a conspiratorial tone. "I bet trouble is ahead."

A twinkle danced in his eyes. "Oh, there will be mayhem. You may take my word for it."

"I agree. The world succumbs to mayhem in all novels, and that is why we enjoy them so." She followed him upstairs to his room, then once he was settled, she knocked on the door to Lily's room.

"I know it's you, Meta. But you cannot help me in this situation. I don't need your assistance."

Meta entered her sister's room and found her sitting in front of her vanity, reading Mr. Drexel's brief note. "Are you fretting that the letter will fail and James will not change his mind and resume his addresses?" She sat in the window seat and attempted to read Lily's expression, but her sister must have realized her intent and turned her head to hide her face. Meta waited, unsure if Lily needed the time to formulate her words.

Minutes later, Lily finally faced her, her eyes red and swollen with tears. "Please, Meta, let's forget this whole incident. I'll put Mr. Drexel's letter in my drawer with my other personal correspondence and that will be an end to it."

"I don't understand. You cannot hide your true feelings from me. I know in my heart you love James. You always have, for years and years. Why do you not want to send this note immediately? It should clear up something that was nothing more than a little misunderstanding." Meta knew Lily and James belonged together. They seemed happiest in each other's company and even on occasion they finished each other's sentences—a perfect match.

A tear finally fell, and Lily brushed it away. "That is my point. The note is useless, a false exercise. I mean, if James truly loved me, he should have known in his heart that it was not my name in that field guide."

Meta silently agreed, then leaned over to hug her sister around the shoulders. "Please, let's pay a brief call on James to show him the note. What harm could there be in that?"

"You were not present, Meta, when he called off. You didn't see his…face. He couldn't even look me in the eye. There will be no reconciliation; you must take my word for it." She arranged her woolen, straw-colored shawl even tighter around her shoulders.

"I know you have been hurt—"

"Hurt!" Her eyes dried, and she jumped slightly in her seat. "Hurt is not the right word. Betrayed is more like it. I was eighteen when the guide was published. Eighteen! Oh the insult."

"If we just speak—"

"I have nothing to say to him. It seems to me he has something he wishes to say to *me*." Lily straightened in her chair. "I feel truly jilted and fear society will hear of it. Everyone anticipated our wedding, but it will never come to be." A few seconds passed, and her shoulders slumped. "I'm sorry, Meta. I no longer trust him. How could I?"

Meta rose and stood behind her sister. She then caught Lily's gaze in the looking glass. "You and I will speak of this again sometime in the future, maybe a year or two after your marriage. By then you will realize that gentlemen are sometimes unpredictable, and it is sometimes difficult to understand their position on a subject. That is why you must speak to him. Give him a chance to clarify his objections. You owe him that."

"No." Lily pursed her lips. "He can pay me a call to apologize, and I will hear him out. I can give him nothing more."

"This is not like you—you have a kind heart. Are you telling me you no longer love James?"

"No, I am not saying that…exactly. I'm saying he must apologize to me first, on principle."

She recognized the appearance of her sister's innate stubbornness, mixed with the mortification of rejection. "Well, come and join me then. Together we will pay a call at Codlington House, and you and James can have a word in private. Show him the letter, and all will be forgotten. We can then celebrate together."

The smallest of smiles finally broke across Lily's face. "Thank you, I really mean it, but I must refuse. James must come to me."

Meta sometimes failed to understand her father or her siblings, leaving her anxious, unable to sleep, and even ill from too much worry. Unfortunately, these feelings proved to have little effect upon the final outcome. Now her mind only registered the fact that Lily needed her. Not only that, but she had great affection for James and worried that he too might be unhappy.

They both needed her to facilitate a reconciliation.

An hour later, Meta found herself standing in front of the home of Lady Codlington and her only son, James. The Codlingtons' town house was at least twice the size of their home, and it possessed a lovely view of the park from the front rooms. While the size and situation of the house matched the elevated status of the Codlington family, it stood merely three dozen houses away from the more modest home of the Broadshams. Indeed, the two families frequently met during evening walks in the park. As a result, the Codlingtons' butler greeted her warmly and showed her to the large library overlooking the private side garden. A climbing old rose grew next to the open window. The day was a warm one, so the scent of roses overwhelmed the normal smell of old books.

Meta hurried over to examine her favorite object in the room, the jovilabe orrery—a mechanical device the size of a tabletop that showed Jupiter and its four Galilean moons. The clocklike mechanism controlled the slow orbit of the four moons around a stationary Jupiter. Both the planet and its moons were made of polished semiprecious stones. The pretty green color of little Io's malachite was her favorite, so she stroked the cool green stone. Upon her touch, she realized a desire to show the orrery's gears to Mr. Drexel. Because of his obvious admiration of all things mechanical, he would delight in watching the tiny gears advance ever so slowly, causing the moons to dance around the great marble Jupiter.

The moment she saw Io move a fraction, Lady Codlington entered the library and greeted her. "Well, my dear, I do not know what to say to you about this business." The older woman slowly moved to sit in her favorite chair by the fire and spread her black bombazine skirt out in front of her.

"Good afternoon, your ladyship."

"I imagine you have called to change my son's mind about his broken engagement. But I will speak plainly, since I am well-known for my frankness. The situation will not change. I insist you drop the matter. Thanks to that field guide, my son has come to his senses at last. In the future, he'll make a match that will prove useful to a young man destined to have the highest office in the Court of Common Pleas—not become shackled for life with a young lady who blushes every time someone speaks a sentence in her direction. No, to advance his calling, he needs a spouse with social skills, like myself, to further his ambitions."

"Mother, enough."

Meta turned to find James entering the cavernous library. A short, broad-shouldered gentleman of twenty-two, James wore a lovely velvet jacket the color of the strongest claret. He strolled over and greeted Meta warmly. "I'm sorry I was not here to greet you upon your arrival."

His mother interrupted. "I was just explaining to

Mrs. Russell that the engagement between you and her sister is rightly called off. I mean—"

"Thank you." He moved to stand in front of her and held out his hand. "I know your intentions are good; however, I must insist upon speaking with Mrs. Russell in private."

Lady Codlington dropped her jaw before narrowing her eyes. "Now, son—"

"Please, dear." Beaming affably, James picked up his mother's hand and exerted gentle pressure to pull her to her feet.

She frowned, pulled her hand away, and rose without assistance. "Very well. Although I do not expect any change in the situation. I think—"

"I really must insist this interview be private," he said.

Her ladyship shook her head and said her farewells. Her spirits remained benevolent enough to express her best wishes to Meta and her family.

Meta curtsied, and the older woman left the library.

James paused and watched his mother slowly leave the room, her gait revealing the effects of her age. "I apologize, Meta. She means well, truly." He smiled, then held his hand out in a motion for her to sit. "It is difficult for any young man to convince his mother of his independence. I should've left this house and set up a residence of my own upon my coming of age. I am quite capable of independent living, but I reside here now solely to give her company and comfort, since she took to her sickbed for so many months after my father's death. Unfortunately, there are consequences of remaining in your childhood home. And you just witnessed an example: the well-intentioned, but odorous interference in a grown man's affairs."

Meta gave him a wistful smile. "Mothers believe their children are always in need of their advice and assistance. I'll probably treat my siblings like children for as long as they live. Fitzy will be old and toothless, but I'll still believe I might be able to help him. Oh, that sounds just terrible, doesn't it?" Her cheeks warmed. "I really don't mean to interfere, but I want to be present if they need me in any way. I would hate to see any one of them suffer or be unhappy."

"Don't distress yourself. I have noticed you sacrifice your own comfort for the sake of your siblings. You left your husband's lovely house in Sussex and moved back here to care for the entire household. As an only child, I truly believe the attention from a sister must be a wonderful thing, even if it might tire"—he winked—"on occasion."

"Oh, James, I do wish you will become my brother." No gentleman had ever impressed her more by his kindness and amiability.

He reddened slightly.

"Please allow me to speak on the matter."

He shook his head. "Nothing can be gained by it. My aspirations to become a justice and hold higher office means my wife's character must be beyond reproach. Later this year my name will be put forward in consideration for an important appointment at court. I think you fail to understand the scandalous tittle-tattle the rumor of a second edition has caused. The members of my club plan to spend endless hours trying to guess the identity of each new lady, under the assumption that the names differ by a letter or two. Even if the public did not immediately relate the initials in the book to Lily's, they might someday, and a scandal would arise. I'd be passed over for appointment and my judicial career ended."

"You are expecting the worst that could happen, James. I truly believe your fears are unreasonable." She glanced toward the door. "Did your mother come up with this…" She did not want to unjustly accuse his mother of interference or causing the situation in the first place. She faced him and implored. "Lily deserves better than being jilted."

His eyes widened, then he let the silence stretch. He brushed his thinning hair across his forehead. "Yes, on principle I agree with you. I apologize and wish to make amends by any means other than marriage. But I have no wish to remain a junior lawyer. Gentlemen have a great desire to succeed, Meta—a strong ambition that women are not fully aware of." He walked to the fireplace and stared at the ruby-like coals. "Tell me, how is Lily? What does she think of me?" His cinched fist rested on the mantel.

Meta rose and placed her palm on his back.

He turned and smiled at her.

"I do not wish to betray a sister's confidences, but I am concerned about her welfare. Lily loves you dearly and is deeply hurt by your refusal. I hate to pain you, James, but you must be aware of that?"

He nodded, lips pursed. "It will be for the best. I *must* believe that."

She pulled away and placed her hands on her hips. "Well I do not. The two of you are in love. And that is a rare thing, indeed, rare enough to celebrate and fight for. Right now I feel like a governess in charge of naughty children. So to set the situation to rights, I had a word with Mr. Drexel, the so-called author of the field guide you mentioned."

"Meta! You did not mention my name, did you? Involve a stranger in my personal affairs?"

She blushed. "I-I do not remember what I said precisely. I did, however, call in the company of Lily and Fitzy. After requesting a private interview with Mr. Drexel, I discussed Lily's happiness and the great injustice of his field guide. After some protestation of nonsense about men and feelings—"

"You didn't." Once again, wide-eyed horror graced his features.

She never realized before how touchy gentlemen could be on the subject of feelings. "Mr. Drexel was kind enough to give us this note." She reached into her silver chain link reticule, pulled out the white paper folded into a small square, and held it out for him to take.

He snatched it out of her hand. "I would hate to falsely condemn you, Meta, but please do not concern yourself with my personal affairs in public."

"You have no concerns on that score, James. Mr. Drexel is as reticent and sardonic as they come." After yesterday's excitement, she realized her interest in Mr. Drexel had not faded in the least. Even this morning during her ablutions, she couldn't help but wonder what he was doing that very moment—an unsettling thought.

James unfolded the note and read, "*Mr. Codlington…*

*Miss Lily Broadsham is not a female of my acquaintance…
not in my field guide…mistake her initials for Lady Lynette
Bearsham. Regards, Geo Drexel."*

"So you see," Meta said, "you were quite wrong
to believe Lily's name appeared in this man's book."

His brow smoothed as he returned to his seat. "The
note provides little explanation and is rather terse."

"It provides the necessary information, surely. Now
that you understand this whole nonsense is just a mix-
up, please speak to Lily again."

"Lynette Bearsham? That name is fictional, don't
you agree? I'm acquainted with many of our aristocracy, and I am not aware of a family named Bearsham.
It seems this Mr. Drexel cannot be relied upon to tell
the truth."

"James, his field guide is fictional, so the names are
fictional too." She considered James to be one of the
most intelligent of men of her acquaintance. However,
the fact that the field guide was fictional seemed to be
irrelevant to him. It didn't surprise her, since many
gentlemen were blind when it came to the subject of
females and romance.

"I don't understand why this man went to the
trouble of writing this note. I need to know more
about this so-called gentleman. What is your evaluation of his character, his manners? What if word
got out that I sought his assistance?" His eyes grew
wide again.

She finally realized his obvious fear that any whiff
of scandal would harm his future appointment. "I can
assure you, no personal confidences were revealed. Lily
has told me very little about your conversation. I merely

suggested that Mr. Drexel might help a young couple by clarifying an unfortunate situation he caused. The man is a gentleman, although perhaps not a normal one. His manners can turn dreadfully bearlike, and you're correct, his conversation can turn a little terse in seconds. Otherwise, I was pleasantly surprised. He is not at all like a scoundrel who would pen a book like the field guide. Behind his bluster is a gentleman who does care about setting the situation to rights for the sake of his reputation, if nothing else. He is an engineer, working on Mr. Marc Brunel's Thames Tunnel. Personally, I believe his brevity is because he has taken on too much work for himself and shoulders serious responsibilities."

"The Tunnel!" James smiled, and for the first time in their interview, he seemed to relax. "I know one of the lawyers overseeing the endeavor, and I do so admire Mr. Brunel. He is our greatest engineer, although it would not suit to say that in front of some members of my club, since he is a Frenchman. Still, his tunnel is important, and we all eagerly anticipate news of the latest progress."

"I'm delighted to hear that. Perhaps now you will take Mr. Drexel as a man of his word and resume your attentions to Lily."

He glanced at the door, presumably in the direction of his mother. "I'm sorry, Meta. While I do admire Mr. Brunel, I have never heard of this Mr. Drexel. My future is too important to rely upon the word of—now here I must disagree with you—the word of a man who could pen that book, a true rogue."

"But here is your chance to correct your mistake and prove your independence to your mother."

"There is another reason you are unaware of. If I did as you ask, there is every chance she would deny me my living. I'd be forced to live like a pauper. No, Meta, I understand you mean well. I just do not see a pathway to happiness that will please everyone. I cannot help but be conflicted." He hung his head slightly, revealing his thinning hair on top. "I know you must hate me. Indeed, the whole family must hate me. I dare not even imagine what Lily must think of me. Instead, I must believe a girl with her beauty and sweet nature will undoubtedly find a husband worthy of her."

She tried to lighten his mood. "Together you'd be happy paupers. Besides, a respectable living is a moot point. Lily's fortune is sufficient for two responsible adults to live on. Therefore, when you wed, you will have a living adequate for any lawyer with higher aspirations."

He paused. "I'm glad to hear that, but it's not just the living. This perceived scandal in her past might harm my future ambitions. Chief justices, judges, and Polite Society are not so forgiving as you would imagine."

"Seems to me a career is a small price to pay to marry the woman you love. Surely if your advancement fails due to some misconception about Lily's reputation, there are other professions available?" For the first time, she became aware of James's stubbornness and unsure if he was indeed worthy of her sister. He seemed to value ambition over love. But she knew Lily loved him, loved him enough to be terribly hurt by this whole affair. "What can I do to change your mind?"

He gave her a direct stare, his eyes wide. "I don't know…"

His intransigence forced her to speak without reserve. "If you resolve to abandon your engagement, your actions may reinforce society's belief that the initials are Lily's. She'd be wrongfully judged by the public. She was eighteen at the time of the first publication. Eighteen! If you do love her, how could you put her reputation in jeopardy like that?"

He jumped to his feet, horror crossing his features. "I-I-I had not considered that."

Meta waited for a reply, but he just stood there. "Perhaps if this Mr. Drexel paid a call and explained the situation, you'd gain confidence that the scandal you believe might happen in the future can be avoided."

"If only that were true." He shook his head, sighed, and collapsed onto his chair. "But I don't see how."

"You must give Mr. Drexel a chance to explain the situation. Maybe there are facts we are unaware of, like only a few copies were printed."

"No, no, they were all laughing about it at my club, you understand."

"Please think of how happy you both will be together with this misunderstanding put behind you."

They exchanged heartfelt smiles.

"Please give my idea a chance," Meta said. "I will go and speak with him again. Maybe together, and with Mr. Drexel's assistance, we can find a way to change society's perception and find our way out of this unfortunate muddle."

~∽◊∽~

A day later, Meta sat in her carriage, her palms damp, all because she journeyed to the south side of the Thames to meet George Drexel again. This time she understood his attractiveness to females, so she should easily be able to steel herself from his charms or at the very least ignore her own response.

Before she reached the Thames Tunnel site, she glanced out the window at the crowded streets and mulled over the best method to persuade him to visit James in person. She could plead, demand, attempt tears, ask kindly, or bribe. Perhaps, "Mr. Drexel, I must insist you consider the feelings of…" No, that plea would fail. Meta knew any mention of *feelings* would bring out the appearance of the bear. Then the angry beast would refuse to join her in convincing James that Lily's name was not in the field guide or help devise a plan to counter the public's erroneous perception, such as removing the initials from the book entirely. If he refused to join her, it would end her last hope to rob James of his excuse to call off his engagement. How about, "Mr. Drexel, since you are a gentleman…" No, she doubted that tactic would work either, since he impressed her as a man who might achieve a certain thrill from considering himself *not* a gentleman, a most perverse individual.

She had plenty of time to formulate her request in a manner Mr. Drexel could not possibly refuse, since it took her over an hour to cross the Thames. This wait was not news to her, but it brought into focus the advantages of a low-cost tunnel to travel to the south side of the river.

Once she reached the tunnel site in Rotherhithe,

she observed a large, round brick pit, similar to the model she had observed in Mr. Drexel's rooms. The spectacular iron-ringed pit impressed her immediately, since it was much larger than she had imagined. She watched sixty or so men hard at work: bricklayers, ironworkers, men hauling bags slung over their shoulders, and at least twenty men surrounding a structure that must be the twelve frames Mr. Drexel had described. The sounds of hammers, whistles, and shouts filled the air around them. Awed by the sight before her, and thankful that the day turned out to be a warm, sunny one, she stood and watched the workers for at least twenty minutes.

During this time, she noticed Mr. Drexel amongst the gentlemen directing the men who levered one of the twelve frames of the great shield into place. She had failed to recognize him at first, because he dressed like one of the workmen. His sleeves were rolled up, his waistcoat unbuttoned, his hat removed, and his white shirt quite stained with soot.

The first time she saw him standing in his drawing room, his sturdy figure reminded her of a well-dressed, upside-down pile of coal: a dark figure wider on top and narrower in the hips. But here with his sleeves rolled up, forcibly shouting instructions, he resembled a man who took charge of his world. Her heartbeat raced again, and she enjoyed watching him.

Only when he looked up at the crowd, holding his hand up to shield his eyes from the sun and glancing in her direction, did she realize he must have seen her. The expression on his face was unreadable; however, he neither smiled nor waved. He said something to the man next to him and then started for the pit's staircase.

Deciding his lack of acknowledgment meant he was displeased with her presence and not desiring a full dressing-down in public because she interrupted his work, she fled from the approaching bear and started back to her carriage. She'd postpone her request to a more suitable time and give him fair warning of her arrival. The second she turned the corner on Lilypond Street, she heard her name called. She ignored it and quickened her pace.

"Mrs. Russell!"

She heard the tone of the angry bear. Should she turn to face him or run away?

"Madam, please stop."

Any lady of good manners could not resist the power of the word "please." She stopped and steeled herself for a possible confrontation.

He reached her in several long strides, then glared down at her.

Luckily, she wore her largest poke bonnet. She tilted the angle of her head slightly downward, so she could respond without catching sight of the bear's snarl on his lips. "I am so sorry—I didn't mean to interrupt your work. I mean, you are always busy. Please excuse me, I..." She held her breath.

He laughed. "Bear got your tongue?"

She glanced up to his face and found him grinning broadly, his dark eyes gleaming.

He extended his arm. "Come, come, I want to show you the tunnel."

She exhaled and relaxed. If she did have any fears

about her reception, she certainly was not going to reveal them now. She took a deep breath, focused on the compliment of his desire to show her the tunnel, and took his offered arm.

He bent down sideways to catch her eye, winked, and gave her a smile.

She couldn't help but smile in return.

Together they headed back to the edge of the pit and the tunnel entrance.

Thankfully, he carried on the conversation with nothing more from her than a general comment offered now and then. He spoke with more eloquence than she expected. With patience, he described every feature in great detail, but only after she conceded an interest in the subject. So she did not become bored with a long recital of features that failed to interest her, like engines and power. He explained the carriage entrance and pathways where people would enter the tunnel in a manner that she could easily imagine. Without doubt he believed this tunnel would spur England on to a glorious future.

After the first ten minutes of his tour, her nerves were fully restored, and she realized her error in fearing a dressing-down. In fact, he was so amiable, she might bring up the subject of paying a call on James after all.

"Providential, madam, that you have visited the site today, since it spares me a journey to Broadsham House." By then they had reached a storage area behind the brick engine house in front of a pile of bricks. Since the bricks were the only place available to sit, he removed a handkerchief from his waistcoat pocket and carefully placed it on the pile.

She recognized the well-practiced gallant and supposed any successful seducer must possess that quality in abundance, as well as natural charm. Her cheeks began to warm, so she looked up at the sun, planning to use that as an excuse if he noticed her blush.

"Your brother, Fitzy—a great gun you have there. The young man reminds me of myself when younger, a fresh and eager learner, anxious for success just around the corner in five years or so."

Pleased by the compliment, she faced him squarely. "Ah, I do see the similarities. Fitzy could speak of nothing else other than the amazing Drexels after our visit. I wish to thank you and your father for your generous attentions to him."

"Your brother mentioned something about engineering drawings to my father. We have use for a young man to take some of the drafting burden off of me. He will even get some time down in the pit, delivering and copying the latest plans. We will of course pay him for his help. It won't be much, but he'll gain valuable experience—skills that might come in handy when he studies to become a member of the Royal Academy. Would you consider allowing him to assist us?"

She jumped to her feet. Nothing could make her happier than for Fitzy to leave the isolation of his old schoolroom to join these men actively toiling here. He'd gain a valuable lesson about the effort needed to create a major achievement. "Yes, I will put the matter before him. I really don't see any reason he should refuse…"

She spontaneously reached to shake his hand in a

gesture of thanks. Once holding on to his palm, she did not let go. Instinctively, she examined it closely. When they had first met, she noticed his palm was unusually large. Now she noticed the strength visible in every sinew of his fingers, his wrist, and his lower arm. All this power lying just underneath a covering of tanned skin marked with a few healed cuts. A canopy of dark hair shadowed his forearm and traveled up to become a visible shadow under his white linen shirt. More heat stole up from under her collar and warmed her face.

"Do you need a hand, madam?" He gave a low chuckle.

She instantly dropped his palm. "I have never seen a gentleman's hand that dirty."

"Apologies, I…" He immediately brushed his hand numerous times on his trouser.

"I came today to request your assistance on another matter." She glanced at him and discovered a raised eyebrow but no expression that might give her alarm. In fact, he seemed slightly bemused. "You see, the letter you wrote had no effect on James whatsoever. He became skeptical of your intent due to the letter's brevity and lack of specifics. You were correct in that the note conveyed all that was needed to be said, but for some reason, James decided you could not be trusted."

He rolled his dark, fathomless eyes.

She recognized that this was an opportune time to appeal to his good will. "I was hoping you would join me, and together we can pay a call upon James. First, your very appearance will show him that you are a gentleman and your word is to be trusted. Then you can explain to him that your book is fiction and that all of London knows this fact. No misunderstanding could ever come about. Once the truth is placed before James by the author himself, he could no longer willfully believe anyone should think those initials were Lily's. Moreover, a scheme may be hatched between us to ensure the public could never believe the initials were hers. I have great hopes this will come to pass, and James will resume his addresses soon."

"I disagree." He slapped his thigh. "My presence will not change his mind. This James should have come around. If he refused, it means he had a reason to call off. Perhaps one you are unaware of?"

They sat silently watching the busy men toiling around them.

How could she change his mind?

She doubted any tactic would work other than the absolute truth. "I don't pretend to know everything about my sister, but I do know she loves James. I also believe he loves her. I can have no other goal in life than to see my siblings happy in love. It is my greatest dream."

"Right. You have now reached a subject I know nothing about and refuse to discuss."

"Your greatest dreams?"

"No, happy in love. Don't mistake me; I know it exists. My two best friends fell under its spell. But it doesn't happen to everyone. Your sister and her James may have been emulating their friends of a similar age. It's a time in life when all of their friends are choosing spouses, I mean. There is a distinct possibility that love had nothing to do with their doomed relationship."

What a pitiful individual, deprived of understanding.

She needed to forgo the love argument and devise another tactic to persuade him. "I once said that I might plead to the Learned Ladies Society for funds on the tunnel's behalf. If you join me to call upon James, I promise you at least one new investor for the tunnel."

He inhaled deeply and stood. Wearing a broad smile, he held out his hand.

She took it eagerly, since perhaps his smile meant he would grant her request. Only once again, her stare fixed on his hand. This time, her thoughts weaved a desire to feel a caress from these very fingers. Then her mind wandered even further, into a dangerous, forbidden territory of intimate masculine touches she had forgotten. She licked her lower lip, lost in imaginings of how his caresses might feel on her neck or her shoulder. She shook her head in hopes of dislodging these reckless desires.

His fingers tightened around hers. "You are obviously not examining the dirt, since I brushed it off. Perhaps you are dreaming about the power of touch?"

She dropped his hand like a hot coal. Why had her mind wandered? What was wrong with her today?

He picked up hers and turned it over. "If not a touch, perhaps a pleasing stroke in just the right place?" His warm forefinger touched her in the center of her palm and then leisurely trailed up the inside of her wrist.

Her cheeks flamed as she searched for an excuse for fantasizing about his hand. "If you must know, I was admiring the strength of the hands that will one day build England's future."

Wearing an expression of half pleasure and half guilt, he dropped her hand. "Pardon me."

She let out her breath; her ruse appeared to work. Her—what must have been blatant—physical attraction she managed to disguise for the moment.

"Thank you for the compliment," he said, beaming and executing a deep bow. "Come. Let me escort you back to your carriage. I will do as you wish and speak to the man, if you promise to deliver one new investor in the tunnel. If it comes to pass, I would be grateful, as would my superiors. But I prophesy your James's heart has spoken the last word, and he will still refuse."

Four

THE GRAY PAVEMENT STONES GLISTENED FROM THE recent rain as Meta approached the London home of her friend and current president of the Learned Ladies Society, Lady Sarah Stainthorpe. She pulled her hands out of her spencer's warm fur-lined pocket and knocked on her friend's door. She then crossed two fingers for good luck.

Meta had always eagerly anticipated the society's meetings: a group of intelligent women discussing books, discussing their families, planning their latest benevolent works, telling the latest jest or *on dits*, or all of these at the same time.

Today, however, Meta needed to ask her friends for a rather significant favor: new investors for Mr. Marc Brunel's Thames Tunnel. Without Mr. Drexel's knowledge, she made discreet inquiries into the cost of shares, hoping her friends could persuade their husbands to make a significant investment or even a helpful donation. If her efforts proved successful, she'd pay her debt of gratitude for Fitzy's employment and further obligate Mr.

Drexel to enthusiastically persuade James to change his mind.

Stepping inside Lady Sarah's personal drawing room, Meta glanced around at the pretty yellow Chinese papers on the wall. Willowy tree branches with sweet little sparrows flying or sitting on branches decorated the papers. On the blue ceiling, white plaster swags complemented the yellow papers. In the center of the cheery room, numerous gilt wooden chairs formed a large circle around a peach-colored marble table. She exchanged greetings with her friends, and they all took a seat to hear the latest news concerning their varied philanthropic efforts.

Lady Sarah, a tall, young blonde whose personal fortitude was immediately recognized by everyone who met her, stood and described the Society's recent success in the rescue of London's destitute governesses. Many of these ladies possessed a higher level of education than most. Yet for various reasons—lack of marriage, old age, or illness—these intelligent women found themselves destitute. The Learned Ladies Society was established to house and feed these governesses so their last years would not be spent on the streets or in the workhouse.

Lady Sarah faced the twenty or so women present that day and began the meeting. "I am pleased to say that we found adequate placement for three governesses this month."

The ladies politely clapped in unison.

Grizel, a black-haired Scottish lady who lacked all reservations about speaking her mind, said, "Clara, how does this good news affect our current finances? I am worried we may not have enough funds to keep all of our women housed during the winter."

Clara's disorderly blonde curls suggested an air of frivolity, but under those curls was a tidy mind especially brilliant with numbers. "I must say, I too have concerns on that score. At our current rate of expenditure, we should save our funds for the time being, until we can guarantee that they will last through the winter with our current number of governesses."

Almost all of the benevolent ladies nodded or verbally agreed.

"But if we do not rescue them now," Bethia said, "more poor women may be required to spend the cold winter on the streets." The oldest lady in the group, her varied life experiences had propagated a tolerant heart.

Grizel countered. "Agreed, but if we're daft and overspend by saving more women than our funds will allow, then all of our governesses may find themselves in difficulties this winter. Sometimes we must make sacrifices to keep those we've already saved."

This discussion ended when most of the ladies caught a whiff of the Spanish almond cake and China tea seconds before it was brought into the room.

While her friends silently ate cake, Meta gathered her courage before standing to address the ladies. "May I take this moment to speak on a personal matter?" Since giving a speech during such an important event as tea was a rare occurrence, she instantly grabbed everyone's attention. "Thank you. You see I have a favor to ask all of you. Without going into details, except that it involves the happiness of my beloved sister, Lily, I would like to request your assistance."

Several ladies resumed eating their cake.

Meta took a deep breath. "Tonight when you speak to your husbands or fathers, I would be so grateful if you could ask them to support the Thames Tunnel project currently under construction by Mr. Marc Brunel."

Whispers broke out amongst the ladies.

"Next week they will start to dig under the Thames, and everyone is excited about the prospect of England being the first country to dig a tunnel under a navigable river. Can you imagine it, strolling *under* the Thames."

Several ladies gasped.

"Oh, I'd be too frightened," one lady said, with a shiver.

"I'm not a mole," said another.

"I think it's exciting, wondrous even," Lady Sarah said, clasping her hands together.

Meta smiled at her friend. "It *is* exciting, very much so." She turned to address the group. "What I request is that you consider funding this remarkable achievement. Profits are expected when the tunnel opens and reaps the tolls from traffic. You have all seen the congestion around London Bridge, so you understand that investing in shares, or even a helpful donation, could benefit all of London. What I ask is that you bring the necessity of funding the tunnel to your husbands' or fathers' notice." With any luck, she'd achieve at least one promise of support today. She blushed upon theorizing what Mr. Drexel would do when she told him of her success. Whatever his response—shake her hand, waltz her around the room, a tender gesture—the thought excited her.

Lady Sarah spoke first. "I fail to understand what the happiness of your sister has to do with Mr. Brunel's tunnel."

Meta feigned a smile. "The situation is a private matter, but I must admit a rather urgent one. So if you would be so kind, please take my word upon the subject."

Several ladies nodded.

"Of course, Meta, dear," said Bethia. "You need not say any more upon the subject."

Clara put down her teacup. "I do agree that something must be done about London Bridge. I myself have been held up by a rabble of not very polite people. Persons of the most disagreeable manners."

"I thought a tunnel had been tried before and failed," stated Sybella, the newest member of the group, who was memorable for her rather daring short, tight spiral curls. "The soil is too damp or loose to build a proper tunnel." Her brows furrowed. "It was several years ago, but I do remember something about it flooding. Can you imagine, the horror of being drowned in a tunnel? Digging under water is clearly a great risk."

"My dear Meta," Clara said, "personally, I must refuse your request at this time. Perhaps we all can come to an agreement that more information is needed before we make such a significant request for funds from our fathers. I can speak for myself when I say that my father feels put upon with each shilling I ask for." She colored slightly. "You must all admit, he has been very generous to our ladies in need."

Most of the women nodded.

Sybella, her dark red hair catching the light from a tall window, stated, "If we donate to the tunnel, it might cause our loved ones not to donate to our governesses. Our ladies would then be in direct competition for funds."

Meta shook her head. "The tunnel is different, because it can be a future investment of your capital." Since her explanations failed to gather her needed support, Meta carefully explained a few of the details of her sister's situation. She expected an empathetic response centered on Lily and James's misunderstanding. But to her disappointment, the ladies only wanted to discuss the field guide.

"That man," Grizel started, then turned to Meta, "is he really a gentleman, my dear? Think of the lack of empathy for womankind a man who could write such a book must possess."

Unfortunately, almost to a lady, they agreed that Mr. Drexel must be a scoundrel toward women.

Meta sighed. They were right, of course. After all, she did not know him well. The naughty innuendo and flirting came to mind first, but he had helped Fitzy and at least tried to right the situation in regard to James. But his behavior could turn unpredictable and contradictory, like all gentlemen's. "The book is a work of fiction solely to amuse gentlemen who frequent places like the Coal Hole. Mr. Drexel is an educated gentleman and a dedicated engineer."

"How did a very proper young man like Mr. Codlington come by the field guide?" Grizel asked.

"Fiction?" asked Bethia. Her gray hair appeared

almost white from the strong sun streaming in from the windows. "Are you sure, Meta? I read the book years ago and thought my initials were in it. To think that someone sixty years of age could be considered 'Eager Out of the Gate.'" She turned to the lady next to her. "Brightened my whole day."

The lady patted her hand. "I understand, dear."

"Yes, it's fiction—truly," Meta said, "and written for the amusement of gentlemen only. Mr. Drexel wrote the book after his friend Lord Boyce Parker, a London publisher, wagered he could not do it, or could not best another man. I know very little of the details, except that he made a significant profit and it proved to be a bestseller." She stopped, curious about why the busy, driven man of today could do something so frivolous. "All young men can be fools. I wonder how old he was at the time?"

"A repulsive book like that," Clara said. "He should've known better. Why he must have had the brains of a mooncalf in leading strings to pen such a scandalous book." As she put her teacup down, it hit the rim of the saucer. Her tea spilled and quickly became a river heading for the lady next to her. "Oh, I do beg your pardon."

"How significant?" Grizel said, ignoring the fuss of spilt tea across the table from her.

"Pardon?" Meta clutched her napkin, eyeing the approaching river of tea.

"The funds," Grizel continued. "How significant are his earnings?"

"I would never dare ask such a question."

The ladies began to speculate widely upon the

profits of the field guide. Their guesses ranged from the equivalent of a new bonnet to funding the King's peccadilloes for a year.

"Think of what we could do with funds like that," said Lady Sarah.

Everyone nodded and spoke to their neighbor.

Meta stood to address them. "Ladies, please, the field guide is not the issue here. Mr. Drexel too, by his profession as an engineer, works to help London's disadvantaged. The tunnel will increase commerce, which means increased employment and less poverty. His profession is building public work projects, like bridges and piers...everything, really. He is currently working on several smaller projects too, one a steam-powered printing press and the other a card shuffler."

Lady Sarah nodded. "Meta does have a point. All of this Mr. Drexel's endeavors will be to society's advantage. I know I certainly wish him well. We could use a card shuffler for our whist parties too." She called in a housemaid to attend to what remained of the spilt tea.

"Oh, I agree, worthy inventions," Clara said, standing and hurriedly wiping up as much of her tea as she could reach before the housemaid entered. "Yet it does not explain why a gentleman wrote such a questionable..." She lowered her voice. "Might I say *vulgar* book? Why doesn't he write a treatise on engineering instead?"

Meta laughed. "Would you purchase such a book? I think we all know the reason: young men need to impress other men."

"Oh, twaddle," Lady Sarah said. "I've seen a copy of his book, and the field guide is not nearly as questionable as some of the books written in the last century. *The Monk*, for example."

Gasps erupted.

"Now that is a questionable book," Lady Sarah continued.

"I may faint." Bethia let her head fall backward slightly.

"I beg to disagree," Clara said, shaking her head and handing her wet, tea-stained napkin to the housemaid. "*The Monk* is lurid, not vulgar. Truly vulgar, filthy, and vile books exist. I found an old book like that in my father's library. The title is *Fanny*…something."

Collective gasps echoed around the room. From the many guilty expressions, clearly most of the ladies knew of the book Clara mentioned, but good manners prevented them from speaking about it.

"What is this Fanny book about?" Sybella asked in all seriousness. "Should we add it to our list of books for discussion?"

Most of the ladies stared at their laps.

"No," Clara said. "Clearly our ancestors must have been wild, uncivilized beings. That book is the most obscene book ever penned."

"Oh dear." Sybella's knitted brows and wrinkled nose spoke of confusion. "You mean it describes"— she lowered her voice to almost a whisper—"*congress* between a man and a woman…in detail?"

"Yes, dear," Lady Sarah said, "and not only in metaphor."

"What do you mean in metaphor?" Sybella tilted her head, appearing like an eager puppy.

"I remember our discussion now," Clara said, her gaze darting around the table. "Authors use metaphorical tricks, secret messages to say something without saying something directly, and this something is a thing that only some people understand."

Blank stares appeared on the faces of several ladies.

Clara tried to clarify the situation. "The metaphor alludes to when a young lady becomes...becomes *fallen*." She lowered her voice to a barely audible whisper. "Carnal knowledge."

The ladies either gasped or giggled.

"Let me explain," Grizel said, turning to Sybella. "When a single man and a woman are destined to be lovers, the author foreshadows this event by..." She too lowered her voice.

All of the ladies around the marble table leaned toward the center to catch her words.

Grizel whispered, "The lady will bleed at some point in the book. A small amount of blood is a metaphor for the blood sometimes found when a virgin becomes *fallen*."

This time more giggles than gasps were heard.

"I remember that now." Bethia smiled, appearing younger than her gray hair implied. "You clever ladies discovered that in all novels of the romantic type, the heroines always bleed in the vicinity of the young man they are destined to wed. Of course, if there is no young man standing about, then it's just bleeding."

Lady Sarah laughed. "Yes, but in a scene with a young, single gentleman nearby, the lady might prick her finger at a picnic or hit her head at the opera—"

"Yes, yes," Clara said. "Young women are extremely clumsy in most three-volume novels and spend a great deal of their daytime hours bleeding all over London and the countryside."

Each lady replied in turn.

"Remember when the young man's horsewhip hit her in the leg?"

"Or the one that tripped over a rake?"

Ten seconds of silence followed.

"An *it* rake and not a *he* rake, of course."

"Of course."

"Obviously."

"We knew that."

"Actually," Clara said, "any poking object is dangerous to virgin ladies with an eligible man nearby."

"Not poke bonnets," Sybella said.

Lady Sarah frowned at Sybella, then placed her hands on the table. "Remember that lurid one we discussed last year, where the lady pricks herself on the gentleman's sword?"

Bethia's eyes widened. "Oh dear, oh dear, I'm going to faint."

"You don't tell people you are going to faint," Grizel said. "You just faint. Otherwise, it's not fainting, it's acting."

"No, it's lounging," one lady corrected.

Bethia appeared quite pleased with herself. "I tell people I'm going to faint, so they will be sure to catch me."

Meta's impatience grew. "If you warn people, it's not fainting, it's purposeful reclining." She checked herself. Her request was too important to lose her temper.

Lady Sarah straightened in her chair. "I firmly believe that one day in the future, women novelists will be able to forgo metaphors and write freely—about any subject—even the subject of amorous congress."

Several gasps were heard.

"If true," Grizel remarked with a certain tinge of northern fatalism, "I think those vulgar books will then mark the end of society as we know it."

"Authorial freedom to that extent will never happen. Too dangerous," Clara remarked.

Several ladies added, "That's true."

"Will never happen."

The newest member of the Learned Ladies leaned over the table and remarked, "I never imagined how amusing a book discussion could be."

"Or how fast they can disintegrate into nonsense," Grizel said.

"Ladies, please," Meta said. "The field guide does not resemble these vulgar books. It's merely satire, an exaggeration of feminine romantic behavior for the amusement of men. Mr. Drexel is a gentleman. His cause is a good one and the tunnel will benefit many. That is the main purpose behind the Learned Ladies Society, is it not? All I request is that you put the matter before your husbands, fathers, or man of business if you are a widow, for their consideration."

"My dear Meta," Lady Sarah said, "from your defense of the man, it sounds to my ears that you are taken by this Mr. Drexel. I wonder—"

"No. I can honestly say that I am not. I doubt he'd make a suitable husband for any woman, since he lacks constancy. Besides, I loved Charles and have no need for another husband. I ask this favor because my sister's reputation and happiness are at stake.

Well, hers and James's. Please, just put the matter before your spouses. That is all I ask. Can I depend on your support?"

The ladies answered in turn. "Yes."

"Of course."

"Yes."

"Yes, indeed, my pleasure."

In total, Meta heard eight affirmations. "You all have my sincerest thanks." She needed to tell Mr. Drexel this news as soon as possible. Perhaps the end of this muddle was within reach.

Grizel spoke last. "I will ask my husband, but I cannot make any promises now, you understand. Hamish must approve first."

Bethia hung her head. "What if he takes it out of my pin money? I did not consider that."

"No, you have no worries on that score," Lady Sarah said. "Your husband loves you dearly and only wants to please you."

Everyone knew of Mr. Valpy's devotion to his wife of forty years, so they all agreed about his dedication to ensuring her happiness.

Bethia generously thanked everyone.

"I speak for every lady here," Grizel pronounced, "when I say that none of us should actually make any promises today. You must give us time to convince our spouses and fathers."

Meta froze. Her good news for Mr. Drexel had evaporated within a minute. She gulped. What else could she do to persuade them?

"I have an idea." Lady Sarah jumped to her feet. "Why don't we all visit the tunnel site together? One of my friends has already done so and considered it remarkable. Maybe we will even meet this Mr. Drexel for ourselves. At the very least, we can determine the size of the operation and the chances for the tunnel's success. We could have a picnic afterwards to discuss our contributions. What do you all say?"

The majority of the members clapped and agreed to the plan.

Meta smiled at the thought of the ladies' reaction when she provided introductions to Mr. Drexel. How would they respond to his charming "bear" expression? Or his conversation that on occasion consisted of a single sly word or vulgar innuendo? She chuckled. Some of her friends might be shocked or offended. Some ladies would laugh. Then again, some of them might fall under his seductive spell the way she had. Or perhaps some ladies, especially Bethia, might act like Lily and flee his presence to hide behind the nearest building.

"Fabulous idea, a picnic," Sybella said. "I'll be delighted to consider the tunnel for investment purposes and to be introduced to this notorious Mr. Drexel in person."

Five

Meta sat in front of a large oaken desk, waiting for the arrival of her man of business, Mr. Cole. Her appointment was for eleven o'clock, but her concern about keeping her promise to Mr. Drexel to obtain at least one new investor propelled her to arrive early. Since none of the ladies had immediately agreed to invest, she decided that if she could afford it, she would buy shares at the tunnel's next offering. Lily and James's future happiness might depend upon it. So she sat and waited, listening to the tall clock chime on the quarter and the coals hiss in the grate.

The numerous papers on Mr. Cole's desk appeared in distinct piles, and his five pens were laid next to each other in an even line. Meta believed the order of a person's writing table reflected the order of their mind. Her orderly desk resembled Mr. Cole's, except for her collection of enamel boxes with painted flowers on the lids, tokens of thanks from her friends for her assistance.

Mr. Drexel's unusual desk by the bow window came to her mind next and the pile of papers and models strewn over every inch of the surface. She did not know him well enough to determine if the disarray was caused by a lack of mental discipline or the natural disorder of an inordinately busy man. Perhaps he needed someone to sort his papers, if his housekeeper failed to do so.

The scent of sandalwood wafted in the air a second before Mr. Cole entered the room. "Good day to you, Mrs. Russell. I am delighted to see you again. How long has it been? A year and a half? I hope all is well with that large family of yours you have taken on." A plump gentleman with quick movements, his blue plaid trousers, coat, and waistcoat all seemed to bounce into the room.

"It's a pleasure to meet you again, sir. Yes, my family is well. Most of my family, as there is no change in my father's condition. However, he is a happy man who does not complain, so I must be satisfied with that."

Mr. Cole took a seat behind his giant desk and donned a pair of gold spectacles too small for his large round face. "Now to what do I owe the pleasure of your company today?"

She removed a folded piece of *The Times* newspaper from her reticule and handed it to him. "Have you heard of the Thames Tunnel?"

Mr. Cole took the piece of newspaper, spread it out on his desk, and carefully read every word. "Well, well, how about that. Very impressive, I must say. How does the construction of this remarkable tunnel affect you, my dear?"

Mr. Drexel came to mind. Not the man who

needed investors for his tunnel, but the memory of his handsome demeanor and physical attractions. Blushing, she turned toward the fire, hoping that the firelight masked her red cheeks. "Without going into great detail, I wish to invest in Mr. Brunel's tunnel. So I came to inquire about the current state of my fortune. Since my late husband trusted you as his man of business, your opinion on the amount of capital I may commit to the project would be invaluable."

He peered at her from over his spectacles. "Mrs. Russell, did you not believe me two years ago when I told you that you need not worry on that score? Your late husband left you well provided for. You have enough capital for all of your wishes."

"Yes, but when we spoke of it before, my only wish was to provide for my family—not to invest in a grand scheme that might be a failure."

He paused. "If I use that criterion then, the loss of the principle, I would advise you to invest no more than five thousand pounds."

"Five thousand! Can I lose that much money and still provide for all of my family members, if necessary? Not to mention providing for myself and funding my charity work for years and years to come?"

"Without a doubt. Your husband had diverse holdings and no new investments have depleted the accounts, so your fortune has escaped all of this current reckless speculation. Within the last year, the shipping investment alone has provided a large amount of new funds. I can assure you without any reservations that you have become a wealthy woman." He nodded.

Her heart lightened with the thought of bestowing

a large donation for the governesses. "Please do not mention my fortune to anyone. I prefer privacy in the matter."

"Of course."

Meta rarely considered her fortune. She knew it was enough to keep her in comfort for her lifetime. Then when she had decided to move back into her family home after her husband's death, Mr. Cole assured her that she had enough funds to benefit every member of her family. She could purchase military commissions for the boys, if they so wished it, and complement her sisters' dowries, so they would be able to marry solely for love. But she never dreamed she would have enough so that five thousand pounds could be considered expendable.

Mr. Cole smiled and removed his spectacles. "I, of course, do not think that any person, regardless of their wealth, should waste five thousand pounds. But if I were you, I would initially invest two thousand pounds. That amount should go a long way to back the project."

"Thank you, Mr. Cole. I will take your advice." She rose and made her farewells.

Before she left the room, Mr. Cole said, "Frankly, with your excellent luck in investments, I would not be surprised if this tunnel paid off handsomely and made you even wealthier."

She turned and smiled at him. "Thank you again. Good day, sir." Standing just outside the closed door, she decided to visit the tunnel next. She could observe Fitzy's situation and see the tunnel for herself. Hopefully, she could keep her planned contribution a secret while she told Mr. Drexel the exciting news of a new contributor. The day was a cold one, but this thought warmed her all the way over the river to the tunnel.

Two hours later, she found herself standing at the tunnel site, overlooking the round pit at least three stories deep. Except this time, at least twice the number of men toiled down on the riverside of the pit. Meta recalled that today was the day the giant shield would start digging its lateral journey of over thirteen hundred feet under the Thames. Of course, the ladderlike structure would probably only move forward several inches by nightfall, but that did not diminish the excitement emanating from the men scurrying around the bottom of the pit.

She became excited too, gifted with a chance to witness London's future—the possibility of roads under the Thames. Then she regained her senses. The tunneling had only started. So whether it would be London's future or a future disaster, nobody knew. Her investment she considered expendable—she could lose it without any deleterious consequences. But Fitzy toiled down in the site too. Her excitement faded, and she resolved to ask Mr. Drexel whether or not he could guarantee her brother's safety.

Despite the day's chilly air and stiff breeze, many of London's citizens lined the bank to witness the progress. Some of the older men mocked each move of the workers in the pit. Someone in the crowd shouted, "Tunneling in the wrong direction, gov? The Thames is over there." The fellow pointed south, in the opposite direction of the river.

By now Meta had recognized Mr. Drexel standing

apart from the workers amongst a group of gentlemen. All of the men were dressed in black, so she assumed it would be difficult to pick him out from the crowd, but that was not the case. First, he was taller than most and possessed a significant build. Moreover, he was easily identified because his hands always seemed to move, gesturing as he spoke or drumming his fingers on a nearby object. Her heartbeat escalated, a most disconcerting event.

From engravings in the newspapers, she recognized the older gentleman next to him as Mr. Marc Brunel, the tunnel's brilliant architect. Several other men gathered around a makeshift table, consulting numerous drawings. Meta concluded these must be the tunnel's engineers. Mr. Drexel appeared to be in a heated argument with a short man puffing on a pipe. The two of them broke away from the group to climb down and examine the front side of the great shield.

The man with the pipe held up a wooden measuring stick and engaged Mr. Drexel in animated conversation.

The boisterous crowd repeated another quip. "Got water on the brain, sirs?"

The laughter and hubbub on the rim of the pit caused Mr. Drexel to glance up. Within seconds, he recognized her amongst the crowd and acknowledged her presence by a slight nod.

That is, he might have acknowledged her. Standing to her left, however, were several beautiful ladies. Perhaps his nod acknowledged one of the lovely brunettes or the short blonde lady instead of her. Since their acquaintance had been short, these ladies were a better choice for the object of his gallantries. Common sense dictated that a gentleman with enough expertise to pen the field guide must be acquainted with a large number of females. Unfortunately, this thought failed to calm her heartbeat.

Glancing at the giant shield again, she saw Fitzy sitting near the miners. He held a large sketchbook and seemed to busy himself drawing the shield in action. She called out and waved. "Fitzy, over here."

Her brother waved, closed his sketchbook, and scampered up the staircase. Within a minute, he stood next to her, his cheeks a full pink, his light brown hair windblown, wearing the happiest expression she had ever seen. "I say, Meta, isn't this the most amazing sight of all time?"

She didn't want to dash his hopes by discussing the risks. "Yes." She discreetly returned her focus on Mr. Drexel toiling below.

Her lack of an enthusiastic reply did not slow Fitzy's eagerness. "I spent the last two hours drawing the action taking place around the shield. I do believe this tunnel will be one of the most important accomplishments made by man. Important enough to become a wonder of the world and remain significant for years and years. And, Meta, I am the artist lucky enough to capture it." He tucked his thumbs into his waistcoat pockets. "Quite a few other fellows are drawing from the top looking down, but I am the only one given access near the great shield. My drawings might become the official record of this outstanding achievement. Think of it, my acceptance into the Royal Academy must be ensured now."

Meta threw her arms around his bony frame and

hugged him. She truly hoped it would be an achievement, but if the previous attempt flooded, why wouldn't this one too? She did not know the details of the new scheme in relation to the old failed one, but sometimes she lacked faith that man could actually build a tunnel under deep water. The premise seemed too ambitious for mere mortals.

Fitzy chatted on about the day's activities, pride animating the tone of his voice.

Ten minutes later, Mr. Drexel started to climb the stairs, two at a time, heading in their direction.

She gulped, straightened her bonnet, and checked that the ribbons had not become tangled from the strong breeze.

He wore an expression identical to Fitzy's, bright-eyed excitement beaming from his tanned face. He held his hands in front of himself, rubbing his palms together. "Delighted to see you again, madam," he said with a slight bow. "Can you believe the public attendance we have here today? I must admit I'm surprised."

"Pleasantly surprised?"

"Decidedly—that is, if our efforts go well." He surveyed the crowd. "Spectators can either be a benefit or a curse. A benefit if they become excited enough to contribute." He inhaled. "Or a curse if we experience some dramatic catastrophe like a water intrusion."

"You mean a leak?"

"Yes, if we experience a significant leak, more than a few silk shoes will suffer and investors may decide the project is too risky. And believe me, we need every shilling."

As he spoke, she surveyed the crowd lining the pit. Even though the day was unseasonably cold, the spectators numbered in the hundreds. Every social class seemed to be represented, from aristocrats to blacksmiths. "Look around you, sir. With the obvious popularity of the tunnel, I suggest you collect a shilling in order to view the site. The additional monies might help the tunnel's bank account remain flush."

He turned and focused those unfathomable dark eyes upon her.

She looked away and stammered, "Ah…well…I really cannot promise significant funds from my idea. I don't know the number of workers, your capital expenditure, the relationship between the funds needed versus total shillings." She stopped babbling, completely irritated with herself for doing so in his presence. After a long pause to regain her composure, spent adjusting the ribbons on her bonnet, she inhaled sharply and faced him again.

Then the most radiant smile she had ever seen broke across his dark face. "Capital idea, madam. Your suggestion is a good one. I will put the matter before Mr. Brunel tonight."

His animated features made him more appealing than she thought possible for a gentleman. Her desire quickly became a raging fire, impossible to extinguish, with its subject fully aware of her condition.

Oh, the mortification.

She turned to face Fitzy.

Her brother repeatedly stepped in place. "The two of you must excuse me. I have to return to my drawings. Meta, I can talk to you at home." Without another word, he ran back to the pit and soon disappeared into the crowd at the bottom.

Mr. Drexel's gaze followed Fitzy's progress. "Tunnel or sister? Smart lad."

"Sir," Meta said, "I do not wish to delay you any more than necessary. I have come today to inform you that I've held up my end of the bargain and obtained—"

"Drexel," shouted the fetching blonde, approaching in the company of the lovely brunettes. "Well met, sir. What fortunate circumstance. We are dying for you to charm…enlighten us with a description of the workings."

Meta had taken a couple of steps back, so as not to seek an introduction or intrude upon the conversation. This movement also gave her time to regain her composure.

The three ladies giggled. The two brunette ladies moved up next to Mr. Drexel and, without hesitation, slipped their arms under his.

The expression on his face resembled a dark cloud rolling in front of the sun. The beaming enthusiasm fled. In its place sat a feigned, well-practiced smile, lifting only one corner of his mouth. He turned to catch her gaze and shook his head.

"After all," one lovely brunette said, "my husband is in the country for two fortnights." She paused. "Did you hear me? Two fortnights. So I have no gentleman to explain the tunnel to me." She flipped a curl over her shoulder.

The blonde lady spoke next. "And my husband is… is…missing."

"Spain," her friend added at the same moment.

"Don't you remember, dear? He's in Spain." She turned to Mr. Drexel. "Yes, that's it. Her husband is missing in Spain."

"Ah, yes, silly me." The blonde nodded her head in an exaggerated up and down. "Spain it is."

Now sporting his wicked smile, Mr. Drexel turned to the third lady. "Let me guess. Your husband has been…transported?"

The lady stared at him for a second, then nodded too. "Transported to Spain. Yes, well, not Spain, but transported, gone, fled. Well, not fled exactly, but gone, missing too."

The blonde wiggled her way to face him directly. "It appears all of our husbands are missing. So we have no gentleman to…show us the tunnel."

The other two ladies nodded vigorously. "Yes, show us."

"Please show us."

"Nothing would please me more than helping to enlighten you ladies." He shook his head and lifted a corner of his mouth. "But perhaps some other day." He stepped aside and held out his hand in Meta's direction.

Meta stepped forward.

"Ladies, allow me to introduce Mrs. Russell."

The ladies exchanged curtsies.

"Mrs. Russell and I have private business to discuss regarding potential investors for the tunnel. So unless you too have acquaintances or missing husbands willing to invest…"

The three ladies glanced at each other and shook their heads.

"If not, I must beg your pardon today. Perhaps we may meet again at the Cornish's ball in three weeks." After a bow and a feigned smile, he held his arm out for Meta. "Madam."

All three ladies appeared crestfallen, their gazes downcast.

One audibly sighed. "Farewell."

"Yes, farewell then."

"We must meet again soon."

"Yes, soon."

"Before our husbands are found."

All three ladies tittered, while two hid their grins with their fans.

Meta placed her arm on his and felt the hard muscle lying just below the serviceable wool sleeve. Together they strolled down the block looking for a suitable place for a private conversation. They turned the corner and stood in front of piles of white tiles used to line the tunnel's walls.

Mr. Drexel carefully pulled several tiles free from under the others, brushed off any dirt on the edges, and assembled a small, stable place for them to sit. He held out his hand. "Madam, please take a seat." He glanced around. "Yes, this will do, very private. Now I can at least hear you without that clamoring noise."

She grinned. "I disagree; all three ladies had very sweet voices."

"I meant…" The smile that gradually crept across his face marked his realization of her jest.

She laughed. "As I was saying, I do not wish to delay you on this important day. I have held up my end of the bargain and have obtained an investor. At the present time, the person wishes to invest capital in the amount of two thousand pounds."

He raised his brows. "Capital." He grinned.

She stifled a small chuckle. "Yes, capital."

He glanced upward and laughed.

"So now you must hold up your end of the bargain and speak—in person—to James Codlington. The young gentleman who called off his engagement with my sister because he mistakenly believed her initials appeared in your field guide."

He frowned and tapped his fingers on his knee.

"Remember, you have another good reason to pay a call on James," she said. "Once this muddle is resolved, a possible threat to your reputation will end too."

"Right, tell me, exactly which category did your sister appear under? It must have been a notorious one to cause this young man to call off. Did this James believe your sister was under Widow Makers Tied Up?"

She blinked several times. "No, no, he believed her initials were under Happy Goer, and that is bad enough. Frankly, I am not sure I don't blame him. I'm sure this book of yours has caused plenty of turmoil, and perhaps many ladies feel misused."

"I've never misused a lady."

She tried to frown or give him a witty set-down, but she could not hold a serious expression—even if she tried. The worst part of it was that he *knew* she couldn't keep a straight face.

Appearing absolutely roguish, he winked.

She expected further teasing or outrageous flirting,

so she resolved to get his interview over with. "Now that you have one new investor—"

He picked up her gloved hand and held it in his large palm. "Thank you. Now is this new investor someone I know?"

Her heartbeat galloped. *Would it appear rude if she pulled her hand away?* Since she still considered him a relative stranger, she decided to keep her participation in regard to the tunnel a secret. "Let's just say the investor wishes to remain anonymous. The identity of this person is irrelevant. What *is* relevant is that you stop evading the subject and agree to call upon James."

"How do I know the funds are real and you are telling the truth?"

"What!"

"Perhaps this *investor* does not exist. You expect me to make a fool of myself in front of this Codlington fellow. Then you claim your new investor decided against a contribution at the last minute. All in the name of revenge upon me for your sister's difficulties." His fingers beat upon his thigh in rippled waves. "Sounds plausible."

"Really, sir, I must object."

He scooted several inches toward her, until his thigh and arm touched hers. Then he whispered in her ear, "Confess."

Now her heartbeat careened out of control. She leaned back to put distance between them. "Confession implies something is a crime or wrongdoing. I have done neither, so I have nothing to confess."

He placed his arm around her shoulders and pulled her closer. "Calm yourself. You misunderstand me.

The word 'confess' can mean you are merely reluctant to admit to something. Embarrassment perhaps, from telling a tall tale."

"Sir, once again I must object." Her cheeks burned. "I have never told—"

"Right, my talent of understanding females has not failed me. You really are in the field guide under Rabbit."

She experienced a sudden urge to push him off the pile of tiles. "Yes, watch me hop away." She stood. "I'm sorry I ever—"

"I cannot think of anything that would give me more pleasure than to witness you hop. Do you have a fluffy tail?" He swiftly peered in the direction of her backside.

She whipped around to stare at him, knowing full well she should be affronted. Thirty seconds later, they exchanged smiles and burst out in whoops of laughter.

He stood too and held out his hand. "After bestowing upon me that delightful sight, I will repay your efforts by joining you to speak to this Clod—Codlington. No promises, understand? He is a gentleman and there is a line that all gentlemen will not cross in discussing personal affairs. So no promises and no—"

Shouts and screams were heard from the crowd just around the corner. A mighty whistle cut through the air, drowning out every other noise.

Mr. Drexel grabbed her hand and almost pulled it off as he led her to the viewing area.

Down in the pit, most of the men gathered around the great shield, while a bucket brigade had formed leading up the staircase, hurriedly passing buckets of water hand to hand.

"Mr. Broadsham," Mr. Drexel yelled down to the pit. "Up here this instant."

Meta watched Fitzy turn and comprehend Mr. Drexel's orders. He glanced wistfully at the bucket brigade and then climbed up the steps.

When Fitzy reached them, Meta rushed forward to embrace him. "Never go down there again. Please, I'm frightened. The risk is too great."

Fitzy pulled himself free. "Naw." He straightened and approached Mr. Drexel like he was the man's adjutant. "Don't worry, sir, it's a small leak. The straw will stop it. I'm sure I can be of use on the brigade. May I join them?" He glanced back at the commotion in the pit, eagerly waiting for permission to descend.

"You are needed up here, Broadsham, to take care of your sister. This accident has upset her to such an extent, she is hopping around like a rabbit. You must see she gets home safely. Understand?"

Fitzy sighed and with a final glance at the pit, walked toward the family's carriage.

"Mrs. Russell," George said, "my attentions are needed elsewhere, but first let me escort you back to your carriage." He held out his arm.

She placed her hand on his arm and they started back to her carriage.

They walked in silence for a minute and then turned the corner onto an isolated side street.

He stopped and glanced around him. "I must also thank you for finding us a new investor." He then swooped down to kiss her lightly on the cheek.

Caught by surprise, she embarrassed herself and muddled the situation by placing her gloved palm briefly on his cheek the same moment his firm lips touched hers.

He stilled.

Her hand still remained on his cheek and their lips remained an inch apart.

Sharing an awkward pause, the seconds ticked by.

A whistle blew in the distance.

She gathered what remained of her wits. Their glances met, causing her to inhale sharply and pull away.

Why did her heartbeat race so?

He winked again.

She glanced at her half boots. *Heavens.* Her blood raced through her veins faster than the winning horse at Ascot.

He took a step closer, almost touching her with his broad torso, his glance one of masculine intimacy. "Madam, this is an emergency. This leak could cost us thousands. Please do not paw me now."

"I'm not—"

"Good day, madam." Sporting his wicked grin, he spun and ran toward the staircase. "The Thames must be stopped."

Six

Damn the woman.

At their arranged meeting a week later, George turned the corner and saw that infernal Russell woman standing on the steps of a London town house grand enough to take up half of the north side of a prominent square.

Mrs. Russell, a rather fetching, petite woman, smiled and waved as he approached.

He readily admired her steadfast willingness to "help." Even when he responded with the full bear treatment, she retained her wit and courage—irresistible traits in a female. Irresistible enough that it led to the moment when he impulsively kissed her cheek. She had surprised him by not pulling away or feigning offense. No, clearly the widow enjoyed being kissed. Today, however, the meddlesome female deserved the bear treatment for hauling a gentleman out of his study, away from important work, just to testify before some Romeo who got cold feet at the thought of his upcoming leg shackle.

"Good day, Mr. Drexel."

"Humph."

"I am delighted that you appear to be your normal self today." She held out her hand.

Feeling guilty about his grumpiness, but not enough to apologize, he took her hand and gave the smallest of bows. "Likewise."

She paused and examined his countenance, most likely trying to determine if she should apologize too. "The normal bear and rabbit. All is in proper order in the animal kingdom." She gave him a coy smile instead.

"Humph, if it were in proper order, the bear would've eaten the rabbit by now."

"Oh no, rabbits run much faster than bears," she beamed.

Upon her smile, George realized she was quite the stunner. Her walking dress appeared to be of expensive, shiny bronze fabric, and her bonnet was all the crack, covered in ribbons and fruit thingamabobs. All of these attractions were nothing more than a fine setting for the most intense blue eyes he had ever seen, their intensity no doubt highlighted by the contrast to her dark hair. Her expression too bespoke of her personal desire to attend to his welfare. This resulted in an urge to lure her to his cave and pleasure her until she begged for more—a thought that caused his body to stir, an inappropriate event for an afternoon call. So he hibernated the bear for the time being and sighed. "Yes, I am delighted to see you too, Mrs. Russell. You are looking togged out to the nines this morning."

Ready compliments must have been rare for her, because this one left her quite unsettled. "Thank you…ah…and…thank you for agreeing to clear up this confusion about the field guide with James. This interview should not take long. Once you explain the simple misunderstanding, he will admit his mistake—"

"Ha."

"Then you can plead—"

"Ha."

She stiffened her spine. "Plead for him to resume his addresses to Lily."

George admitted to himself that he found her more attractive than most women. This morning she really did resemble an innocent rabbit: bright blue eyes and a spencer trimmed in soft fur. But the woman must have gone stark raving mad. She belonged in Bedlam. "May I ask you a private question?" He gave her a brief pause to respond.

She batted her eyelids in confusion.

He softened his tone. "How many years were you married?"

She stepped backward, almost a hop. "I don't understand."

"Yes, I know. That is my point."

She shook her head. "I married at eighteen years of age and lost my husband sixteen months later. While we had only a short time together, I can assure you that we were as close as any husband and wife."

He bowed his condolences. "I was right then. You have little experience with men."

She huffed.

"You just mentioned," he said, eager to correct her error, "this James Codlington would admit to his mistake. A gentleman—*admit*—a mistake. Gentlemen rarely admit mistakes. I never do. And lastly, you are under the false impression that I am going to *plead* with another gentleman concerning his choice of a wife. The fact that you believe gentlemen admit mistakes and plead with other men about their lovers leaves me convinced that you know very little about men."

"Don't tell me that instead of clearing up this meddle of your making, you are going to stand fixed, like the proverbial suit of armor—no—the proverbial stuffed *bear*, and not say a word?"

"Of course not. I am grateful for your effort to discover new investors for the tunnel. Therefore, I will do my best to clarify the situation. I will explain… *explain* that Miss Broadsham's name is not in the field guide, that I never had the pleasure of meeting Miss Broadsham, and that he must take my word as a gentleman. This simple explanation should be enough for any man." He nodded once and pulled the doorbell.

She glared at him.

He chuckled, knowing full well that if she were a rabbit, her little pink nose would be moving up and down rapidly. He laughed aloud at her pursed-lipped reticence and decided that of all the rabbits he knew, Mrs. Russell was his new favorite. When younger, he would've set the fetching widow within his sights, her seduction guaranteed. But today the thrill of the chase seemed boring and dissolute in comparison to the excitement of building England's iron future. He had even failed to visit his longtime mistress for several months now. He wondered if dear Lydia would be offended by his time away from her bed, or if she would even welcome him for an

evening visit. "Madam, you will do me the courtesy
of letting me speak."

Mrs. Russell finally smiled and shook her head.
"You are *unbearable*."

He laughed. "No, I am just a very busy gentleman."
Of course, he really should thank her for the opportunity to right the misunderstanding created by his field
guide. After all, if the Codlington match failed, the
rumors of his involvement could expand, become out
of control, and stain his reputation even more. But he'd
save his gratitude for a later date, if at all. Right now
he needed to save his breath for this wayward Romeo,
since there was only so much talking a man could do in
one day. "Let's get this interview over with. Then you
and your sister can return to your reason for living—
planning a wedding—while this James can purchase leg
shackles and resume fawning over your sister."

She marched up beside him. "Indeed."

Minutes later, they were shown into the library.

One glance around the room, and he became
fixed on the jovilabe orrery in the center of a large
mahogany table. Made of gleaming brass, except for
the precious stones of Jupiter and its moons, the small
gears for each moon grabbed his complete attention.
He first examined the moon closest to Jupiter, the one
with the shortest orbit, in hopes of detecting the gear
movement. A minute later, he thought he might have
seen the gear turn forward, if only slightly.

He glanced up to find her standing directly across
from him, wearing that ravishing smile that changed
his thoughts away from the orrery to something more
intimate. "Do you admire machinery, Mrs. Russell?"

"Oh yes, not only for its beauty, of which this orrery is an excellent example, but for the skill and knowledge acquired to construct such a machine."

Her enthusiasm created a desire to give her an all-encompassing hug, leading to something much more. He struggled to suppress these annoying wayward thoughts. "I see we have something in common—the appreciation of machines. I'm impressed."

She gave him a slight nod.

Mr. James Codlington walked into the library and welcomed his guests.

Codlington impressed him as a drumble sort of fellow, a man suited to waste away his life as a civil servant or in government. "I say, Codlington, this orrery is magnificent. Can you tell me about the gears? Are they accurate, so that each moon rotates at the right speed in relation to the other moons?"

His host appeared pleased by the compliment. "You must have experience with these machines, I see, Mr. Drexel. Unfortunately, the answer is no. The outer moons rotate too fast, but it takes a trained eye to observe the flaw."

They spent the next twenty minutes discussing all varieties of gears and clock mechanisms before the conversation naturally turned to the tunnel.

Mrs. Russell returned to her seat, and for the first time in his experience, remained perfectly quiet.

Exceptionally wise woman.

By the time tea arrived, he and Codlington had a passing respect for the each other's knowledge in relation to engineering. Codlington was not the dull sort of cove he initially thought, but the sort of man who does not show well the first time in the ring. He gulped half a cup of the strong heather-scented brew to fortify himself. Best to get this over with.

His favorite rabbit eyed him with a fixed stare and nodded.

"Right," he began. "Now, Codlington, I'm here today to clear up a point of confusion I created unbeknownst to me. My field guide, you understand, is nothing more than popular fiction. A book to amuse gentlemen like us, sophisticated, town gentlemen desirous of a good laugh or two." He winked.

Mrs. Russell cleared her throat.

"As I was saying, the initials L. B. in the field guide do not refer to Miss Broadsham's. I have recently had the pleasure of meeting Miss Broadsham for the first time and she, in no way, resembles a Happy Go…"

Mrs. Russell's eyes widened to the size of the orrery's Jupiter. "Mr. Drexel did not mean—"

"Excuse me," he continued, "Miss Broadsham is a happy…*person*, but not at all happy in the way presented in the field guide." *Damnation*. He had just made a perfect hash of that explanation.

In stunned silence, Mrs. Russell poured everyone another cup of tea.

"Right. The thing is, Codlington, Miss Broadsham is not in the field guide, so there should be no impediment for you to resume your addresses." *He stated the facts; promise met*. Eager to exit this stage of masculine mortification, he shifted forward in his chair.

"Are you sure?" asked Codlington.

"I am the author."

"I see." The young man took a minute to leisurely

sip his tea. "I apologize for taking your time away from the tunnel." He frowned in the direction of Mrs. Russell. "You must understand. I've been…advised that my living will be cut off, unless I wed a wife my mother feels will be respectable beyond reproach."

A situation George understood well. He possessed a sufficient living to keep himself in the manner of a gentleman after his parents' death. However, he might need additional capital for his engineering proposals. Or just to remain solvent, if one of his projects failed to reach the expected profits or an invention was stolen.

Codlington addressed Mrs. Russell. "I must marry a wife suitable for a lawyer with aspirations for the highest office in court. Right now, I suffer from conflicting obligations, and I don't know what to do. Please understand, Meta."

"You mean you hope *Lily* understands," she said. "James, you are aware that Lily has a…significant dowry? Greater than even she is aware of."

George wondered about the exact amount. Perhaps he should make addresses to Miss Broadsham, if this James fellow withdrew his cards from the game.

Mrs. Russell spoke in the well-practiced, irritating tone of a wronged female. "How could you be so unfeeling as to endanger her reputation?"

George stifled an urge to flee the room.

Their host did not reply; he seemed to be considering the situation. He closed his eyes and tilted his head down. "A member of my club asked me if the initials were Lily's—asked me directly, to my face."

She ignored the man's distress. "How can you break her heart?"

Feminine manipulations depending heavily upon guilt did not surprise him. Time to set the matter to rights and move on. "I believe you missed my point, Codlington. Miss Broadsham is *not* in my field guide, so there could never be any scandal attached to the young lady. Moreover, I will do everything within my power to make sure those initials are removed from any second edition. I promise."

Codlington nodded. "I have been at court for only a short time, but from what I have observed, the facts seldom matter in regard to public gossip." He glanced up and sighed. "I believe you, sir, but I still believe her initials in a second edition will start a scandal, regardless of the veracity. And it might be even worse if her initials are removed altogether. People are clever and will notice. Then all sorts of speculation will arise about why they were removed." He shook his head. "Whatever actions we take, I'm sure they will be misrepresented in the newspapers too, because people enjoy that sort of thing. They thrive on the latest *on dits*. Consider my circumstances. I cannot take that risk."

"Right." Like a great number of men, he and Codlington were in the same boat. "You must retain a spotless reputation to gain support of the superiors in your profession, a situation I know all too well." If Mrs. Russell's mawkish pleadings to spare her sister's heart failed to change his mind, perhaps a reverse tactic on this reluctant Romeo might work. It was worth a try. "If I were a lawyer with higher aspirations, I certainly would not wed a sweet, young wife like Miss Broadsham. I compliment you, Codlington. What did you have in mind? Some ol' harridan, plush in the pocket, to organize your life to the minute, who would be a skilled conversationalist around lawyers." He turned toward Mrs. Russell and gave her a quelling look. Her eyes widened, and since she was no slow top, he felt confident she would not muddle the situation.

"Well," James said, "I would not go that far—"

George caught Codlington's gaze and then nodded his head sideways in the direction of Mrs. Russell. "I'm sure Mrs. Russell will forgive us for speaking in the common language of men."

Thankfully, she remained silent—a probable first.

George's confidence in the eventual success of his scheme grew. "A gentleman with ambitions like yours needs a skilled wife, skilled in Polite Society, skilled at handling the politics of the Court of the Common Pleas. Am I right?"

"Well, it never hurts to—"

"Mrs. Russell, once again I must apologize for my vulgarity, but as you are a widow, I consider you a woman of superior understanding. The subject of a wife is an important one to gentlemen like Codlington and myself. I too have no need for a beautiful, sweet wife that would never nag a fellow. A gentleman can always satisfy his desires for that elsewhere."

She choked on a sip of tea.

"I would never—" Their host straightened.

"We both need a plain wife that will further assist our advancement. A hostess with expertise at seducing any gentleman to open his purse or advance her husband's career. Of course, it goes without saying that she must have a flawless reputation. Therefore, all intelligent, beautiful women with these skills cannot be trusted." He turned to address James in a sham lowered voice. "Likely a rake or two in her past, I dare say. That means you must search London's older—and beg pardon—uglier widows. Then there would be no doubt whatsoever of a scandalous past."

Mrs. Russell hiccuped.

George didn't even glance in her direction. "I too will marry for wealth. Love has nothing to do with a choice of wife, not in the least. If I were you, Codlington, I too would take the easy route and not stand up to my mother. Standing up to Mater is serious business for a son. What is the importance of a lifetime of love anyway? Success in one's profession wins over romance every time."

Codlington narrowed his eyes, but George could not determine if his hard stare was a fulminating one, expressing protest over his indelicate feelings, or a censorious one, expressing condemnation over his vulgarity.

Codlington strode over to the orrery and stared at a small moon.

George winked at Mrs. Russell. Her expression did not change, a sign she must be aware of his intentions to goad this reluctant Romeo into action. His plan might work. Codlington may indeed have the stuff to defy his mother. But to wager it all on romantic love? An impressive gesture, but thankfully, a wager he would never have to take.

Much to her credit, Mrs. Russell continued to remain silent.

He appreciated her reticence, but her expression of

tight-lipped disapproval left him uneasy, like the sight of black clouds on the horizon.

James finally walked over and took the woman's hand. "I apologize, Meta, but I have an appointment to keep in court, so I must be on my way. Mr. Drexel—I beg pardon—seems to lack a loving heart. Upon reflection, my decision to end my engagement to your amiable sister was a hasty one. I shall pay a call on her as soon as possible to resume my addresses, because I truly do love her. I'm confident that because of her sweet temperament, she will forgive me."

Mrs. Russell hopped out of her chair. "Thank you, dear James. I know Lily will be delighted." She grabbed both of his hands and gave him a brotherly kiss on the cheek. Then the two of them stood there beaming like idiots.

The young lawyer exhaled. "Do you know, I feel quite restored. I never realized how worried—couldn't eat. I truly believed I'd never be happy again. Now we can move forward and finally announce the engagement as if nothing had interfered." He turned to address George and frowned. "Obviously, Mr. Drexel here is ignorant of the benefits of a loving spouse."

Mrs. Russell smirked. "I must agree with you on that point."

"Humph." They were right, of course, but he failed to see how it was his concern that this young Romeo decided to risk it all for the love of some schoolroom chit.

"Tell Lily," James said, "that I apologize for my hasty decision to end our understanding. Tell her to expect me to call tomorrow. I cannot wait for this incident to be behind us, so we can contemplate our happy future instead."

"Yes, yes." She turned and approached him. "Thank you, Mr. Drexel. Let's be on our way."

After their farewells to Codlington, he offered to escort Mrs. Russell the few blocks to her house, and she took his arm. He whistled as they strolled. He could not remember being this happy in a long time. Upon entering the field of battle with her James, he withdrew the victor. The pressure on him eased, and he felt vindicated. He glanced down at Mrs. Russell and recognized his renewed desire to kiss her senseless or make love until she cried out his name.

She walked straight ahead and remained silent.

He swelled with pride at his great victory, made even sweeter because Mrs. Russell had witnessed it. From now on, whenever their paths crossed, she would remember he was the man who triumphed over this Codlington. With any luck, she'd remember to thank him every time they met. But then he realized that Lily would now accept her suitor, so his acquaintance with Mrs. Russell would likely end. After all, he had no real reason to see the woman again. A disappointing fact, since he'd be sorry to see the backside of his favorite rabbit.

She spoke first. "That went well."

He burst out laughing. "I agree. The question is, for whom?"

Seven

META GLARED AT HIS FLIPPANT REMARK AND REMAINED silent as they strolled to Broadsham House.

Meanwhile, Mr. Drexel whistled and almost skipped, his heels lightly tapping on the stone pathway. Looking for all the world like a man who just won every hand at whist.

What did he mean when he said it went well for whom?

It went well for everyone, surely? James summoned the courage to defy his mother's wishes, admit his mistake, and marry the woman he loved. He would apologize to Lily, while her sister must overcome her resentment of being jilted. Together the couple would announce their engagement in the immediate future. Meta did not see any other possible outcome. All this field guide twaddle would be forgotten and life would return to normal. A life without the Drexels, she supposed, unsure of her feelings upon the matter.

A block away from Dover Street, they passed an entrance to a block of mews.

"Come," Mr. Drexel said, glancing both ways. "Shortcut."

She stopped and shook her head. "No, this leads to—"

He gently pulled her several feet into the mews, so they were hidden from any foot traffic on Hay Hill. "Mrs. Russell, you held your tongue. What an exceptional, brilliant female!" He lifted her off the ground and spun her around and around and around.

Finding herself in a dizzying whirl, she tried to focus on the dark blue wool on the top of his shoulder. For at least a minute, all she could see was a hazy mixture of brick wall and navy coat. "Put me down. Someone will see us. Have you gone mad?" Her heartbeat escalated and she clung to his broad shoulders.

Without any apparent effort, he flipped her sideways.

She found herself carried in his capable arms. Glancing at his face, she discovered a very self-satisfied smile. "What was that about?"

"Well?"

Still dizzy, she could only manage. "Well?"

"Right." He lowered his head and kissed her square on the mouth.

Caught by surprise, she balled her fist to pound him on the chest. Only she failed to do so. She neither lifted her head away nor struggled to get out of his arms.

Astonishing.

Deciding not to worry about it overmuch, she blamed her lack of response on his remarkable attraction and gave herself the freedom to relish the intoxicating moment, nothing more than pure pleasure. She forgot everything else and dissolved in the blissful feelings of his warm lips caressing hers in the traditional dance that stoked the inner fires of pleasure.

He stopped and lifted his head, the wicked smile firmly planted on his lips.

Thoroughly charmed and utterly surprised from the sensual delight of kissing a handsome, powerful man, she was not quite ready to stop. Desiring him to continue, she twisted slightly, then kissed him full on the lips.

Her unspoken desire was clearly a language he spoke fluently. He righted her, lifted her a foot higher, and then pressed her against the brick wall. His firm body provided support, while he cupped his hand behind her head to protect her from the rough stone.

He surged forward to grant her wishes and kissed her again in a deep, erotic, and altogether naughty kiss. The movement of the kiss soon escalated without control, a crescendo of gasping for breaths in between the fluid caresses of wet lips and tongues. The flared passion eventually melted until their kisses became an extended, languid moment of thoughtless bliss.

A feeling she missed.

Her fleeting pleasure ended when she heard the clacking sounds from the wheels of an approaching carriage.

A curricle came into view and drove toward them.

Mr. Drexel concealed her with his figure as best he could, providing anonymity by holding his hat several inches in front of her face. As a result, the curricle driver would suspect nothing more than lovers stealing a kiss and would be unable to identify her.

The minute she spent incognito, listening to the wheels clanging on the cobblestones, brought her back to reality and the impropriety of her situation. She watched his intense desires smoldering within his gaze as the sound of the carriage faded into the distance. This interruption allowed her to regain her fortitude, so she pushed his shoulder hard. "Put me down now."

He stilled; only his chest moved from his rapid breathing.

"Please."

Following a nod, he gently lowered her feet to the ground and steadied her until she could stand by herself.

She righted her crooked spencer and brushed her skirt into some order.

The wicked smile grew. "Well?"

She could play his monosyllabic, single word game too. "What?"

"My performance?"

"Pardon?" She immediately flushed. Did he expect her to comment upon the kiss—in words? She quickly passed off the event as sudden excitement or irresistible physical attraction or a mixture of both. A fleeting, stolen moment, unimportant, and never to be repeated. The sort of behavior normal for a man with Mr. Drexel's reputation, but not a common situation for her. She certainly would never put herself in a position of instigating a kiss again. In the future, she must summon up her personal will and not succumb to the potent allure of an all too attractive, well-practiced rake. Any stain on her reputation could affect her sister's chances of making a respectable match and damage the future of all of her siblings. She must do her best to remember that her family's welfare came before hers.

Ah, but she gained so much pleasure from his kisses.

"Madam, your blush gives you away. By performance, I did not mean my stunning and exemplary technique during our celebratory kiss. I meant my clever scheme to show your James the error of his ways. I didn't know if it would work, mind you. But it did! Spectacularly too. And you! You, madam, remained…mostly silent. Imagine a woman who knows when to hold her tongue. I am honored, Mrs. Russell." He gazed at her with a fierce appreciation in his dark eyes.

While she now realized his motivation had been one of blowing off steam and celebration, she ached to kiss him again. Her continued forwardness utterly shocked her.

What was wrong with her? Had she gone mad?

Unfortunately, her rapid breaths still caused her chest to rise and fall, enough for him to notice, so she tried to divert him. "You *can* string more than one word…"

He stepped closer.

"Word together." She recognized the eminent danger of seduction—another kiss likely foremost in his mind. A gesture of no worth, other than cheap excitement for them both.

Standing imperiously over her, he too was breathing fast.

She summoned what remained of her strength of character and pushed him back. "Indeed, you were articulate and splendid." She stepped back farther. "Quite the performance. I can see why you are so thrilled. But it is time for me to return home." She caught his gaze. "Understand?"

He paused, then squinted. "Right."

She chuckled.

"Very well, madam. It's time for my favorite Lepus to expose her fluffy white tail as she hops on home." He tilted his head, as if to catch sight of her backside when she started walking.

She stood fixed and held out her hand in an obvious motion for him to go first, denying him a chance view of her backside. "After you, sir."

He chuckled. "Very well." He presented his arm.

She placed her hand on his broad arm and, without meaning to, she caught a glimpse of *his* backside—a very attractive one indeed. Shocked by her forward behavior, a pot of tea was needed to recover her wits. "While your tactic to change James's mind was risky," she said, "I do admire its success. I cannot thank you enough for your effort." She glanced up and smiled at him. "You must now realize that pleading your case on the basis of stirring up strong emotions can be successful?"

"Humph."

When they reached the front door of Broadsham House, she turned to bid Mr. Drexel farewell but was interrupted when Fitzy threw open the door.

"Drexel! It *is* you. I saw you walk by the window and thought what perfect timing. Well met, sir. Come on in." He held the door open.

Mr. Drexel hesitated.

"Has luncheon been served?" she asked Fitzy. She focused on pulling off her kerseymere gloves, instead of Mr. Drexel's wide-eyed expression.

"Not yet," Fitzy said. "We were waiting for you to

return. So you see Drexel, you must dine with us. I want to hear all the latest engineering difficulties at the tunnel. That Mr. Marc Brunel is a remarkable man. Please say yes. I would love to hear all about him, and your work too, of course."

Meta hoped he would stay for the midday meal. She was curious to understand the reasons behind his questionable speech about gentlemen marrying rich, ugly wives. How did he know this tactic of describing an imaginary future wife would prove successful with James? Was it solely to motivate James, or was there some personal truth to his words?

Mr. Drexel peered up the street, no doubt formulating a good excuse for taking his leave.

Meta hoped he would agree, for Fitzy's sake, so she whispered to him, "You need not worry. There will be no emotional scenes to make you uncomfortable."

"I don't avoid emotions, in a proper context, just nonsensical conversations about feelings with females."

"Eww, I agree," Fitzy said, joining the male side of the argument. "But please, Drexel, I'd like to show you a wood model I have completed. It is an exact replica of the great shield now tunneling under the Thames. I do believe you will be impressed."

Mr. Drexel focused those wide brown eyes on her, a clear unspoken plea for her intervention. Perhaps for her to devise an excuse for him to leave, which would not hurt Fitzy's feelings.

She wanted him to stay. It would present her with a chance to thank him properly for speaking to James without the interruption of a kiss, so she repeated her brother's invitation.

He sighed and removed his beaver hat. "I must not remain long. How many mewling infants did you say reside under this roof?" He sounded like he expected her siblings to bite him on the ankles.

"Not a single infant. My youngest brother, Tom, is just eight." She smiled and gently pulled him into the vestibule. "The meal will be short, not a grand repast. I promise."

He stared down at her hand clinching his arm. "Very well."

She jerked her hand back, then masked the embarrassment created by her improper touch by asking the butler to inform Cook that luncheon should be served in fifteen minutes.

"Weee!" Tom shouted, flying down the stairs, his little knees pumping away.

Mr. Drexel stepped back and stood full against the wall.

Her brother ran past both of them without a flicker of recognition.

"Tom!" she shouted, but her brother continued to run. "Thomas!" She took a rushed step forward to pursue him, but stopped. By now her brother had run downstairs and out of sight too fast for her to catch him. "That was my youngest brother, Tom."

"Clearly your resident infant."

She grinned. "You have a point." She then led Mr. Drexel to the small schoolroom at the back of the house, near the mews. Fitzy's wooden model of the great shield rested on one of the oak tables in the sunny white room.

Fitzy could barely contain himself. His rapid

description of this model came out so fast; no sane individual could comprehend him. All they heard were mumbled words like "iron," "brick," "water," and repeated "Brunel," "genius," "Brunel," "genius."

"Slow down," she said. "We cannot understand you."

A blush crept up from under his high collar and stained his cheeks. "Oh, I am sorry, sir. But I needn't explain a thing to you, obviously. What do you think of my model? It's a first attempt, so I don't expect it to be up to professional standards. But I am pleased with it, and Meta said it was very fine." He clutched his hands together, anticipating Mr. Drexel's response.

She hoped their guest would not be too hard on an eager beginner.

Mr. Drexel went through the motions of examining the model carefully. He then straightened. "You are correct in that the initial drawings indicated hydraulic screws, but they proved to be too costly. At present, we employ hand screws to move the poling boards forward once the dirt is removed. Other than that one small detail, your model is a perfect rendition. You are quite justified in being pleased with it. Well done."

Meta could have kissed him right then in front of everyone, an irritating urge that unsettled her completely and left her cheeks blazing.

Thankfully, no one noticed her red cheeks, because Fitzy held everyone's attention by gushing about his achievement. "I'm pleased to hear I got the details right." He glanced down. "Except for the very small one about the hydraulics. It is the details that are important in capturing the essence of an engineering design. Isn't it, sir?"

"Yes," Mr. Drexel said, "nothing else matters. Some argue that the drawings must be pleasing to the eye, but for me the details must be scrupulously correct. Great effort must go into it to make sure of this. It is the rendering of details that separates a good draftsman from a brilliant one."

He turned and caught sight of her blush.

Fitzy continued without pause. "I plan to cast one of the great bolts in plaster too. While some may consider it just a bolt, the sheer size, intricacies, and the use in some magnificent construction move my emotions. So for those very reasons, I believe they are true art. I cannot wait to show you my results."

Mr. Drexel grinned, placed his hand on Fitzy's shoulder, and caught her gaze. "Me too."

She silently thanked him with a smile.

He gave her a wink. A simple gesture, yet accompanied by an expression of ardor that made it wicked.

Luncheon was announced and the entire family gathered around the dining table. The light meal of cheeses, fresh bread, and a cold game pie provided plenty to eat for the family and their unexpected guest.

Tom spent his time stabbing a toasted piece of bread with his fork, despite Meta's direct admonition not to do so.

Susanna, age fourteen years, ignored her meal. Instead, she seemed to be either fascinated or frightened by Mr. Drexel, taking turns from blatant stares to looking like she wished to flee at the drop of a spoon.

Meta understood Susanna's apprehension. Mr. Drexel's dark countenance, extraordinary height, and nervous hands did not resemble any gentleman her sister had encountered before at home. He repeatedly tapped the table with one forefinger, a motion that Susanna eyed with some suspicion.

During the meal, Mr. Drexel answered all of Fitzy's questions with great patience, a somewhat surprising event due to his earlier hesitation to accept the family's invitation to dine.

"What is your exact title on the tunnel project, sir?" Fitzy asked. "Is it engineer? There seem to be many engineers at work every day. What exactly do you do at the site?"

"Right now I am a temporary engineer, one of Mr. Brunel's assistants. There are probably three of us performing the same job when needed. Of course, Mr. Brunel trusts his son, Isambard, and rightfully so. He works tirelessly and rarely gets more than four hours of sleep. He truly is a remarkable man. My current ambition is to join Isambard and be promoted to one of the resident engineers. If I'm successful, it will provide additional opportunities to meet influential men who can advance my career as an architect of public works. But of course, if that comes to pass, I will be spending much more time at the site than I do now." He gave her a brief grin.

Then the oddest thing happened. When she caught sight of his grin, electricity shot through her, or at least what she expected electricity felt like. A sudden jolt, not painful, but rendering her keenly aware of being alive. She shook her head. Had other women felt this too in his presence? Was this electricity the reason he proved irresistible to all females? She reconsidered her extreme response and refused to believe it meant anything significant, other than overwhelming gratitude for his efforts on behalf of her beloved siblings.

He lifted both brows and beamed the wicked smile.

Confused, embarrassed, and mortified about her body's unusual response to him, and doing her best to hide it, she gave him a neutral smile and focused on eating her meat pie.

By now her siblings had become adjusted to this large, acerbic man at their table, and they no longer seemed awed or frightened.

Tom amused himself by repeatedly grabbing everyone's attention by shouting, "engineer, engineer, engineer."

Susanna and Lily, who had been absorbed by their own personal conversation, now turned their interest to this unconventional gentleman sitting just several feet away.

Susanna spoke first. "Mr. Drexel, have you ever danced in the ballroom at Almack's?"

Involved in an animated conversation about a suspension bridge with Fitzy, he answered her in an offhand fashion. "Attended once, Miss Susanna—most boring Wednesday evening of my life. My only excitement was relieving myself on…"

Meta gasped, then held her breath, hoping he wouldn't say anything vulgar in front of the children.

Mr. Drexel paused and caught her startled expression. "Right. Relieved myself *of* my male companions of the evening to stand up with every wallflower in attendance." He gave Susanna a courteous nod, then focused on slicing his cheese.

Meta thought Susanna might swoon. She remained staring at the man in a brazen, admiring fashion Meta needed to comment upon once they were alone.

Now emboldened by his response, Susanna continued. "I beg pardon, sir, but I have no one to ask, you see, and I have several questions I'm dying to get answers to. Do gentlemen really admire satin ribbons? My suspicions are that it is only ladies who do so."

He stared at Meta, his dark eyes unusually wide.

She had no intention of rescuing him.

He must have understood her reticence, because he forced a smile and turned to Susanna. "When I was at Almack's, I admired every…ribbon in the room."

"Including the satin ones?"

"Now I must apologize. I am unable to discern satin from…other ribbons, because the blinding effect of a well-placed ribbon is so alluring to gentlemen like myself."

With a deep sigh, Susanna stared at him admiringly.

Tom must have decided that this was his chance too to get a burning question answered. "If a tunnel under water has leaks, why don't you dig one in the sky?"

Mr. Drexel's wide eyes once again pleaded for her rescue.

She flashed him a cheerful smile. "Excellent question, Tom. Mr. Drexel, perhaps you would be so kind as to answer Tom's question?"

The expression of revenge in his eyes revealed that he intended to comment about this once they were alone. He turned to her brother. "Tunneling in the sky is a difficult endeavor. Air does not form very solid bricks."

Tom nodded his little head. "Yes, I see, that makes perfect sense."

Mr. Drexel decided to join the ask-a-question party, in all likelihood to avoid responding to more questions himself. "Mrs. Russell, did you enjoy Almack's during your first Season? I imagine you were very popular with the gentlemen, and not just because of your satin ribbons."

Susanna beamed.

Meta chuckled. "I wed almost immediately after I came out, so no, I have never been to Almack's."

He nodded. "I can say with certainty you would have been sought after for a…dance by all of the gentlemen."

"Ah, I don't believe…" This time the thought of waltzing in his arms brought about the return of the electric feeling, startling her into confusion. His innuendo fueled her fantasies about him, physically feeling him above her, and filling her in an intimate manner. Imagined details of his passion and tenderness embarrassed her to such an extent, she was unable to smile or speak in a lighthearted fashion. She concentrated on buttering her toast. Spreading the butter back and forth many times, she knew all eyes were upon her. Whichever of her siblings spoke first and broke the tension, she promised to direct Cook to make their favorite dishes for a week.

Mr. Drexel broke the silence. "I see you enjoy a lusty appetite for food. Do you read Fielding, *Tom Jones*, for example?"

Cheeks aflame and too embarrassed to speak, she stifled an urge to crawl under the table. He likely referred to the seduction of young Tom by

Mrs. Waters. If she remembered rightly, that lady's promised lovemaking was mimicked during their shared meal by bites and licks of their food. Meta failed to drive his allusion to the seduction of *Tom Jones* out of her mind. As a result, outrage, horror, and quite frankly, desire, spread through every inch of her figure. She looked up at his gleaming eyes, immediately glanced down, then reflexively up again, then down again.

Bother, bother, bother.

"Well, madam, it seems we enjoy similar books."

Within a second, Lily must have caught the jest. "Do you mean when Mrs. Waters—"

"Yes, Mrs. Waters eats food." Meta pasted on a smiled and swiftly rose. "Back to your studies everyone. Mr. Drexel has important business to attend to." She herded her siblings out of the room. Luncheon could not continue with her in this unsettled condition. Catching Mr. Drexel's glance, sure enough, he keenly understood her feelings.

What a bothersome, flirtatious, irresistible man.

No woman could ever be safe in his company. Right now, she wanted him out of the house. It was the only way to regain her composure and stop lusting after him. She needed to focus her mind on safer, happier topics, like telling Lily of James's change of heart. Her sister must be worried sick, so she yearned to tell Lily the news to relieve her troubled mind. "I know you are eager to return to your work, sir. May I show you to the door?"

He chuckled, a low and deep resonance that spoke of understanding her hint. "Of course."

Once she led her guest to the front door, she naturally wanted to thank him for the restoration of her sister's marital future. However, she could not do so with any semblance of composure.

He stood by the door without saying a word, threw his gloves into his hat with a thud, then turned to give her his thanks for the meal, the wicked smile set firmly in place.

She gathered every wit available for rational speech. "No, it is I who should be expressing my gratitude, sir. Although it may have been painful for you to *plead* with another gentleman, those efforts will soon restore my sister's happiness, and for that I cannot thank you enough."

"I have discussed more unpleasant subjects today than I have in all of the previous year. As far as I am concerned, I have met my obligations to right the situation caused by the misunderstanding over my field guide." He took her hand. "I doubt we will meet again, so farewell."

While she possessed no regrets if he left her life altogether, the safest method to avoid further entanglement or kisses was to forgo his company from now on. Then for some unknown reason, she desired clarification of his unusual, heartfelt speech to James. "Is it true you will only consider marriage to a rich wife? Or was that just fustian to force him to change his mind and resume his addresses to Lily? I've heard of aristocrats and people merging estates marrying for wealth, but why an engineer? Surely you are a gentleman with independent means of support. Any woman sympathetic to your profession should make a suitable wife." She froze upon the comprehension that her question might be misunderstood as seeking the position for herself.

He examined her thoroughly once again but kept her hand held tight in his. "Some truth."

She pulled her hand away.

"Society is full of women like you, on the shelf and forced to live with their family due to lack of funds. This type of female would not be suitable for me as a wife. On occasion my profession requires significant monetary support. Oh, it can be very profitable, but there are lean times too. Even Mr. Marc Brunel found himself in the poorhouse once, because his clients failed to pay for their projects or others stole his inventions."

Bother. Heat seized her cheeks and every inch of skin that came within his view. He must have thought she asked the question because she desired to be his wife. That's why he mentioned females like her living at home. All she could do at the moment was stutter, "I se-se-see."

He must have considered her question a compliment, because he swooped down and retrieved her hand for a gentlemanly kiss. Then he put his large palm on top of hers. "Warm, soft fur." He laughed. "Farewell, Mrs. Russell. Perhaps one day we may meet again at the tunnel. I hope so."

"Good-bye, sir," she said in a perfunctory manner, still mesmerized by his large, strong hand.

Wearing a wide grin, he nodded and turned to lightly skip—or was it a hop—down the steps to the street.

She suddenly remembered his promise. "Fitzy's bolt," she shouted. "You will return to see his bolt?"

He turned to face her, his fingers moving at his side. "Best send him and his bolt to me; it's quicker. That way I will not lose my valuable time."

She nodded and watched his long strides carry him away until he was out of sight. Her cheeks were no longer warm—thankfully—but she could not help but wonder if she would ever see him again.

Oh bother.

Unsettled by his flirting and even more unsettled by her strong reaction to his charms, she had forgotten to tell him about the Learned Ladies decision to have a picnic. Since she knew the importance of new funds, she resolved to pay a brief call soon, to arrange the details of the picnic. Her visit would not last long, no more than a minute or two, so he should have no objections.

Tom ran into the vestibule on his way to the drawing room. "Weee."

Meta smiled and chased him. "Weee."

Eight

"I HAVE IMPORTANT NEWS THAT I MUST TELL YOU IN private," Meta said, finding Lily with Susanna in the schoolroom watching the various rocks they had collected attract or repel a magnetic needle.

Susanna smirked. "Is Mr. Drexel going to pay a call again? Will he be at our table in the future? Is he courting you, Meta?"

"No, what gave you that idea?"

"You do seem to like him an awful lot and your cheeks redden in his presence."

Susanna had a valid point. So she decided to avoid his company for the foreseeable future—except for two mandatory encounters, which she'd complete as soon as possible and in the presence of others. First, she'd inform him about the picnic and convince him that the possibility of new investors was serious enough for him to attend. Then her final encounter would be to enjoy the picnic with her friends. Fulfill these two obligations but nothing more. Her attempts to control her romantic imaginings in his presence repeatedly failed and would likely do so if she continued the acquaintance. "Forgive me, Susanna, but you are too young to discuss gentlemen. And I have news for Lily concerning James that I know she will be eager to hear. So if you please, could you leave us alone?"

Lily quickly glanced up. She wore a fleeting expression of surprise, but then hid it under a mask of indifference. She resumed watching the magnetic needle spin. "Whatever it is, it is of no importance. Come watch this rock make the needle jump."

Her sister's indifference in regard to her wayward suitor confused Meta for a minute, but if she waited much longer, she might burst with excitement. Nothing appealed to her more than witnessing Lily's joy upon hearing the news that she and James would marry. "Please, Lily, you'll be delighted; I promise. I really cannot wait any longer."

Lily pursed her lips and then suggested they remove to the privacy of her room. She followed Meta upstairs with the gait of one walking to the gallows. Lily sat on her window seat without fluffing the pillows as she normally would, apparently indifferent about her proximity to the cold, rain-soaked glass.

Meta then poured out the whole story of their remarkable visit with James, including Mr. Drexel's promise to do his best to remove her initials from the next edition. Well, almost the whole story. She left out Mr. Drexel's scheme of describing the perfect wife as a means to force James to realize the consequences of losing a sweet wife such as Lily. "James plans to call tomorrow so you two can discuss resuming your engagement."

Lily jumped to her feet. "Asking Mr. Drexel for a

simple letter is one thing, but, Meta, I wish you had not carried the matter further. I've asked you before, but please do not meddle in my affairs."

"I only—"

"Yes, I know your intentions are good and my welfare your main concern. But good intentions are not a valid excuse for discussing my private affairs with strangers. This time you went too far."

"I expected you to be grateful to Mr. Drexel for clarifying the situation he caused by his field guide. Not to mention delighted that James has finally seen reason. He truly is willing to apologize and risk his mother's censure to marry you."

Lily sighed and then took her seat by the window. She stared at the misty gray yard and leaned over to place her cheek on a window that must have been very cold. "Well, I hope he speaks to me first before his mother," Lily said, still fixed on the gloomy scenery. "Then when I refuse, he will not have to endure that unpleasant conversation with his mother."

"Refuse! Oh, Lily, you wouldn't. Why would you do such a thing?" She felt a sharp pain in her stomach and a general fear of Lily suffering a lifetime of unhappiness because of a single hasty decision caused by a brief moment of mortification.

"I…I don't know, exactly, except James should never have called off in the first place." She paused. "I was shocked at the beginning, but now I have come to accept it. I will never marry. I'm sure once Fitzy or Susanna establishes a household, they will need an aunt to care for them and their family."

Meta seized her sister's hand. "I apologize for

involving Mr. Drexel further. But please, don't make a hasty decision because you are angry with me. Dearest, you deserve a future with the man you love, and I know you love James. Don't let pride stand in your way."

"I think I love him. You have always told me I do, but now I'm not so sure." Her sister shot her a glare. "But no one, not even you, will make me change my mind."

The following day, Meta sat reading *The Talisman* to her father. Her normal enthusiastic reading seemed to be missing, and the character-specific voices that delighted him failed to come to her easily. So she asked Fitzy to finish reading the next chapter, then she headed downstairs.

She felt guilty about Lily's admonition over her "meddling" and dismissal of James's olive branch. She had involved Mr. Drexel against his wishes, and he— eventually—had done as she asked. Now she let down her side of the bargain. Regardless of Mr. Drexel's statement that they would likely never see each other again, she felt she owed him an explanation about why his attempts to rectify the situation caused by his field guide failed, and Lily refused to accept James's addresses. Meta didn't know how Mr. Drexel would respond to this news, but she could envision two scenarios. In the first, he'd use a single wry word to say, "I told you so," and in the second, he might turn into the bear and bite her head off.

Since she also needed to inform him that the

Learned Ladies wished his attendance at a picnic, she decided to not reveal those cards until after she told him about Lily. Maybe if Lily's refusal angered him, she could restore his good will by the news of possible new investors.

Thankfully, the combination of a sunny day and ingestion of an entire pot of tea had put her in good spirits. So when she bounded up the steps of the Drexels' town house, she found herself eager to meet him.

The Drexels' housekeeper, Mrs. Morris, answered the door. A friendly, older woman with bright blue eyes, she explained that the younger Mr. Drexel was not at home, and she did not know when he'd return. In fact, since he had failed to come home last night, he might be expected at any time. If Meta wished to, she could speak to the senior Mr. Drexel while she waited for the son.

"Is staying out all night a usual habit for him?" Meta asked.

Mrs. Morris smiled. "When young, he spent the evenings out more often than at home, if I remember rightly. He's become more serious in the last two years. Come this way then, Mrs. Russell," the housekeeper said, leading her to the parlor and announcing her before taking her leave.

In the room's rear, far from the bow window and the street, she found the senior Mr. Drexel drawing something that appeared to be a gear.

The older man must have difficulty with his eyes, because he held the paper close to his face as he worked. Upon her approach, he stood and greeted her warmly. "Good day, Mrs. Russell. What a delight it is to see you again. George is not at home but should return anytime. In the meantime, please take a seat and tell me all the news about your family. How is that remarkable brother of yours getting along down at the tunnel site? I saw him myself there two days ago, but I was in the company of other board members and therefore not able to have a word with him. Does he like his new job?"

"Yes, indeed, Fitzy spends his time at the tunnel, but when I do see him, he can speak of little else."

Mr. Michael Drexel laughed, a gesture that made his wrinkles fade so he appeared more like George.

Meta enjoyed his company, because the older man always maintained a cheerful attitude. Unlike his son, she harbored no expectations that he might transform into a bear. Now sitting here enjoying a hearty laugh, he reminded her of his son's more charming qualities.

"Fitzy told me he feels like he has fallen into heaven every time he descends into that pit." She took a long step over an iron model of a wheel, then sat in a tub chair with a well-worn ivory seat. "He wakes each morning in delight, anticipating the wonders he will see that day. When he returns home in the evening, he cannot speak fast enough to convey every detail he observed. I doubt he gets more than a few hours' sleep."

Her companion laughed again heartily. "George was like that too when young. Sarah, my wife," he glanced at the ceiling for a fleeting second, "was worried about George's lack of sleep. I told her not to fuss. The boy was young and sleep is specific to an individual. If George needed sleep, he would have taken it."

"I understand your wife has suffered a stroke. Please accept my sympathies. It must be unbearably difficult. My own father has lost his sense, and I deeply miss the man I grew up with. Every day I find something I would like to tell him or say to myself, 'Wouldn't Father enjoy hearing this?' Perhaps on occasion I see a flicker of comprehension in his eyes, but it is always a false one. But a spouse is different somehow than a parent. Had my husband lost his mind, or remained unconscious, instead of dying within days after his accident, I cannot imagine how much harder it would have been for me. Again, you have my condolences and regard."

He gave her a smile bigger than she expected. "You understand, thank you. Jane and I are not unhappy. Unlike your father, she retains full comprehension. She just lost the ability to speak clearly and walk without pain. Those are the facts of our life now, and we make the best of it. When she is sleeping, I tend to my affairs and help George when I can. But during the day, I read to her." He blushed. "I know you will consider me a sentimental man, but we also hold hands. You would think after forty-one years of marriage, holding your spouse's hand would be a commonplace occurrence—like a passing compliment, felt for a second, then lost. But when I hold her hand, she breathes easier, and I do too. Neither of us would rather do anything else. We must appear rather foolish in our old age."

"No, not at all." Meta nodded but could not say anything more.

He winked at her. "To what do we owe the honor of your visit today? Does it concern your lovely sister and that misunderstanding involving George's field guide?"

"Yes, it does. But I don't think your son will be too happy about my news. You see, even though he was hesitant, he did his utmost to explain the situation to my sister's suitor. Yesterday, we were both delighted when James admitted that he regretted his mistake of calling off and would resume his addresses to Lily the next day. Only now Lily has decided against him." She sighed deeply. "She is not normally a stubborn person, so her position is inexplicable to me. Tell me, has George experienced other problems from the publication of his field guide? Or are my sister's difficulties an isolated incident?"

"You must forgive George on that score. His acerbic charm has given him more success with the fairer sex than a man of his age ought to have." He sighed. "His stated motivation for publishing the field guide was money for an expensive model bridge he was building at the time. But his real reason was more a young man's pride, a lark, a cock crowing, showing off his familiarity with females to his friends. In a word, he is spoiled by attentions form the fairer sex. I am glad—and quite surprised actually—that he exerted himself to consider the feelings of others, like your sister, not to mention set the situation to rights before it escalated out of proportion to reality and harmed his reputation irreversibly. I hope this can be resolved to everyone's satisfaction and, in the end, teach him a valuable lesson."

The drawing room door opened with a bang. A whoosh of people entered the room, including George Drexel followed by Mrs. Morris and a housemaid. George Drexel was soaking wet and covered in mud. His dark hair appeared matted on his head, dried muck streaked across his cheeks, and wet mud stained all of his clothes. He had no coat, his waistcoat was unbuttoned, and his shirt was rolled up to the elbows. He seemed in a trance, because he failed to register her presence. Instead, he careened by everyone and collapsed on the sofa, his arm flopping to the floor.

"A leak?" the older man asked, running forward to attend to his son.

The younger Mr. Drexel nodded. "Water started coming from two of the poling boards in number twelve. I thought the straw had contained the leak, but suddenly four boards shot out of the frame and a massive amount of water entered the tunnel. It was foul water too, full of London sewage, a veritable liquid privy. Several men cast up their breakfast at the smell. We've fought it for at least ten hours." He turned his head to address his father. "Duff even went down in the diving bell to pull sandbags over the leak."

"What about the new chain? Was there enough time to test it properly? I hope Mr. Duff has survived and is not left behind in a watery grave."

"The chain was tested by lowering the bell once before Duff entered. I would have preferred a more thorough test, but under the circumstances, Duff being the only man on the barge at the time with experience going down in the bell, he decided not to wait. The straw and clay bags have finally stopped the water for the moment, so I returned home." His head fell back on the sofa, and he breathed heavily. "I must return soon."

Another housemaid entered the room, carrying a large tray full of towels and a bowl of hot water. Mrs. Morris attempted to remove his soiled, wet shirt by pulling his torso upward, but his eyes had closed, and he turned into a dead weight.

Meta quickly stepped forward in front of his father, grabbed him by the collar, and with the combined efforts of Mrs. Morris, pulled him up into a sitting position. "We must help you, sir. Your wet waistcoat and shirt must be removed, for your own health." For a brief second, the stench from the Thames overwhelmed her, but she held her breath in intervals to make the odor more tolerable.

He opened his eyes; a flicker of recognition brightened them for an instant. "What in the devil are you doing here? Be off, madam. I have no time today for your tomfoolery." He groaned as Mrs. Morris lifted his arm to remove his shirt.

Together the two women removed his soaking wet boots, shirt, and trousers. In unison, they grabbed wet towels and started to wash him. While Mrs. Morris gently brushed his face free of dirt, Meta lifted his left arm and began to wipe it clean. His forearms were a mixture of brown dirt mingled with a light covering of dark hair. Once the dirt was gone, for some reason, with each stroke of the cloth, she smoothed the hair into an orderly direction.

Frankly, his arm fascinated her, from the strength of the muscle underneath his hair to the bulge in his wrist where those large, active hands began. She marveled at the thought of these very hands holding back the mighty Thames for ten hours. She inhaled and started to clean his fingers. Her attention fixed on their strength and dexterity, delicate enough to create intricate detailed models, yet possessing the power to keep pressure on a poling board for hours.

She recognized her unnecessary admiration of his arm and hands, so much to her disappointment, heat stole across her cheeks. The room seemed unnecessarily warm. Thankfully, everyone focused on getting the mud removed, so they failed to notice her wavering attention. That is, until she discovered him staring at her.

Her admiring glances—oh, he noticed—understood them too.

"Right. Why are you here, madam?"

Of course he noticed. Her mind still swirling in a heated fog of sensuality, she began to babble. "I called to tell you—bad news, I'm afraid—not bad, but—well, disappointing—you see…" She stopped and stared, eyes wide, as he pulled on a new shirt. Her brief glimpse of a broad expanse of chest lightly covered with brown hair caused her to gulp loudly.

He caught her staring. "Stop wasting my time and your time. Do you understand my meaning?"

She looked down at her skirt and nodded, thoroughly chastened.

A housemaid entered with a tray piled with cheese and ham and placed it near him.

"Thank you," he said, addressing his servants. "I don't know what my family would do without you ladies."

His father moved to the opposite seat next to the fire. "How long do you plan to stay?"

"I'll be off in a minute. The next soil samples should be available within the hour, and I must inspect them. Hopefully we are still digging through the layer of blue clay."

His father nodded.

"Leave? Again?" Meta failed to understand the urgency. All she recognized was the danger. "Is all this tunneling worth the exhaustion and possible illness from foul water?"

Both men stared at her as though she spoke in a foreign language.

"Madam," George Drexel said, "I have done what you asked in regard to your sister. Now, if you please, take leave. Go embroider something, read someone else's diary, or discuss *ribbons* with Miss Susanna."

She must tell him about the picnic before she left, even though it meant poking a stick at the bear. "I must tell you that the Learned Ladies Society is interested in buying shares in the tunnel at the next issue. They plan to gather at the site next week for a picnic, so they can see the amazing tunnel for themselves. If all goes well, the ladies have significant connections that could benefit the tunnel in ways you cannot imagine. I came today to tell you about this. Although no promises of support can be guaranteed."

He turned to his father. "Learned ladies are having a picnic. How exciting. What gentleman could possibly resist."

"Now son, we all know you are clearly exhausted, but Mrs. Russell is only trying to help you." The father addressed her, "Please, Mrs. Russell. When a leak happens, the entire tunnel project is at stake. He must return as soon as possible, because every hand is needed. Return another day, and I'm certain he'd be delighted to hear your news."

Meta watched the bear inside him grow: his eyes narrowed, and his chest expanded.

"Right, Mrs. Morris, would you *kindly* show Mrs. Russell the door. I'm incapable at the moment. Good-bye, madam."

"But—"

"I have important work to do. Shove off!"

"Of course," she said and hurried out of the room.

Nine

META CONFRONTED HER SISTER. "ADMIT IT, YOU LOVE James. Stop pretending you don't wish to go to the picnic just because he will be there."

Lily's countenance grew mulish. "No, perhaps not love, but I do not hate him either. I question whether I'm ready to spend several hours with him staring at me, recrimination written across his face, without me being able to throw something at him."

"Ah, maybe he agreed to join us at the picnic because he too wishes to see the tunnel, not stare at you. Everyone in London seems to be talking about the tunnel, and James has met Mr. Drexel, so he has reasons to be curious. Don't worry. I won't let him pester you during the picnic. *Promise.*" An easy promise to make. After James learned of Lily's refusal to reconsider his suit, he left the room without saying a word. During the weeks that preceded the picnic, he made no move to contact her in any manner. Today would be the first time they would be in each other's company for an extended length of time. She had no doubt that James would behave like a gentleman. Lily's behavior, on the other hand, was more uncertain.

Meta glanced out of the salon's tall windows. "It promises to be a wonderful day to spend across the river. The sun is out, and we'll picnic in the gardens of St. Mary's. It is only a few steps from there to the tunnel workings."

Fitzy yelled, "James's carriage is here." He bounded out the front door.

Meta grabbed her straw bonnet and tied the cornflower blue ribbons under her chin. "Come on." She snatched Lily's bonnet and fixed it on her sister's head, pulling the pink ribbons tight with a tug.

"You owe me a favor in return, Meta."

"Indeed I do." She bent to peek under her sister's poke bonnet. "But what do you owe me if you enjoy yourself?"

Lily's face broke into a feisty smile, the first one to appear naturally since her engagement ended. "You're right. I'll enjoy watching James closely so that I may put down his actions as a character in a novel one day—the wishy-washy lover."

Meta sighed. "You will do no such thing. Cheer up, for Fitzy's sake, if not mine."

Lily tossed her head; the mulish expression on her face returned.

The family soon settled into the carriage for the short journey to Lady Sarah's house in Royston Square. Once all the guests, their carriages, and the carriages carrying Lady Sarah and several members of the Learned Ladies Society were assembled, they all headed for the tunnel. An hour later, quite a number of bonnets poked out of the carriage windows as the ladies, and James, passed the tunnel site in Rotherhithe. They passed the inn, The Spread Eagle and Crown, and disembarked next to the gardens of St. Mary's church. The grooms and footmen stayed behind to set up the picnic things, while their party walked the hundred or so feet to the tunnel location.

Meta had previously confirmed that Mr. Drexel would be at the works today to receive the Learned Ladies, but she had no idea how he would receive her personally. Perhaps the presence of so many ladies would make him behave with all politeness and keep the bear in hibernation. Moreover, the presence of potential new donors might bring out his natural charm around ladies. She knew him well enough to understand the charmer was not his normal habit but one employed only when needed. Her pulse quickened. She eagerly looked forward to the skillful charmer plying his wiles upon her friends—an amusing spectacle, nothing more.

As their party joined the crowd of spectators, Meta explained to her friends what she knew about the tunnel from Mr. Drexel. She pointed out that the fifty-foot-wide iron cylinder was built on the ground and then lowered by removing the dirt from under it until it reached its current position. They walked to the far side next, directly opposite the spot where the lateral tunneling began under the river. At this location their party could look down and marvel at the twelve men, standing three men above each other, on the giant shield.

Fitzy recognized Mr. Drexel in the crowd first and called out to him.

Mr. Drexel looked up to their party and waved.

Fitzy scampered down to address him directly. They chatted for several minutes before Fitzy ran back up the steps. Her brother ignored her and approached James instead. "Drexel asked that I invite you down to see the workings. He expects that since you are an engineer by inclination, if not by practice, you would enjoy seeing some of the tunnel's features up close."

Meta wondered if the invitation included them all. "Did he invite—"

"He expressly said no females," Fitzy informed them, lifting his chin. He waved his arm for James to follow him down into the pit.

The two climbed down the staircase and conversed with Mr. Drexel.

Ignoring her irritating envy, Meta could not help but speculate. Did the men discuss James's broken engagement, the possibility of additional funding, the workings of the tunnel, or all three? Whatever the answer, it vexed her that she could not be there too. By the time the gentlemen and Fitzy climbed up to greet their party, she had reached the end of describing everything she knew about the tunnel to her friends.

The group then strolled to the church's grounds to enjoy their picnic.

Mr. Drexel greeted her with lifted eyebrows and a satisfied smirk. "Madam."

He must have known how eager she was to see the great shield up close, so he probably withheld the invitation on purpose to punish her.

She answered his greeting with a toss of her head. "I am disappointed we were not allowed down into the pit. Especially, since I know other ladies have been given a tour of the shield."

He laughed and reached for her hand. Then he stared into her eyes until she met his gaze, and the wicked smile broke out. "In regard to our last meeting, my mind was focused entirely on the leak, but that is no excuse for my rude behavior at the time. I apologize."

She tugged her hand free. "Yes…of course…I interrupted… Bad timing…sorry." She turned away.

He laughed again. "Please do not hop away on my account."

She spun to formally address him. "Sir, let me make the introductions, and then we can all take our seats."

After everyone had been introduced, they sat on oilcloths with several picnic baskets spread out over a large lawn.

Meta chose a seat surrounded by her friends.

Mr. Drexel made a motion to sit next to her, so Clara graciously—albeit wearing something of a smirk—moved to another position. He lowered himself to the ground next to her, almost touching. "This grass is a perfect spot for rabbits to frolic. Don't you think so, Mrs. Russell?"

She gulped, then glanced up. "I hope this brilliant sunlight does not prove unbearable."

He chuckled.

Keeping herself busy making sure everyone had the food they needed, she tried to ignore him just inches away. She failed, of course. Instead, she caught every

movement, chuckle, and word, a heightened aware-
ness of him that left her unsettled and breathing faster
than normal.

As they ate their lunch, she noticed James had
become reticent after his conversation in the pit with
Mr. Drexel. James glanced one or two times at Lily,
but nothing more. James sat next to Clara, one of the
unmarried ladies of the Learned Ladies Society. Did
James and Mr. Drexel discuss Lily's refusal down in the
pit? Perhaps the two were now scheming to devise a
clever, masculine plan to change her mind. Without
drawing notice, she watched Lily's reaction to this
event. Her sister had noticed James's attentions, since she
appeared more interested in his conversation than the
one she was engaged in with Grizel sitting next to her.

Mr. Drexel quickly ate his cold meat and bread,
likely eager to return to the tunnel work. When
finished, he stood and addressed the group, while the
rest of their party continued to eat. "I would like to
thank Lady Sarah"—he nodded—"and all of you for
visiting our site."

The party briefly clapped.

"Today I have had the privilege of being introduced to ladies of great intelligence, and from what
I understand from Mrs. Russell, benevolent ladies, as
well. I"—he focused on Meta—"commend you all."

She instantly turned away, not wanting to blush or
reveal that personal confidences existed between them.

Lady Sarah explained their purpose. "Yes, our little
group does our best to house London's governesses
when they are no longer employed. It is a small effort,
but a much needed one, I can assure you."

"I do not doubt it," Mr. Drexel said, oozing deference and charm. His perfectly tailored pepper-colored coat and shiny black boots presented his irresistible masculine figure to advantage, as confirmed by many appreciative stares from almost all of the Learned Ladies.

Grizel provided further explanations in a clipped Scottish accent. "We have also come at the request of our dear member Meta to see for ourselves if your tunnel is a worthy project. If so, we plan to speak to our husbands and fathers about supporting your endeavors."

He paused. Then he retook his seat and leaned back, resting on one arm. With his great height lessened, his casual attitude added to his appearance of amiability. "Thank you, madam. What kind of support did you have in mind?"

While Grizel and several others discussed shares and projected profits, his two fingers on his right hand "hopped" through the grass close to her arm.

She ignored him.

The two-finger rabbit then hopped on top of her hand resting on the grass. His two fingers easily slid into the space between hers. She jerked her hand away.

Lady Sarah hid a smirk. "Did you prick your finger, Meta?"

Several ladies chuckled discreetly.

One whispered, "On a rake?"

As the Learned Ladies laughed, Meta glared at her friends.

Lady Sarah appeared genuinely sorry for her comment and endeavored to quickly change the subject. "Clara, tell Mr. Drexel about the children."

Clara brushed her curls aside, then smiled at James

and said, "We have also come here to inspect the school for children of lost seamen, just over there by the watchhouse." She pointed to a tall building across the street. "Our governesses don't need schooling, of course," she reddened, "but we do appreciate learning new ways to house them and keep our costs down."

After that remark, conversation lagged and everyone randomly glanced around them.

Mr. Drexel unsettled Meta by his continued unwavering stare in her direction, one that the others must have noticed too.

Lady Sarah broke the silence. "I understand from Mrs. Russell that you earned a significant profit from the sale of your field guide. Is that true?"

Mr. Drexel sat upright and turned to Lady Sarah. He clenched his teeth slightly, enough that Meta thought that she might be the only person aware of it. Then he raised a brow. "A *tolerable* amount."

"Ladies," Grizel said, "think of what we could do for our governesses with a tolerable amount of additional funds."

Mr. Drexel remained calm. "Not as much money as you think, I can assure you." He turned to address the group. "I hope your journey today is a success and that you will consider buying shares in the Thames Tunnel Company when issued next month."

"Please, sir, I think you have changed the subject," Lady Sarah countered. "How many copies of the field guide have you sold?"

He sighed, stood, and waited a minute to answer. "A few."

Clearly, he would never reveal the details in relation

to his profits. So Meta switched the conversation back to the tunnel and the schedule for completion.

After several more questions tendered by her friends, and answers he fielded in a lazy, confident attitude, Lady Sarah and several others admitted that they were very impressed and indeed would speak to their relatives about financial support.

Grizel withheld her immediate approval and decided to obtain as much information as possible. She then grilled Mr. Drexel about every detail.

Throughout it all, he remained standing, a smile lingering on his lips.

His explanations appeared to please Lady Sarah. "I cannot tell you how impressed I am with this tunnel. I have always appreciated science and mechanical progress more than any other woman I know. In fact, more than any other person in my circle of acquaintance. My father in particular seems adept at keeping his head under a rock."

The company chuckled. Many of the ladies spoke of their amazement and approval too.

Following praise for the tunnel, Lady Sarah became quite animated. "Indeed, sir, I have been so impressed by Mr. Brunel and his tunnel, I may have a surprise in store for you. I will arrange things, in coordination with Meta, of course. If my plan comes to pass, I promise you will benefit greatly and be very pleased with the result."

"Thank you, Lady Sarah." He bowed in her direction. "I am exceeding grateful that I have made your acquaintance."

Grizel appeared hesitant. "I really do not see what

is so impressive. Ladies, please forgive me, but you all seem too taken with your admiration of the site and fail to consider the risk of such a project. Need I remind you that we are taking about investing in a tunnel *under* a river. A feat that has never been successful." She addressed Mr. Drexel in a forcible manner. "What about water leaks? There are rumors that the band of blue clay fluctuates in depth and may become too thin for the size of the tunnel. So when you reach the end of the clay and enter the quicksand, you will become inundated, like the Travistock project. Have you had any significant water leaks, sir?"

His brilliant, wicked smile bloomed. "We are splashed now and then."

A small, very dirty boy of about twelve ran up to Mr. Drexel. "Brunel needs you now, sir. There's a leak in number three." The boy almost hopped in place.

Mr. Drexel did not even blush. "Right, here's an example of a splash." He stood and bowed. "Forgive me, ladies, Codlington, my services are needed elsewhere. Believe my sincerity when I say it has been an honor to meet you all." He moved over to Meta and reached for her hand.

She gave it to him, and he pulled her to her feet. Then he lightly squeezed it a few seconds longer than considered appropriate. "Thank you for inviting your lovely friends to visit our little dig." After a quick bow to the group, he spun and ran after the boy in the direction of the tunnel.

"Well," Grizel exclaimed, "splash, indeed. He appears a little loose with the facts. I wonder if we can trust anything he said?"

"Ah, I believe him," Meta said. "I'm sure a little water is a natural occurrence, like rats in the cellar. They use straw to stop these leaks on regular occasions, but it does not mean the project will be a failure."

Lady Sarah stood. "I agree with Meta. From what he already told us, water appears on the dirt face when the miners remove the three inches of dirt. But take note of the drainage plans, and the massive steam pump, and cistern. I think Mr. Marc Brunel is a genius. We are very lucky to have his services applied on our behalf here in England."

"I agree," Meta said, clapping first.

"Well said, Lady Sarah," James replied, joining in the applause and turning to Clara. "A most impressive fellow."

Sybella spoke to Grizel. "Your concern, however, may become justified. Too many leaks might prove costly to complete the tunnel in the long run. But I'll have to check the numbers first."

Now that the picnic ended, and their guest of honor had returned to the tunnel, everyone gathered their belongings and headed to the carriages for the return journey across the river.

Meta noticed James offer his arm to Clara, instead of Lily.

Her sister's frown and wide eyes suggested Lily noticed his compliment too.

Ten

"OH, HOW WONDERFUL," META EXCLAIMED, SITTING in Lady Sarah's private drawing room. She leaped up and gave her friend a hug. "I cannot thank you enough. Mr. Drexel works very hard, you understand. He has also been so kind to both James and Fitzy, I'm delighted that we can give him this moment to impress his superiors. But how can we keep this event a secret? Surely with the involvement of such a distinguished personage, our surprise might be prematurely revealed."

Lady Sarah motioned for Meta to take her seat again on a small gilded sofa and glanced toward the door.

The housekeeper entered with an ornate silver tray filled with various sweets and a sterling tea server resting on a large hinged stand.

Once the housemaid had closed the door behind her, Lady Sarah picked up a sugarcoated puffed treat filled with clotted cream. "Forgive me." She stuck her finger into the sweet and swiped a large amount of cream on her forefinger. Briefly glancing somewhat guiltily over her shoulder at the door, she licked the cream off in a single motion. "You should have no worries that our surprise will be revealed. I expressly told His Grace's secretary that we would like to keep this a secret. Given the regimental nature of our interested party, you must put your fears of our surprise being spoiled behind you."

Meta took a bite of her confection. The melting sweetness of the cream's vanilla flavor on her tongue could only be described as divine. She softly moaned in pleasure. "Please compliment your staff. I have never tasted a finer sweet."

"I will," Lady Sarah said, pouring tea for both of them. "Mrs. Wilson makes these when Father leaves town to visit Swithin. It seems there is a competition between her and Mrs. Handbury in the country." She giggled. "Both cooks know that when I write to his lordship, I always mention the culinary treats served in his absence. My letters make Father jealous, hungry, and eager to return home to London. In other words, it is a competition between the two cooks to best one another in tempting my father to return."

Both women laughed.

"I'm delighted your father is away then," Meta said, smiling. "I must remember to call whenever I hear he is not in London." She attempted a sip of tea, but it was too hot. So she blew air across the surface of the satin black brew lapping on the side of a pink floral teacup.

Lady Sarah put down her empty plate on the tea table. "So what do you make of Clara walking off on James's arm? Lily looked as mad as a March hare."

Meta giggled. "It will do her good, as far as I'm

concerned. She has been hurt; I understand that. But I still believe both James and Lily love each other without reservation. My guess is that Mr. Drexel put James up to paying his attentions to Clara. Some sort of manly scheme to bring Lily up to scratch."

"I thought you said Mr. Drexel would rather cut off his arm than deal with emotional subjects like romantic love."

"Indeed, I know for sure he would do so. Any words like feelings, plead, love, and affection bring out his masculine defenses. But in this case, I have a hunch James's behavior is a result of some sort of pact between the two men. Once gentlemen have interests in common, they bond in such a way that they will readily team up to oppose whatever they consider feminine nonsense. The two of them will engage in any far-fetched scheme as long as they consider the result to be to their advantage."

"Silly creatures," Lady Sarah said, focused on another confection lying undisturbed on the tea tray. "Why does Cook put so many of these on the plate? She knows I lack any hope of resisting temptation when these are in sight." A long sigh escaped her.

Meta smiled. "I lack the ability to resist treats too. So let's divide this one in half. Then we will feel quite satisfied for not eating the whole thing."

"Excellent idea," Lady Sarah said, cutting the sweet into two pieces and handing Meta one. "And then when we are finished, we will cut the last one in half too."

Meta burst out laughing. "Of course, that way we can congratulate ourselves on our rectitude."

"Of course."

Both ladies giggled and consumed the entire plate of sweets.

Later, when Meta stood by the door putting on her straw bonnet and kid gloves, Lady Sarah asked her, "Do you think Mr. Drexel will do as you ask? Our guest will be disappointed otherwise."

"You mean ensure that the tunnel's board, including both Mr. Brunels, is at the site that day?"

"Yes, it is a tall order, since the board of the Thames Tunnel Company would have to assemble at a moment's notice. Does Mr. Drexel trust you enough to do your bidding?"

Meta did not know the answer to her friend's question. But if she dwelled on the negative side—that he would refuse—she'd become upset. Besides, the promise of new investors was at stake, so she decided his response would likely be an eager, positive one. "I'll call upon him at home today. So I guess we'll be able to judge what he thinks of my request soon."

That afternoon, Meta decided she couldn't wait to have a word with Mr. Drexel to arrange for the Learned Ladies' surprise. Fitzy had mentioned he would like to examine more technical drawings, so she invited him to accompany her. While she would normally be more circumspect, and had no desire to raise false hopes, she was too excited not to tell Mr. Drexel the good news. After all, she wished to assist him in any way possible for many reasons. Besides easing her guilt over Lily's stubbornness, she needed to thank him for his efforts in regard to Fitzy's interactions with professional men—not to mention her interest in the outcome of the leak.

She found Fitzy in the schoolroom. His sleeves were rolled up to his elbows, and his arms appeared almost white from a thin layer of plaster. His expression seemed far too serious. "Ah, what have you cast today?" She could only see the smooth plaster layer at the top of the mold, which gave her a good excuse to not realize this was the treasured bolt. "From the size, I'd say it's a cast of a hand."

"No, don't be silly," Fitzy said, poking the smooth top of the plaster to determine if it had dried.

"An apple?"

He looked at her like she had become a simpleton. "I have more imagination, and more skills, than to cast something as easy as an apple." A streak of plaster across his cheeks moved with his broad smile. "It is a bolt used on the tunnel's shield."

"You used all that plaster just to cast a bolt?"

"Ladies are ignorant about bolts and mechanical whatnots. This bolt is the size of Drexel's fist, maybe larger. Honestly, Meta, you have never seen anything like it. Truly amazing. I cannot wait to show him the final result."

Meta had never seen him happier. "How long before it sets?"

"It is set now, but I'll probably need another hour to trim it properly. I don't want you to see it until it is presentable and professional." He grabbed a towel and tried to wipe the lingering plaster off his forearms.

Meta took a cloth too and dampened it in the nearby washstand. While he struggled with removing the large amount of plaster on his arm, she gently wiped away the streak and little spots of plaster on his cheeks, forehead, and chin. "Let's pay a call on Mr. Drexel in an hour then. You can show him your bolt, and I can inform his that the picnic was a success. Indeed, at the monthly meeting, at least three ladies promised funds for the tunnel. But most of all, Lady Sarah spoke with her father and arranged a surprise. I know this news should please Mr. Drexel."

Fitzy's eyes brightened. "Oh yes, let's do. I want to show his father my bolt too. Both men will appreciate it equally, I'm sure."

Later that day, Fitzy and Meta entered the Drexels' town house and were shown into the drawing room. Young Mr. Drexel stood by the large desk, tapping his pencil on a drawing. He wore his greatcoat, so he had either just arrived or was ready to leave.

"Right, Mrs. Russell," Mr. Drexel said as he bowed in proper greeting. "Why am I not surprised to see you here? You have become a fixture, have you not? Greetings, Fitzhenry, always a delight. Exactly to what do I owe the honor of your visit today?"

Meta could not get the words out fast enough. "Well, the ladies were so impressed, you now have three more people interested in buying shares at the next offering. Well? Well?"

His eyes widened, and he shook his head in disbelief. "Excuse me?"

"New subscribers—your tunnel—funds—fathers—husbands—they said *yes*."

He turned his head sideways and peered down at her feet. "Did you just hop?" He turned to her brother. "Fitzhenry, can you translate your sister for me?"

Before Fitzy could open his mouth, she explained. "The Learned Ladies Society was so impressed after the picnic, three of them will be confirmed subscribers. What do you think about that?"

The smile that broke across his face was not the wicked one. No, this smile had warmth as the main ingredient and could likely charm any observer at twenty paces. "Thank you." He nodded. "Right, I must admit I had my doubts. Thought I was on a fool's errand. But it appears I was in error. Thank you again, madam."

"Oh, but there is more news. Lady Sarah and I have arranged a surprise for you—for the entire Thames Tunnel Company. We would like to schedule a meeting with both Brunels and most of the board present. Can you arrange that?"

"What sort of surprise?"

Fitzy broke into the conversation. "Then it would not be a surprise, sir. Would it?"

Mr. Drexel frowned at Fitzy.

"Oh, sir, I have brought a casting you might be interested in." He started to unwrap his bolt, but Meta stopped him.

"Let me finish my request first, dear." She turned to Mr. Drexel. "In fact, I do not plan to leave this residence until I get a promise for what I seek, a meeting with all of the board at the site to receive…visitors."

"I'm skeptical about this plan. Do not mistake me. I'm delighted you managed to obtain more investors. But as I have noted before, if you bring investors by to observe the workings and something adverse happens, like a leak, it may damage our reputation even further. Just yesterday I saw a caricature by Robert Cruikshank mocking our efforts."

"Please. Trust me."

He stared at her for at least half a minute.

"I'll consider it."

"Thank you. You will not be sorry."

"I said consider, madam, not agree. Fitzhenry, how do you manage to live in a household full of females?"

"Um, I never thought about that subject before. But now that I'm thinking about it, it's a great advantage. The food is likely better, isn't it?"

Mr. Drexel laughed. He then asked to see Fitzy's bolt and admired her brother's work without reservation. "Now if the two of you will excuse me, I must be on my way. There is a meeting of the board in an hour, and I am presenting a new plan for a drainage system."

The door to the drawing room opened, and the older Mr. Drexel entered. "Mrs. Russell, Fitzhenry, I am delighted to see you both. To what do we owe the honor of your call?"

Both Meta and Fitzy eagerly greeted him, but Meta got her words out first.

"We are here to inform your son that we obtained three more investors for the tunnel."

"Well, I'll be." Michael turned to his son. "Congratulations, that should help your promotion."

Meta had never heard a promotion was at stake. She turned to George. "You did not tell me about a promotion. Is that why you are reluctant to arrange a meeting of the tunnels primaries for our surprise?"

"There is more than my promotion at stake."

Michael Drexel chuckled. "Ignore George. He sounds surly when something is on his mind. He is just on his way to a meeting of the Tunnel's board of directors. He sits in my place, since I do not wish to leave my wife alone. She is eagerly looking forward to continuing the ghost story we started yesterday."

George appeared peeved. "You only need be away for a few hours."

Meta understood George's wish to have his father's presence at board meetings. Then whenever George proposed a change or improvement, his father could support him and provide the benefit of his experience in discussion with the members. "I don't understand, sir. Why can't a servant read to Mrs. Drexel? I know your son would appreciate your presence at these meetings."

The younger Drexel raised his brows and turned to his father. "See? Even Mrs. Russell thinks it is not necessary for you to stay at home."

His father shook his head. "My wife believes the servants have far better things to do. In fact, we are constantly short staffed due to the muck and dirt George brings into the house. They are overworked as it is."

Meta saw two gentlemen who needed her assistance. Nothing could make her happier. "Please, let me read to Mrs. Drexel. I read to my father daily, so I'm well practiced. Besides, Fitzy has come to show you his plasterwork, but he can stay too and occupy himself with drawing." She turned to her brother. "Can you stay a couple of hours to help out the Drexels?"

Fitzy beamed and turned to the younger man. "Can

you provide me with paper and pencil? I have been meaning to make drawings of various model bridges in this room."

Mr. George Drexel beamed, while the older man remained hesitant.

"Mrs. Russell," George said, "I must leave immediately or I shall miss the meeting." He turned to his father. "Please. We plan to discuss my suggestions for the new elevated drainage today, and your opinion carries weight with so many members of the company's board. I could use your support."

His father studied his son but remained silent.

Fitzy unwrapped his plaster cast of the bolt again and held it before the older Mr. Drexel. "What do you think of my casting? You of course will recognize it as the bolt holding the shield's footings. Perhaps the size does not amaze you, but I have never seen anything like this. It is beautiful."

Mr. Michael Drexel smiled and slapped Fitzy on the back. "Congratulations. You really do have an innate sense of beauty that can be found in the commonplace. A true gift for an artist."

Fitzy's chest swelled with the compliment. He turned to Meta. "I will stay, of course. Mrs. Drexel may even want to see my bolt too. And I can read to her, if you tire."

Meta patted his head, and he leaned sideways to avoid it, probably not wanting the grown men to see his sister treating him as a child.

The older Mr. Drexel laughed. "Very well, I give in. We have been reading *Redgauntlet* by the author of *Waverley*. Have either of you read it?"

Meta mentioned her sister was the only one that could finish the book.

"Well," the older Mr. Drexel said, "come with me and I will seek her approval and make introductions. No promises, mind. I want you to know that my wife retains full capabilities, except the ability to speak or move her right side. If she falls asleep, you can stop reading and...I hold her hand, but I suppose you need not do so." He turned to his son. "Introductions will take no more than ten minutes, and then I'll join you and we can head off to the board meeting."

The younger man smiled. "Right, I'll wait. But we will have to bustle—don't want to set a bad example by being late."

His father agreed and the three of them climbed the stairs, the younger Drexel remaining behind.

Michael opened the door of his wife's bedroom. "Stay here for a minute. I need to ready her to accept visitors." He entered the room and shut the door.

Meta whispered to Fitzy, "Thank you. I promise you your favorite roast chicken tonight for helping me."

Fitzy's eyes brightened. "Roast chicken for just drawing and reading. That is a most excellent deal."

A little more than two minutes later, Mr. Michael Drexel opened the door and invited them in.

Meta first noticed that on every square inch of the walls in the large, green room hung paintings of flowers. Most pictures had a black background that accentuated the flower's brilliant colors. The stuffy, heavy air smelled faintly of lavender, suggesting the windows were seldom opened.

Mrs. Drexel lay in bed wearing a small smile on her

face. She did not appear old, as no wrinkles had yet to grace her countenance, but she was almost entirely hidden by a long lace cap. She sat up in bed, one hand holding her husband's. Their joined hands rested on a small table standing next to the middle of the bed. The large chair next to the table suggested the table was placed there on purpose, so that the couple could hold hands for an extended time.

Meta bit her lower lip. Watching Mr. Drexel attend his wife, every movement between the two of them expressed nothing but the deepest love. Her heart almost broke at the affection in Mrs. Drexel's eyes and the tender care her husband rendered her.

Michael patted her hand and made the introductions. "Look, Mother, Mrs. Russell has come to read to you, and young Fitzhenry will make some drawings of George's bridges."

"I say, sir," Fitzy pronounced. "I just noticed these paintings. They are not really paintings, are they?"

Mrs. Drexel wore a frail grin.

Mr. Drexel dropped his jaw for a second. "I am impressed, young man. You're correct. The flowers are constructed using small pieces of cut paper. Not many people discern that; you have quite the eye." He obtained some paper and a pencil from a table under the window and motioned Fitzy to join him. "You can draw here or anywhere else in the house if you wish to." He then walked over to the nightstand, grabbed a book, and handed it to Meta. "We've reached the part where Wandering Willie is telling a bang-up ghost story, so you may want to start by reading that part again."

Mrs. Drexel smiled weakly and nodded.

Before Michael Drexel took his leave, Meta asked him to speak to George about the Learned Ladies' surprise. Especially about how important it was to have both Brunels, Marc and Isambard, and the Thames Tunnel Company's board members present that day.

Mr. Drexel smiled. "I do not see any harm in your plan, Mrs. Russell. I will discuss it with George for your sake. I think it can be managed without too much difficultly. I must admit your surprise has me rather intrigued."

Both Drexels left the house and she sat in the stuffed chair by Mrs. Drexel's bed. The older woman clearly felt no distress over having strangers in her room, because while Meta read to her, she wore a smile of gratitude. She did not seem perturbed and even made a noise like a giggle when Fitzy bounded in and out the room, eager to show both women his drawings.

As the afternoon wore on, Meta's heart broke a little more upon her full understanding of the woman's condition. Other than the effects of the stroke on her speech and one side of her body, she retained her full faculties. How could the younger Mr. Drexel blame his father for giving his first priorities to remaining by his wife's side? Meta stifled an urge to make him understand his father's feelings on the subject when he returned, because, without a doubt, that discussion would prove unsuccessful and unwanted.

Close to six o'clock in the evening, Meta sent Fitzy home for his dinner. It wasn't until seven that the men returned. Michael Drexel praised her generosity for reading to his wife, thanked her profusely, and immediately left to visit the invalid upstairs.

Mr. George Drexel stood in the drawing room, one elbow on the hearth, puffing a cigar. He blew the smoke upward toward the ceiling.

Meta joined him by the hearth. "Shall I stay while you greet your mother and then return?"

"Mother can wait. I've had some wonderful news." His chest expanded as he inhaled.

Meta considered giving him a scold for not thinking of his mother, but refrained. She did not want to dampen his current enthusiasm. Indeed, every part of his person seemed alive with happiness, expressing itself through rapid movements, joyous smiles, and laughing words he could not quite get out in any coherent order. "Mrs. Russell, you…you fabulous female. I cannot fully express my thanks." He puffed on his cigar. "Thank you for being the instrument that let my father attend the board meeting of the Thames Tunnel Company tonight. It is through your good offices that I owe you my deepest gratitude." He threw his cigar into the fire, then reached for her hand.

She stared at their joined hands, marveling at the sudden transfer of warmth. Her hand had not felt cold before, but now encased in his warm skin, she enjoyed the pleasant, heated sensation.

"It is because of you, dear madam, that the board plans to offer my name up at the next shareholder meeting for one of the positions of resident engineer. Do you know what this means for me?"

She smiled and shook her head. "No, not in the least."

"It means the possibility of advancement and a higher salary. But of more importance, this recognition also means more exposure for my inventions. One board member even expressed interest in my card-shuffling device. Imagine the potential earnings once the machine is patented and put into production." He threw his head back and laughed. "And all of this because of you, dear lady. I must admit my father is rather taken with you. He says you help others in need without expecting something in return—a true gift to others, surely? Well, you have decidedly given me a gift."

"I'm pleas—"

"My father and I also discussed your request in regard to your *surprise*. I believe I can accomplish what you wish. Give me a firm date, and I will arrange for the members of the board, and both Brunels, to be on the site within the next couple of weeks." He gave her hand a swift kiss. "Would that be acceptable?"

"Yes." She managed to hold her hand steady and not offend him by jerking it away.

"My concerns remain, however, because the stakes are high. If a water intrusion or accident happens when everyone is assembled, and the public has full view of the accident, it may hurt the tunnel's chances of drawing further investors. Even worse, if a major leak happens in front of an elevated personage, Parliament and all of London could turn against us. The resulting bad press might end the tunnel's chance of being completed forever."

She nodded and pulled her hand free, missing the warmth of him immediately.

He focused on her hand as it was pulled away, his brows knit.

She took a step backward.

Upon her movement, he stared at her until their gazes held.

Holding her head high and stepping backward again, she neither shook nor stumbled but continued to hold the stare. Her retreat formed a message loud and clear: *I may desire you, but I can resist you too.*

A corner of his mouth lifted, and he draped his arm on the mantel. Quite the vision of a gentleman at leisure, despite a few mud spatters on his shiny black boots.

Stepping back again, she neared the wall across from him and realized his power to move her with his physical presence had been greatly diminished. She took a deep breath and gave him a carefree smile. "Will Tuesday next be suitable for the Learned Ladies' surprise?"

He drummed his fingers on the stack of white cards on the mantelpiece. "Tuesday next then. I'll get back to you by tomorrow, if that date proves impossible." He took a single, large step closer.

Her heartbeat became noticeable. Forcing her voice to remain calm, she said, "Thank you. I know you will not be disappointed."

"Women rarely disappoint me." He took another step in her direction.

She almost laughed. "Indeed."

He stepped forward again. "By persuading my father to join me today, you've helped me in ways I cannot adequately describe. My career may turn on this chance."

Now only a couple of feet away, she considered holding her palm out to stop him from advancing further.

He paused. "Madam, may I have permission to kiss my favorite pet? You have no worries I will come closer. I will not force my attentions on you. This time it is you who must take the step."

His meaning was perfectly clear. Since she had instigated a kiss in the mews, he was giving her another chance to do the same.

For some unknown reason, she wanted to kiss him—desperately. Desire spread through her, while on the outside she could only stare.

He shifted his weight to one leg in a more casual stance. "I repeat. May I express my gratitude by having the honor, the pleasure, and the celebration of my victory complete, by kissing you?"

Ready words failed her.

"No kiss then?" Good to his word, he remained fixed in place.

"How many women have taken you up on your… unusual offer for a kiss?"

His chest swelled. "All."

"All!" While the word "all" was an English word used by humans, she heard a cock crow instead.

"I promise you, none of the ladies ever regretted it in the least."

"I do not doubt you, but I do not need a kiss, thank you." She struggled to make her laughter sound carefree, but she knew she treaded on dangerous ground. "Do you always express your happiness by kissing the nearest female?"

Why did she ask him that question?

Did she seek confirmation that he was not angry over her refusal or that she had lost his interest altogether? She inhaled deeply and steeled herself against the appearance of the bear.

"May I ask why you have refused me?" He remained calm, the bear kept in check.

"You know why. I have no expectations of a relationship between us and do not seek one. My situation in life is settled and happy." The full danger of her situation hit her. She found him as appealing as an irresistible sweet, even though any alliance would likely be about bodily desires only. The other option—and the real danger—was the possibility that she might fall in love again, fall in love with a man who likely never considered marriage. Besides, if she did wed a second time, all of her fortune and property would belong to her husband, thus limiting her ability to freely help her siblings. No, another marriage would never do, but a kiss would certainly be nice. Should she reconsider, take her fill of him while he offered himself? If so, could she steel herself against falling in love?

They stood in silence for a minute or two, listening to the chimes from the tall clock in the hall. During this time, his fingers remained surprisingly still, a first in her presence. He kept his eyes focused on her, a wry smile upon his lips. Today the magnificence of his figure, dressed in a scarlet waistcoat and those shiny black boots, attracted her more than she dared to admit.

He broke the silence with a chuckle. "I had hoped I could move you into a higher category, and I'm quite disappointed on that score. Surely had we kissed again, you could have reached the exalted honor of Wilting Flowers or Eager Out of the Gate or…" He gave her the wicked, sensual smile. "Perhaps your performance would be up to a Happy Goer?"

Meta's first response centered on indignation, embarrassment, and the type of surprise similar to what Lily must have felt when she found herself classified as a Happy Goer. "Ah, the honor is my loss, sir. I believe it is time for me to leave. We will meet again when the Learned Ladies deliver their surprise." She gathered up her gloves and bonnet. Before she left, she turned and said, "No, I prefer my original category, thank you. I like rabbits, so I'm quite happy to remain a rabbit in your book."

He came near, lowered his head, and dropped his eyelids a fraction.

Any female with a brain would've fled. She stood fixed, indulging in the memory of his kisses. Then she let her thoughts tumble even further into forbidden territory. First, she itched to reach up and remove his snowy cravat and rough coat. How long and hard would it be for her to fully remove his garments? Was there a private place where they could remove their clothes and spend the day in lovemaking? These amorous desires caused her body to respond in languorous preparation. She started to pant.

He spoke in a silky baritone, "Very well, you will be my favorite rabbit. My rabbit who I cherish hopes that one day I will call my special Happy Goer rabbit."

That moment, the words that tumbled from her mouth reflected her sexual desires. "Are you so sure I'm not a goddess rabbit?"

He approached close enough to place his foot between her legs; his thigh touched hers. Then he tenderly dragged the back of his hand slowly across her cheek. "My dear Mrs. Russell, is that a promise? I must say I am intrigued."

Eleven

GEORGE GLANCED UP TO THE PLATFORM WHERE HIS father stood in conversation with Mr. Marc Brunel. With the ease of one familiar with soliciting funds, his father had arranged a meeting with the majority of the tunnel's important personnel. Without their knowledge of a pending event, the tunnel's principals now gathered at the site on Cow Court. While his father and others poured over the account books on a wooden platform next to the giant pit, George and several other engineers, including Mr. Isambard Brunel, Mr. Beamish, and Mr. Gravatt, conversed below at the bottom of the pit.

Twirling his pencil between his fingers, George wondered if Mrs. Russell's surprise would indeed take place. If it did, and proved successful, his promotion might be sealed. He would be given more responsibilities than he had at present. Moreover, the one hundred and fifty pounds added to his salary would go a long way toward helping pay for the construction of models for his proposed projects.

However, he considered himself a realist, so failure

could be in his cards too. His acquaintance with Mrs. Russell had not been long enough for him to have complete confidence that she could deliver upon her promise. After all, she had guaranteed success once before. She had promised that if he performed the onerous office of setting James straight on the initials in the field guide, James and Lily would resume their engagement. Decidedly, that did not happen. So today, would she and her "Learned Ladies" come through with their surprise? Thankfully, if she failed, no one would be the wiser. Most of the tunnel's principals were engaged in normal duties, so a failure to deliver on her part would have little detrimental effect upon his chances of advancement.

In the middle of an argument with the cement supplier about the latest lot's inability to dry within the specified amount of time, George heard a commotion above him. He and the other engineers looked up to the platform. As if orchestrated by an unseen conductor, all of the men working on the tunnel also turned to look up to the street.

So Mrs. Russell must have come through with her surprise.

His spirits lifted to a remarkable degree, and his current opinion of her softened from fetching busybody to possible benefactress. He mentioned an upcoming honor to the other engineers standing near him, so everyone ascended the staircase to join the others already assembled on another wooden platform built for the public to view the workings.

At least five black traveling coaches had pulled into Cow Court, and their passengers disembarked. His father quickly informed the other tunnel personnel that they might expect the privilege of a visit by a person of significant importance.

George scanned the passengers as they exited their carriages. Mrs. Russell, Lady Sarah, and several other "Learned Ladies" disembarked from the first carriage, while at least fifty gentlemen exited the other carriages. The guests greeted each other as they all moved to gather around the platform.

Mrs. Russell caught his eye and waved.

He enthusiastically waved back but immediately lowered his hand. In his excitement, there was no need for him to turn into a tomfool schoolboy.

She seemed to understand this, because she covered her mouth to hide what must have been a short burst of laughter—the irritating female.

Glancing over the assembled guests, George spied a tall man in a black suit and a recognizable hooked nose. His heartbeat escalated wildly. The man was the "Iron Duke" himself, the Duke of Wellington.

What an honor!

She had mentioned connections, but this was beyond even his wildest expectations. Besides a great war hero, the duke's opinions also had significant influence on Parliament. George wanted to jump off the platform and kiss that astonishing Mrs. Russell right in front of everyone. Instead, he caught her glance again and gave her a deep bow. He could be generous. She deserved it—the brilliant woman.

It didn't take long before all of the guests stood on the platform and introductions were made. The tunnel was represented by members of the Thames Tunnel Company's board, two of their bankers from the Bank of England, and one of their solicitors. The guests included the Duke of Wellington and the Dukes of Cambridge and Somerset. Also amongst the visitors of distinction were the local MP and Nathan Rothschild, the financier. Mrs. Russell's party included Lady Sarah Stainthorpe along with her father, the Earl of Royston.

Mr. Marc Brunel began the festivities by giving the assembled guests a tour of the workings, including leading them down into the pit to examine the giant shield.

George stayed behind and swiftly culled Mrs. Russell away from the herd following Mr. Brunel. Dressed in a sapphire blue walking dress with a straw poke bonnet, she looked like an angel recently descended from heaven. "Madam, if we were not in company, I would...kiss you right now." He chuckled. "Perhaps more. I expect that you understand my meaning?" He gazed at her with fierce appreciation.

She giggled, but as soon as their gazes met, her smile vanished and she began to take rapid breaths.

Could she discern his amorous intent that very moment?

Of course, he knew she was no slow top. "Yes, if there were no consequences, I'd pull you into the steam engine house and kiss you senseless."

This time she broke out in a ravishing blush and looked away toward the pit.

Had his expression of spontaneous ardor inadvertently insulted her? "Right. I apologize, madam. I hope no offense was taken."

While keeping her gaze on her feet, she nodded. "I've enough experience with your physical need to celebrate that I understand you completely."

Oh, he wanted to lick every inch of that blush. "My sudden desire to express my gratitude arises because, frankly, I did not think your promise would come to fruition."

She whipped her head around to look directly at him.

"But, *madam*, now I could just sing—you wonderful woman."

"I don't think bears sing," she said, her humor returned and smile radiant. "Although I'm a bit miffed you didn't trust me."

"You once indicated that if I enlightened James your sister would resume her engagement. However, you must admit that never came to pass. But this surprise… From now on, I'll trust whatever you say."

"I wouldn't go that far," she said, laughter playing about her blue eyes. "You must thank Lady Sarah. She made the arrangements with His Grace."

"Ah." He tilted his head and nodded to show his respect.

After the distinguished guests returned to the platform, chairs were placed in a semicircle, so everyone took a seat to listen to a few speeches.

He led Mrs. Russell to the side and held out his hand to offer the chair next to Lady Sarah. "Madam."

She sat and adjusted her bonnet to shield her beautiful face from the bright sun.

This gave him the privacy to take her in, the lovely figure ending in fetching ankles—nothing like a slim ankle to set a gentleman on fire. Taking the seat next to her, he moved his chair close to hers, so their thighs lightly touched.

Would he get away with his impertinence?

She flashed him a look of surprise, but she did not pull away. An audible breath escaped from between those rose-colored lips.

Next a representative of the tunnel's board gave a brief welcome and introduction.

George appreciated the brevity but squirmed in his seat nevertheless. He needed to move about, felt an urge to do something else.

When she finally glanced his way, he lifted his eyebrows. "I can think of more interesting things to do than listen to this boring fellow."

She rewarded him with a soft giggle.

The first speech, given by a junior MP, proved to be a tedious speech about his "questionable fitness to address you" because he considered them such an eminent gathering.

George leaned close to her ear. "I don't question my fitness to dress you."

"Hush!" She blushed quite prettily.

The MP did, however, please his audience at the end of his speech by praising the tunnel. He even ended his speech by calling it "one of the proudest ornaments in England."

The audience cheered and clapped.

He leaned close again. "May I say that wearing that blue gown, *you* are one of the proudest ornaments in England?" He took and squeezed her gloved hand, then laced his big fingers between hers.

A small gasp escaped her. She turned to look at him, then grinned. "May I say you are proving yourself quite the charmer?" She pulled her hand free.

He bowed his head. "Honored."

A hush then claimed the crowd, as the Iron Duke himself rose to speak to the assembly. Wellington described the tunnel as "the greatest work of art ever contemplated." His words delighted the audience and everyone cheered loudly. From that moment on, repeated cheers unreservedly followed every comment the old warrior made.

While the Iron Duke continued his remarks about the importance of new routes of commerce, George caught Mrs. Russell staring at him. So, still obsessed with amorous thoughts, like kissing her senseless, he gave her the best wicked smile he could conjure up at a moment's notice—a gesture proven to be an irresistible treat for most ladies.

She blushed and whispered something in Lady Sarah's ear.

The Iron Duke then spoke of the tunnel's military advantages.

The audience clapped, and several "huzzahs" filled the air.

The next time he caught Mrs. Russell glancing his way, he flashed his stare of polite admiration. If for some reason the wicked expression failed, his charming look had always proved successful with the ladies. He shifted to press his hard thigh slightly harder against hers.

Meta glanced down to her kid shoes but did not shift away.

Lady Sarah noticed his thigh and frowned at him.

He countered with a feigned innocent smile.

During his final words, the Duke of Wellington

asked the crowd to buy further shares at the next offering or donate directly to the tunnel's funding.

The crowd cheered and eagerly agreed to invest.
Everyone stood and began to gather around the carriages for the journey home.

After exchanging a few pleasantries with Mrs.
Russell and the Learned Ladies, Lady Sarah took Mrs.
Russell's arm and led her away. After several steps,
Mrs. Russell glanced back at him.

Next his father approached.

His father squeezed his arm. "I must rush home to
tell Mother the news. It will mean so much to us both
to share this celebration. Would you like to join me?"

"Not now. There are still some gentlemen I would
like introductions to."

Michael Drexel nodded. "Very well."

George watched the back of his father's coat disap-
pear into the crowd, off to tell his mother the good
news, rather than take a little time to join the celebra-
tions with any of the other principals.

"Drexel, my boy."

He turned to see Mr. Marc Brunel approaching.
The Frenchman pushed up his round spectacles and
held out his hand.

They shook hands.

"Sir," George said.

"Quite a triumph, eh, Mr. Drexel? I tell you, at the
next meeting of the Thames Tunnel Company's board,
I plan to vigorously insist upon your promotion to
resident engineer. Your assistance has proven invaluable in so many different ways. I can honestly say I am
truly grateful for your efforts." Mr. Brunel slapped him

on the shoulder. "Keep the line, understand? No more publishing books or public imbroglios. If you stay out of trouble, I do not see how the board could refuse a good man like you." Mr. Brunel waved at the Duke of Somerset. "Please pardon me, His Grace desires a word. Congratulations again." The short, active man smiled and headed in the direction of the duke's party.

George could not stand still another minute. He must share his good news. He strode off in the direction his father had taken, but he failed to catch him in time. While his friends spoke of the successful speeches, he decided to tell Mrs. Russell about his potential promotion. She would keep his secret and perhaps appreciate what this promotion meant to him.

As he approached her, she excused herself from her companion and walked up to congratulate him.

With a silly grin no doubt planted on his lips, he said, "You initiated this, so I am quite aware of where I should place my gratitude. This is all your doing. Thank you." He then whispered, "My name will be put forth for a promotion. I must give my farewells to our guests, but then I'd like you to stay until they leave."

She repeatedly blinked.

George let her read in his fierce expression exactly how he planned to thank her. Thank her in a way they would both find pleasure and satisfaction. Thank her in a way that would remove his building frisson between them, once and for all. He had practiced this look so many times, no woman could fail to understand its meaning. Besides, this female was a widow and likely missed intimate relations. He whispered into her ear, "Please allow me to thank you by giving you the benefit of my skills to bring you to bliss and hold you there. Afterwards, we will resume our separate lives." He raised his voice. "I'll escort you home safely. You have nothing to worry about on that score. It's just…I wish to give you the full expression of my gratitude—in private."

She started, made a nervous little jump. Then her demeanor changed to a happy one, and she gave a single nod. "I'm surprised to discover that I would welcome your—attentions." She started to breath hard. "We will celebrate together, is that right?"

"Yes." He chuckled in a mixture of surprise and delight. So his favorite rabbit possessed courage as well. "Thank you. I have a feeling I will be saying those words to you many times in the next couple of days."

The corner of her mouth lifted. "Perhaps I may find an occasion to say that too."

He stepped closer. "I can decidedly promise you that. After the crowd has departed for home, I'll engage a room at the inn across the street." He pointed to the right.

"Yes." She stiffened, nodded, and her features became overwhelmed by an alluring blush. She probably never contemplated such naughty behavior before.

"I will enter the inn first and arrange to let the room. When you are ready, enter the door on the side so no one will see you. To your left, you will see a staircase before the main public rooms ahead. I'll engage a room on the first floor, leave the door ajar, and wait for your arrival." His words had a stirring effect upon his person and that rush of expectation that warmed his sense of masculine satisfaction.

She nodded but failed to look at him directly.

"The public house is called The Spread Eagle and Crown."

She giggled. "Oh no."

"Oh yes. I guess that means I represent the crown, while you represent—"

"No, no, no, don't say it. You are, indeed, the only man in London naughty enough to have written the field guide."

He laughed aloud and slapped his thigh. "I'm going to enjoy showing you exactly why, madam, your observation is a correct one."

Twelve

META HEARD THE CROWD BUZZING AROUND HER, heard her friends speak words like "success" and "tunnel." A slight breeze had chilled her during the speeches, but now her entire figure became overheated.

This time, when he offered something decidedly more than a kiss, she had said, "Yes."

Yes, her response decided before her brain was given the question. Yes, the word spoken by some unknown aspect of her character. She became agitated and impatient. Her excitement escalated; she began to perspire; her breathing rate increased—all from the mere anticipation of the shared act of passion to come.

On her wedding night, her mother delicately described the event to her as "amorous congress" and said very little else. It did not take long after her marriage until she started to enjoy sexual relations with her husband. She learned to relish the variety, the happy, celebratory relations, the giggling, silly relations, and even the panting relations of seemingly detached, mutual need. Today she wanted to give herself to this man. Give herself as she suspected she desired from their first meeting. Give herself to a man known for his famed skills with women. Would the action itself be different from that of the inexperienced twenty-year-olds she and her husband had been?

Of course, she faced the possibility that the mere deed might lead to pregnancy or romantic love, but she dismissed those concerns. She had never become with child in the months she spent with her husband. And as for as falling in love, George had, in his own way, let it be known that this would be a single, shared moment of passion. Yet the possibility that her heart might be vulnerable remained. She shook her head, dismissed her concerns. Today she'd join him in celebration, bestow upon this irresistible man her most intimate regard, celebrate together, share the victory, and relish the moment.

Stifling her embarrassment, she excused herself from returning home in Lady Sarah's carriage and indicated Mr. Drexel would escort her home, once he had become free of the lingering guests. If her friends suspected something amiss, they hid it well. Meta stood there, watching the ladies enter their carriages and leave. All the while, she felt like a schoolgirl about to enter a room after being told not to do so, hoping to find an unguarded treat.

When the time arrived to join Mr. Drexel, she became anxious and almost ran to the inn. The surroundings on the way blurred. She could not catch her breath. She easily found the side door, like the doors found in many physicians' offices, discreet entrances hidden from the main street.

She entered the inn and let her eyes adjust to walls

of dark wood, a probable relic of Elizabethan times.
The sour smells of ale, smoke, and the river wafted
in from the inn's ground floor. The loud voices of
the workmen in the taproom masked the sounds of
her arrival. She climbed the stairs out of the haze and
onto a bright landing with an open window on the
far end. Here the sun shone on a vase of open-form
red peonies placed on an old wooden table, a modest
effort to brighten this one corner of the world.

Meta soon discovered the door left ajar and entered
a small room with a single leaded window. A shaft of
low afternoon light reached across the entire room,
illuminating a cupboard with strong iron hinges reaching across the entire front. Besides the cupboard, bed,
and washstand, the room contained a dark oak spindle
chair almost black with age. Above the bed hung a
rather crude oil painting of a prized cow, charming
regardless of the painter's lack of skill.

The room also contained one very tall and dark
engineer. He rose from the chair and moved to hold
out his hands. "Come here. Let's celebrate."

Somewhere in her mind, she realized that if her
courage failed her, now would be the time to make
polite excuses and leave. Instead, she struggled to mask
her excitement and appear calm. Calm in the face of a
gentleman of well-practiced allure. There was no sign
of the bear, only a handsome man standing before her
in polished black shoes, black trousers, and a white
lawn shirt. His hat, coat, and waistcoat were piled on
top of the dark cupboard. His loosened cravat hung
like a white silk snake around his neck, while the
three buttons on his white shirt were open, revealing

a strong neck and tanned skin, all set upon impossibly broad shoulders.

"You're a courageous woman, Mrs. Russell. Allow me." He moved slowly to first embrace her in a standing hug before he began to kiss her. He kissed lightly. Mere fleeting touches repeated many times, escalating waves of joy. Smiles mixed with giggles and punctuated by chuckles in between. "I've planned this single moment to express my complete thanks for your efforts. You will enjoy this, believe me."

"With your reputation, I have no doubts on that score." His kissing talents had abolished any uneasiness she possessed when she entered the room and left her with a happy anticipation of the lovemaking to come.

"You see, the secret to pleasuring a woman requires many traits unique to engineers." His wholly wicked smile appeared on a pleased countenance. "There are steps to consider for maximum satisfaction. It's like building a bridge: first you must find the right site. In this case"—he locked the door—"the site needs to be secured."

Meta found herself pleasantly surprised that from his lighthearted words, "single moment," neither of them would take this any further than just this one time. And while she anticipated enjoyment in the act, she now firmly believed she would remember this stolen moment of passion forever.

This voice took on a low seductive tone she had not heard him use before. The deep rumble sounded like an approaching thunderstorm, causing within her a resonance of languid ease.

The wholly wicked smile frolicked just above that

deep cleft in his chin. "Of course, the site must also be removed of existing structures." He took her hand and led her to the bed.

She sat, waiting.

He moved to stand in front of the cupboard. "Of course, the gentleman must go first." Swiftly removing his socks and white lawn shirt, he pulled his cravat off and flung it on the bed.

She stared—she couldn't help it. Never had she seen a man with a more broad, sculpted chest. His torso, lightly covered with dark chest hair, seemed too perfect to be real, like the marble statues of Greek warriors in the British Museum. Then she remembered him working alongside the Tunnel's miners in manual labor, the likely cause of his large, smooth undulating arm muscles. Her throat dried. Upon the realization that he had allowed the exact amount of time needed for her perusal and physical response, she blushed.

He slowly moved his hands to the four buttons on the top of his falls.

She glanced upward to his face.

He wore a smirk of promised satisfaction. "The site must be completely bare, you understand?"

Nodding slowly, she licked her lower lip.

Flicking the buttons open with practiced skill, his trousers dropped to the floor. This time he lingered once again, giving her the time to fully take in the sight of his erection.

She had never been granted the opportunity to examine her husband naked. Their lovemaking had always been in bed, under the covers. Now with the freedom to take her fill of him, she couldn't pull her eyes away—she couldn't. She softly sighed.

He picked up his trousers and hung them over the cupboard. "We are only halfway to fully uncovering our building site." Standing in front of her, he held out his hand.

She desperately wanted to stroke him, but she placed her palm in his large hand instead. A gentle pull, and she found herself standing.

He began to disrobe her. "The site must be cleared and laid bare for a full examination." He knew exactly the order of which garments to remove and the method of removal. A swift tug with a flourish for outer garments, but for those items of dress that lay next to her sensitive skin, he pulled achingly slowly, leaving a stimulating trail of pleasant sensation. She had noticed seconds into his "site" examination that his full erection grew between them. But he had obviously trained himself to continue on, without overt regard to his state of arousal.

Soon she found herself naked, except for her drawers, standing still while he alternately moved his hands and lips across every inch of her sensitive skin in a thorough "site examination."

"Hold your arms out to the side." He trailed his finger from the top of her ear, down along the curve of her neck, and then out along her shoulder. "So many curves on a woman. Curves are the hardest part of engineering to get right. They must be given special attention. And only the most skilled craftsman can hammer out a curve in iron or carve it out in wood."

The effects of his touch lingered on her skin. Her

languid ease vanished and transformed into a deeper, wetter, urgent sense of desire.

He swiftly removed her drawers. Then his finger started on her low hip and traced the curve of her body all the way up and under the long line under her arm. "So many curves...beautiful curves." He stepped closer to straddled one of her legs with both of his, so she could intimately feel him against her hip. Then he started to rock her slowly between the bed and his thigh. Meanwhile, his clever fingers stroked, circled, and flicked across her sex. He looked down between them at her large firm breasts. "And then the most alluring curves of them all."

She smiled and watched his fingers move up to trace curves from the bottom of her breasts to the top. Then they circled around in even smaller circles until he repeatedly flicked his finger firmly across her nipple. She softly moaned, thoroughly eager for release.

Kneeling before her, he used his tongue and skillful lips to retrace the trail his finger had taken and moved upward. "Any engineer worth his salt knows the nature of these curves. The question is"—he traced the curve of her breast again from the bottom to the top—"the physical forces involved. What we have here is the force of a downward weight seemingly without support."

She dug her fingers through his black locks falling around his neck. "Do you play the inquiring engineer with other ladies?" She glanced down at her breasts currently held upward with both of his hands.

His deep chuckle resonated. "Not when I was young, because I lacked the discipline to collect the relevant...data." He moaned before licking each nipple again, one after the other. "In other words, analysis required a presence of mind that I frequently lacked for *two* obvious reasons."

She sighed and managed to say, "You are a delightfully wicked man."

"On my best days." A bout of leisurely kisses began again, his tongue savoring her entire body from her intimate folds, to the sensitive spot behind her ears. His attention then returned to her breasts. "Now, the two choices for opposing forces to counter gravity are a vertical hold"—once again he placed both hands under her breasts and lifted them—"from a tight stay or some hidden buttress system." He then tenderly kneaded or lightly flicked his fingers along the side of both breasts.

She dropped her eyelids, moaned, and let herself relish the pleasure of his tender touch. "It's the tightness of the stays that provides a supportive shelf, correct?"

"You are a lady of some mechanical talent. But you are getting ahead of the force analysis." A long kiss followed, an escalating dance of lips and tongues. He gasped for air. "So let's examine the problem. On a normal gown, the downward force of weight is countered by an upward force of cloth just about here." He proceeded to lick and kiss her thoroughly just under her neck.

Her breaths came faster and her moans louder. "The force of stays is...different...than...that... piece...of...cloth."

"Correct, so there is little upward counter force in a stay. So what holds these lovely breasts up?" He reached over to the bed and grabbed his long black cravat. "Kneel before me, please." His eyelids lowered a fraction, and he held out his hand to steady her.

With her heartbeat racing out of control, she climbed up and knelt on the hard bed.

He stood directly behind her. With both hands, he wrapped the cravat around her breasts and held them tight from behind. "Stay engineers have two weapons to solve the gravity problem. The first is friction." Wearing his wicked smile, he pulled the cravat tighter and rotated it back and forth several inches.

Heaven. She lost all comprehension of his words.

"The expression on your face tells me friction is the preferred method of force." He chuckled. "Now the second method used by stay engineers is a mechanical force provided by the whale bone, in the center or along the sides." He held the cravat under her breasts and lifted the ends upward, so the cloth resembled a giant U. Then he alternately pulled the ends to cause friction on the bottom of both breasts.

She sighed. If she were in a normal state, she'd probably giggle, but her body had become a liquid pile of warm, reactive flesh, and her brain succumbed solely to obedience of his intimate touch.

He stopped moving the cravat, but still held it tight around her. "Of course, if these two forces, upward and counter, are not sufficient to counter the downward force of gravity, a disaster might happen." He let go of the cravat ends.

The silky cloth fell across her sensitive skin until it pooled on the bed. Her bare breasts a fetching pink due to the lavish attention they had received.

"It would be a great tragedy if insufficient force caused a disaster, and you appear unsupported and bare as you do now, let's say, in a crowded room."

"More." She chuckled. "More please."

He wrapped his long fingers around both her breasts. "You know, I suddenly realize the similarities between these forces and those related to a cantilever beam."

His sentences became too long, her need too great—she wanted him now. "Please stop talking."

He chuckled before lowering her down on the bed, then covering her with his solid, warm body. Then achingly slow, he penetrated her with a single plunge. Holding himself up on his arms, he began to thrust.

She felt the rhythmic lifting, the sense of fullness, her softness filled with his solid, hot flesh. Her need climbed, climbed, climbed, and became restless. "Ah."

"Yes." He grabbed her buttocks and swiftly pounded into her.

Then her bliss came with an abbreviated sigh. "Oh."

He continued as long as he could, before he withdrew at the right moment. A long moan escaped his lips as he released his seed upon the sheet.

They lay side by side, panting.

She had enough wits remaining to consider his control remarkable and not unexpected for an experienced rake. All she desired now was to do it again. How could she have been pleased with the thought that they would only do this once? Now the memory of his passion changed her mind and filled it with an aching desire she might not be able to forget—ever.

They both remained still, breathing hard, and

clutching each other. Then, following a kiss under her ear, he buried his head in the crook of her neck until his panting slowed.

She remained still, relishing the warm slickness he left beside her. Around her the heady smell of sex mixed with the stench of the Thames seeping in through the window.

They held each other close and listened to the rain begin to tap upon the window. He rose, shut the window, and returned to the bed. "Let's nestle. Funny, don't think I've ever really appreciated nestling before. The physical part, I mean. Usually I avoided it, since it is the universal moment desired by all women to *talk*."

She laughed. "It's just words. Granted, not as enjoyable"—she smiled—"but you'll survive conversation. Gives me an idea though. Tell me about the field guide. How it came to pass, the inspiration that spurred you to write it."

"I find I'm not irritated at all over your version of female talk—surprising that. The expected flattery is the worst." He pulled her onto his warm chest, facing him. "The field guide started as a jest between three friends the year we left Oxford. My friend Ross quickly became successful on the exchange, but he could always use more funds to invest. Meanwhile, the jingle-brained Boyce and myself struggled to find professions. At the time, I resisted engaging in my father's occupation. I suppose it was some sort of rebellion on my part."

"Understandable." Her hands roved over his chest, stroking him in the direction of his smooth chest hair.

He smiled. "Boyce's brother owns a publishing firm, so my friend challenged us to pen the field guide to help his brother's business become profitable." He chuckled. "But our reasons were more like a chance to best each other. In the long run, it proved an easy way to make instant funds separate from the control of our parents. The three of us all had experience with women from an early age, so writing the books was easy."

"You had intimate relations with the same number of ladies in your field guide?"

He blushed, a heartwarming, rosy contrast to the dark stubble around his cheeks, the dimple in his chin, and those fathomless black eyes. "No, no, of course not, at least not that many. While every lady is unique, most of the descriptions arise from our previous experiences, hopeful imaginings, or just pure fiction. The book is mostly the product of three young colts with little to do, under the influence of a great deal of brandy."

She laughed.

"After its publication, we received many compliments. It got to the point where strangers would shout at me walking down the street, 'Hail there, my good fellow. Enjoyed your book.' The handbook and field guide amused and entertained a large number of men, which I discovered to be quite gratifying. If you ask me today, I have only a few regrets. At the time, I was too daft and too young to realize the notoriety gained from its publication might affect the success of my future profession. Frankly, I've heard the majority of the ladies enjoyed it too."

"You never became fond of these ladies in your past?"

He stared, wide-eyed. "Fond of them all. Two of the relationships lasted for over a year. Yes, I was devilish fond of them all."

"Fond is the wrong word. Did you ever fall in love?"

"If you expect me to carry on a conversation about romantic love"—he rolled his eyes—"we can leave here this instant."

"Why can't you speak easily about simple emotions like love?" She clung to his chest.

This time he gazed at her like she had instantly become a candidate for Bedlam. Then he shifted his glance to the cracked plaster ceiling for several minutes. Finally, without turning his head, he simply replied, "I'm a man. I do not understand why, but men avoid that like the plague. You must not have been married long if you cannot understand that."

"Perhaps you're right." He fell silent, so she expected him to fall asleep at any minute. "You must have fallen in love with some lady very hard to be so reticent and bitter about it."

He sat up and pulled her along with him. "I'm not bitter," he said, a defensive tinge coloring his voice. "Romantic love has no use, does it? Look at my father. When my mother had a stroke, he walked away from the tunnel. Walked away from the most exciting achievement ever constructed by man. Even when I pleaded, begged, he walked away."

"But the woman he loved needed him more."

"He could afford a servant to look after her."

"Then they both would be alone."

"Pardon?"

"She would be bedridden, ill, and alone. While he could help his son and build the most amazing achievement in England, but it would not signify—not really. How could it? I never witnessed any regrets in your father's word or tone about his current situation in life. My guess is without her by his side to celebrate with him, the achievement became less meaningful. Maybe now he does his best to work on the project, whenever he feels he can spare the time, solely for your sake. You have to give him credit."

"Perhaps a little, when he does provide help. But she is not in danger or pain and spends most of her time sleeping. A servant can be easily engaged to care for her, but he refuses to leave her side and gives irrelevant excuses. I am his only child—his son, for God's sake. Since I am beginning my profession as an engineer, it is a crucial time when my whole future and career depend upon his assistance. He has vastly more experience than I do and can guide me as no other man can." His voice softened on the last word, so he stopped speaking and rolled over to face the wall.

She could not see his face, but he seemed wounded by his father's preference for his mother's company. After this exchange, her previous concern about forming an unrequited love posed no threat. Instead, she found an overwhelming desire to help him achieve his goals by any means possible.

A little while later, they made love again. Only this time, in a slow method more romantic than th exploring engineer. His skills were achingly tend but exhilarating nevertheless.

When she could no longer be pleasured

remained in each other's arms as the rain beat harder, the torrent blurring the small leaded glass windows.

He pulled her onto his chest. "I feel I must hold you, a gesture I've always made because it is required. But today I desire it. Another strange change in my normal behavior, is it not?"

She nodded, not knowing what to say.

"Perhaps the ease of a perfect day, in the company of a beautiful woman, could be the reason."

She smiled up at him. "Thank you for the compliment, Mr. Drexel."

He chuckled. "Time to call me George. And I suspect in the long run I owe you more than I can ever repay."

They leisurely dressed, left the inn by the side door, and, under the gray skies of rain at dusk, walked back to town. Thankfully, the rain had rendered the streets deserted, affording some level of privacy.

Just two blocks from Swallow Street, they happened to meet Grizel and Sybella. Both Learned Ladies had been at the tunnel earlier and stopped to pay a call on a mutual friend. After greetings were exchanged, the two other women fell silent. They merely glanced at Mr. Drexel and then back at her, suspicions of an attachment or an assignation written on their expressions.

Meta thought that if she dismissed them or hurried away, they might become even more suspicious, ⸺ she decided to pretend nothing seemed amiss or ⸺roper. "I stayed so late talking to Mr. Brunel, Mr. ⸺el kindly offered to walk me home. Dusk can ⸺ightening place in London. Would you ladies like to join us? Mr. Drexel can walk us all safely to our residences."

The two women reluctantly agreed, and the party started off.

George winked at Meta, then wore a ridiculous smile the entire journey.

Grizel was dropped off first. Unfortunately, Meta's town house was just around the corner, so she would have to leave the party before Sybella. Thus she would not have the chance to speak freely to George again.

It rained harder; the cold water poured off the edges of their umbrellas.

She turned to give her farewells to George, in case she might never see him again. But she couldn't think of a word to say of any importance or ones suitable to mention in front of her friends.

He must have been in the identical situation. "I'm at a loss for words." He shook his head. "Funny that."

One glance at Sybella's knowing smirk and Meta became more composed. "I'm not, Mr. Drexel. The words are thank you." She gulped. "Thank you for the escort."

"Yes, that's it. Thank you, madam. Everyone involved with the tunnel owes you and the Learned Ladies so much." His active hands twirled the umbrella. "Will I ever see you again?"

She glanced at Sybella—the small smirk had disappeared. If her friend had suspicions before, her matter-of-fact farewell must have vanished them. "I see no reason for it," Meta said. "Unless you can persuade Lily to change her mind better than I can, which I doubt." She held out her hand. "Mr. Drexel, if I don't see you again, I wish you the best of luck with your tunnel. From now on, I will eagerly look forward to the evening's newspaper to hear of news of the tunnel's progress. Farewell, sir."

"Until we meet again, Mrs. Russell."

Thirteen

"SIR, I HAVE DONE IT." GEORGE YELLED, STANDING outside the drawing room door. He received no response. Perhaps his father had not heard him, so he yelled toward the upstairs part of the house again. "The card shuffler, I've solved it." He returned to the drawing room and waited, assured his father had heard him the second time.

Staring at the simple oak box on his desk, he swelled with pride at his accomplishment. The box had been a devilish nightmare to invent. It started as a flip comment made while playing cards with his two best friends, Ross and Boyce. His friends probably didn't recall his promise to build a shuffler, but he remembered. Now years later, fiddling with it in the few precious moments of his spare time he used to relax, he solved the problem of separating the individual cards. The cards had always seemed to hang up upon the metal levers meant to separate them. Today as he studied the problem, his mind wandered to th appreciation of Meta's appealing curves. Then inspi tion struck. The concept of a wheel's curve tv out to be the solution of his card separation problem. Without her knowledge, she had provided him with assistance, which he knew would please her.

His father entered the room, joined him at the desk, and nodded his appreciation.

George considered his father's manner upon hearing the good news far too casual. Considering the importance of the accomplishment, he should show more enthusiasm than just a nod, for heaven's sake.

"Congratulations, Son." Michael smiled and patted him on the back.

George waited for further praise but received none. While he appreciated the pat, he frankly felt a touch more admiration was due, given the years he had worked on the shuffler. He then remembered Parker was in town, so perhaps his friend would better appreciate his success, since he had suggested the shuffler in the first place. George leaned out of the door, called for Mrs. Morris, and asked her to send a note around to Parker, suggesting they take luncheon together. He returned to demonstrate every detail of the shuffler to his father.

"What are you going to do with it, now that it's a practical reality?" His father turned the wheel again, opened the box, and pulled out the cards shuffled into four separate compartments. "I recommend you seek a patent. And perhaps we should put more effort into investigating a possible market."

"Yes, I'll apply for a patent. Perhaps Burns might consider putting it into production."

"I agree—at least it sounds like a good start." Soon after that comment, his father returned to his mother's upstairs.

George sighed and shook his head, frustrated that his father had clearly understood and appreciated his success yet only spent ten minutes altogether admiring the clever little machine. He'd have to depend on Parker to show the appropriate amount of enthusiasm during luncheon. He returned to the large desk and tested various positions of the wheel in relation to the deck of cards.

He traced his finger along the curve at the top of the wheel, eliciting memories of Meta—warm, pleasant memories. Quite different from the many pleasant memories he had following his other liaisons. Those tended to reflect conquest or success in some form. In his relations with Meta, his intent started as a celebration of success. But the second time they made love, on that rainy afternoon, he discovered a newfound desire to express gratitude and give pleasure. Please her, yes, like the other women who shared his bed. Except the act became more tender in a manner he could not quite fathom. It differed too because the memory of their lovemaking stayed vivid with him. Every day a sight, like this curve before him, or a sound, like a sigh, or a touch, like that of soft skin, created a flood of tender recollections. She would surely appreciate his shuffler, and he regretted the fact that they were unlikely to meet again.

"Hallo, hallo," Parker shouted, bounding through the drawing room door. A frequent guest, he never rang the bell, for the stated purpose of saving Mrs. Morris the bother of coming up from the kitchen. "Happy day, what?" Parker bounced over and shook his hand. His friend's green eyes appeared to sparkle brighter than he had ever seen them. Parker had always dressed in the first stare of fashion. His garments spoke of hours spent with his many tailors and boot makers. Today his drab coat and simple waistcoat hinted that his friend no longer had time to spend on his appearance; therefore, his new marriage must suit him very well.

George slapped his best friend on the back. "Cork brain, come look. Remember that day—what is it—three years ago, when I promised to build a card shuffler? Well, I did it!" He held out his hand. "Shall I demonstrate?"

"Yes, yes, please do." Parker moved close to the desk and bent down to watch the machine close up.

George placed a pack of cards in a little compartment on one end and then turned the wheel several times. After he felt no resistance on the handle, he opened the opposite end of the box revealing shuffled cards in four separate compartments.

"Well, I'll be." Parker straightened and vigorously shook his hand. "Congratulations, ol' man. Never thought it possible, but I'm not surprised. You always were a clever fellow with the whatnots. What are you going to do with it?"

"Patent it first. I don't want anyone to steal it."

"No, no, shuffling cards is so troublesome, you'll probably make a packet on it. Mum's the word."

George smiled, delighted his friend understood and celebrated at the appropriate level his achievement deserved. "A packet would be welcome. We could use some extra monies around here at the moment."

"I must show this amazing box to my wife." Parker

closely examined the interior of the machine. "She would understand what a great thing this is, since she is keen on new machines." His friend straightened to his full height and smoothed his hands over his unruly brown curly hair. "But you will have to show this to Eve yourself to explain the technical bits. She will be thrilled like me, of course, but she will understand your accomplishment better. Lucky to be married to such a clever woman. Would have become married in a tick if I had known about this business of connubial bliss. Yes, yes, married in a tick."

"Happy then, married to a lady of science?"

His emerald eyes flashed with delight. "Never happier. Do you know what she did the other day? She organized all of my waistcoats according to the color, or rather the color in relation to what she calls 'the visible spectrum.' Not quite sure myself what that is, but I'm sure it's a bang-up thing to do with a fellow's waistcoats."

George grinned and motioned for them both to take a seat. "You know, I have truly never seen you happier."

"Yes, yes." Parker wore a boyish grin. "Pater is extremely fond of my wife, more fond than he expected, and more fond of her than of any of his other daughters-in-law. The consequence is that he and his friend, the general, call almost every other day. Not surprising someone accomplished like Eve has him wrapped around her finger, what?"

"No, not surprising in the least. Your wife is remarkable," George said.

"Remember how we used to play tough, mock

each other about being leg-shackled? What a bunch of silly schoolboys. I tell you, a wife is just the ticket to happiness. No more dalliances that turn needy, home and servants run like clockwork, and a fellow happy to boot. Not to mention the waistcoats given the scientific treatment. Seems to me now that the rumors spread about being leg-shackled as nothing more than trouble and grief are probably meant as a decoy. Clearly greedy men spread these false rumors to frighten young men, so they can pick all the best wives for themselves. Doesn't signify now though, since in the end I got the best one."

"You sound just like Ross. He seems to be in some sort of heaven up in the North. And everyone I know considers Heaven and the North mutually exclusive terms. Have you had a letter from him recently?"

"Yes, yes, a week ago. He'll travel down to London at the end of July, so we must all meet. You can tell him all about this tunnel of yours, and I can tell him about m' waistcoats. Currently, he's buying furniture for the Mater and planning more sons. I told him it might be a girl this time, but all he wants is sons." He leaned close. "Serve him right to have a girl. Probably turn into a bowl of jelly at first sight of the little lullaby cheat. The toughest men usually do, you know."

"I'll take your word on it."

"How about you? Leg shackle on the horizon?" He glanced in the direction of the story above them. "Or just not the thing at this time with your mother's illness?"

George had been asked about his matrimonial intentions many times. He had even considered it as a young man, solely as a general concept. But when he did, he could never place a face on the woman lucky enough to be his wife. Seconds after Parker asked him that question, for the first time his mind pictured a lady—Meta. Funny thing, that. Since he had no desire to marry, he quickly dismissed it as a consequence of his lack of visitations to his current lover. "Will marry someday, I suppose. Right now I have no time for females. Every waking hour is spent on working toward my future, starting with the tunnel."

"Yes, yes, I want to hear about that. What an accomplishment. All of London is making bets on whether or not it will succeed. I have fifty on it myself at White's. Any chance I can get an inside account? Will it succeed?"

"What was your wager, success or failure?"

Parker feigned a wounded expression. "Success, of course. Know you can do it. Bound to be problems though. Tell me about this diving bell. Some sort of giant bell on a barge out in the middle of the Thames? I don't quite understand what dangling your feet on the bottom the river will do to help you build a tunnel."

"The diving bell was hired in case of a major leak. We do not know the thickness of the band of clay we are digging through. We also know the Thames was dredged recently. So as we dig out the dirt in the tunnel, if we break through to the river, a diving bell will be used to inspect the hole. But most of all, it will tell us where to dump the hundred bags of clay we have waiting to plug up any leak."

"Don't tell me you are going down in that bell thing? Must be dangerous, hard to breathe."

"There is an air pump, you know. I already have been down once without any difficulties. Recently, Isambard Brunel went down in the bell to map a low spot in the Thames. Like me, he's without a wife and kids, while other men have dependent families. It's common practice for only single men to descend in the bell. Let me tell you how much I admire Isambard. I cannot wait to introduce the two of you. No man has such dedication to a project or unceasing courage. Working by his side, I have learned more than I care to admit." He lowered his voice and said, "I'm likely up for a promotion. Don't spread the word, since it may be premature, but if it comes to pass, it will please my father no end."

Parker leaned close to whisper, "Consider it a secret then."

"Have you talked with your brother recently? Is he still planning to publish a second edition of *The Rake's Handbook: Including Field Guide*?"

"Good news on that front. He understood our objections, and said he would postpone the publication. However, he hasn't ruled it out altogether. Because our little tome earned him a small fortune, if his publishing firm has an attack of the duns, he might print another edition. Hope not."

"That's good news indeed."

"Funny that; Ross said the same thing. Seems we all want that book as good as forgotten." Parker stood in preparation to leave for luncheon. "Congratulations again. Suppose you're off building England now. You're tunneling the way to the future, and Ross is powering that future with his small steam engines.

Mighty proud of my friends, yes, yes, mighty proud."
He placed his hand on George's shoulder and patted
it. "Well done."

"Thank you." As he grabbed his coat to leave, an
extreme flash of pride swept through him, replaced
by a pang of regret. Damnation, he wished Meta had
been present to hear Parker's compliments on his shuffler. He then headed upstairs to tell his father the good
news that another edition of the field guide would
likely not be published.

∽

After dinner that same evening, George became
distracted by the sounds of a visitor at the front door.
Hoping the new arrival had no business with him,
since he needed to deliver a new set of plans tomorrow, he tried to ignore the sounds now coming from
the hallway. Unfortunately, the possibility that the
tunnel might flood meant he must be on alert and
available at all times. Even though he failed to recognize the voice chatting with Mrs. Morris, he searched
for his coat and gloves, in case he had to venture out
into the night due to a leak.

To his surprise, Mrs. Morris announced James
Codlington.

George received him and bade the young man to
sit down by the fire.

Once James sat under the light from the oil lamp next
to him, George could discern his ashen skin and sunken
features. James began the conversation before George
had a chance to sit in the opposite chair. "You must
forgive me for bothering you at this time of night. You

see… I don't know how to put this. I realize I may be imposing." He stopped to take a deep breath before sitting fully back into the deep cushioned chair. "I apologize. I must appear mad to call at such a time of night, but my reasons are sound. You see, after a tremendous row, I have been asked to leave Codlington House."

"Pardon?"

"Mother asked me to vacate my rooms. It seemed my continued refusal to choose a spouse of her liking, this time a Miss King, has enraged her enough to order me from the house at last."

George shook his head. "Her own son?" He stood and moved to the drinks cabinet. "Something stiff? A brandy?"

"Yes, much obliged. The fact that I'm her son is the heart of the problem. As the heir to the Codlington estate, she demands obedience in all matters. My steadfast refusal to end my addresses to Miss Broadsham led to an irrevocable estrangement. Ironic, isn't it? Especially since Miss Broadsham refuses to accept my apology over the misunderstanding in regard to your field guide. Still, any gentleman worth his weight in salt must stick to his guns. My choice of wife will not be dependent on a woman my mother deems suitable. I've learned to demand better."

"Quite." Since his friend Parker was a lord, George had been naturally envious of his friend's title. But the trappings of the aristocracy—titles and estates—came with serious responsibilities and a position in society to uphold. George enjoyed his freedom too much to be envious any longer and doubted he could easily wear the shackles of a title.

James took a long draw of his brandy. "On my way out the door, I explained to her that this is the nineteenth century, not the eighteenth."

"Hear, hear."

"All that happened this morning when we argued, and I left in something of a miff. So I spent the day engaging rooms in the new Fenton hotel, but they won't be ready for three days. I could stay with friends or my relatives, but they might share her sympathies or, even worse, inadvertently reveal my whereabouts. So I popped on over to see if you could put me up for a few days. I'll be at court or purchasing items for my new lodgings, so I shouldn't be too much trouble. Any chance you have a spare room?"

He smiled. "Of course. I'll have the housekeeper make it suitable immediately. But you must understand we have only four servants. Will you bring your man?"

"No, I'll leave him at Codlington House until I am ready to permanently relocate. I expect to return home to pack a few things when I know my mother will be absent and then come on over in the morning, if that's all right with you? My needs are simple, just a bed, since it will be for such a short time."

George was frankly delighted to have James reside in the house. His new friend would appreciate his card shuffler and many of his other mechanical ideas. So he looked forward to discussing his accomplishments with a like mind. "I'll tell Mrs. Morris tonight, and the room will be prepared immediately. Do you require any special conveniences? We don't have stables—I stable my horse nearby—so if you have cattle, they will have to remain at home too."

"Thank you for putting me up, but I plan to leave my horse in her nice warm stall. Don't see why she should have to suffer from my decision to live elsewhere. At least for the time being."

"Right." George gulped his brandy, relishing its warmth. "Seems like moving is a lot of bother." How would Meta receive this news of James being kicked out of his house? He could not determine with any certainty what her reaction would be. He did know, however, that she still desired the reconciliation between James and her sister. Maybe if he could smooth the waters on that score, it would go a long way in repaying her for her many successful efforts to further his future. "Is there no hope that your mother will ever accept Miss Broadsham? She seems like such a...pleasant young lady. What is her objection to the match? The flummery about the field guide has been discounted and forgotten, so it should be a moot point by now."

James sighed deeply. A small smile flitted across his lips before he rose to pour himself another brandy. "May I?"

"Of course."

"In the last several days, I have come to understand that my relationship with Miss Broadsham may be permanently severed." This time a longer sigh escaped him. "She fails to reply to my letters or even grant me the chance to speak to her in person."

"You could pay a morning call regardless of her invitation."

James quickly turned his head in George's direction. "If I did, what would I say? We discussed the betrothal already. I apologized for my panic and hesitation. Frankly, I'm disappointed in her lack of forgiveness in regard to the field guide nonsense. Then after I showed appropriate contrition, I asked for her hand in marriage again. I don't know what else I can do at this point, except wait for her to come around."

"Good call. Give her another week. By then she should have forgotten the whole escapade. Then you can propose once more, she will accept, and all will be well."

James shook his head. "No, I have no intention of repeating my addresses. I asked her twice and apologized the second time. So I refuse to make a fool of myself in front of her again." He stopped and took a long draft of his brandy. "I thought she loved me, but I must have been in error. I won't be embarrassed again by her refusal. I'm a gentleman, after all. Codlington gentlemen are known for saying our peace and moving on. Troublesome things, females."

Fully under the effects of the brandy's liquid ease, George waved his hand rather randomly. "For the most part, I agree with you on that score. Never truly know what females are thinking, do you? Besides, a gentleman doesn't need a woman to be successful. You'll find someone else. Perhaps that Learned Lady I observed on the receiving end of your attentions at the picnic?"

For the first time that evening, James smiled. "Clara is a lovely woman. I could eventually find another lady whom I admire enough to propose, but I am in no hurry. I believe time will help me forget my devotion to Lily. Perhaps in a year or two, I ma consider making my addresses to another female of *my* choosing."

"You are a few years younger than I am. My advice is to further your profession at this time. Make the connections needed to be a success in your chosen field. But most of all, avoid all women until you accomplish the success you desire, especially Mrs. Russell and the Broadshams on account of potential lingering resentment over Lily's misfortune. Otherwise, women are brilliant at making a fellow compromise and make sacrifices in that quarter. So I agree with you; you're right. Troublesome things, females."

"I could never imagine Mrs. Russell to be troublesome." James beamed. "I really do admire her so. I wonder if she would consider marriage again?"

Without warning, the bear inside George roared. He tightened his jaw and failed to reply.

Fourteen

"I'M NOT CRITICIZING YOUR ART, DEAREST, BUT DID you notice that this hand has six fingers?" Meta examined Fitzy's reaction, hoping her observation had not discouraged him in any way.

Fitzy scratched his head and carefully examined his latest work in clay. Still consumed by his admiration of bolts, this version had a giant hand wrapping around an even bigger bolt.

Meta waited for his response. Bright light flooded the schoolroom from the tall windows, so he couldn't use dim lighting as an excuse for an extra digit.

"No," he said, "you're wrong. See the knuckles? I count five fingers on the hand."

"Yes, when you look from the top. But below where the hand wraps around the shaft, I count the tips of six fingers. Bolts don't have fingers, so the extra finger must come from the hand." She held her breath.

Fitzy leaned his head close to the bottom of the sculpture for a careful examination. Then he straightened and faced her, his cheeks flushed. "Actually, that is the flange on the bolt, but from your viewpoint, i does look like another finger. I don't see how I can fix it though, since that piece carries the load of the top. If I chop that extra finger off, the weight of the palm will likely collapse the whole thing." He wiped his hands back and forth. "I told you before, Meta, hands are hard. I should give up sculpture and stick to easy techniques like drawing and painting."

She immediately embraced him, and he wrapped his arms around her waist. "Certainly not. In the future, you will be the celebrated, official hand sculptor to the King. Having difficulties is a part of every endeavor, every profession. People who succeed in life are the ones who learn from their mistakes and try again. Never be afraid of failure or criticism. Promise me?"

"Yes, but a fellow can get rather discouraged."

"You can be discouraged, even wallow in it, but not for longer than overnight." She released him and looked at him directly. "Still discouraged?"

He smiled. "A minute more?"

"Agreed. So what did you learn?"

"Never to let you into my studio." An impish smile crossed his lips.

She laughed and ruffled his hair. "Maybe if you added another hand next to the first, the excess number of fingers would no longer be an issue."

"A real man holds a bolt with one hand, not two. No, later I'll pound this clay into a mound and start over, but not immediately. Today I'm going to pay a call on the Drexels to learn a new drafting skill. After all, the elder Mr. Drexel invited me to visit anytime ⌐ wished. Perhaps I'll get his opinion on whether or not the statue can be fixed. He never uses the word 'failure' in front of a fellow."

Meta sighed, acutely aware of the limitations of a sibling's direction compared to a parent's. Now she felt quite guilty about her pontification on failure. "I have a suggestion. Let's visit the Drexels together. Neither of us has seen them for weeks, and I would like to know how the family is getting on. I know George is very busy with the tunnel, so instead we can ask his father how the tunnel is progressing. How about this afternoon?"

"Yes, please. I'll bring my sketching pad, since I always discover an interesting model in their drawing room."

"Excellent. Take off your apron, tidy up, and let's have some of that fish pie before we leave." To her surprise, the thought of calling upon the Drexels made her somewhat giddy. Nothing could please her more than seeing George again. Truth be told, she dreamed about him frequently. In her dreams, she saw him in many different forms. George as the proverbial knight in shining armor slaying the dragon, George as a steely Viking at the prow of his longboat, or George as a red-coated general leading his men into battle. But those were just silly dreams. Dreams paled in comparison to reality. In real life, he was George, the man building modern Britain, a far more significant accomplishment than a typical hero in a novel. Now even the sound of his first name caused her pulse to escalate. She turned to hide her over-warm cheeks from Fitzy's notice.

The door opened and Lily entered the room.

Meta could tell by her sister's stiff posture and

set lower lip that Lily had something important she wanted to communicate.

Lily faced them squarely. "I'm glad to see that you are leaving, Fitzy. Shut the door behind you. I have something I wish to discuss with Meta that does not concern you. Understand?"

Fitzy narrowed his eyes and then waved his hand in dismissal. "Girls." Then he deliberately took his time cleaning up his art supplies.

"Meta, I cannot wait any longer. Please come to my room. I can lock the door too, so we won't be interrupted." She stuck out her tongue at Fitzy.

Meta grabbed her sister's hand. "We can speak here. Fitzy will leave in a minute or two. Then no one will disturb us, I'm sure."

Lily huffed. "This is important, very important."

"All right," she said, smiling. "You lead the way." Minutes later they found themselves seated by the window in Lily's room. Today the sun had warmed the entire area, making it almost pleasant. "What is so important that we must prevent someone from overhearing our conversation?"

To her credit, Lily's expression took on a tinge of guilt.

"I've had a word with my friend, Miss Longacre. Everyone in town is talking about it." She inhaled deeply. "Lady Codlington has thrown James out of the house." She sighed and looked out to the garden below. "He must still wish to marry me, don't you think so? What other reason could she have for throwing her own son out of the house?"

"Poor James." Meta sympathized with James's

troubles, but she did not want to tell Lily that Lady Codlington was capable of throwing him out for a myriad of other reasons, as well.

"Don't you see what this means?"

She watched her sister fidget. "No, tell me what it means."

Lily huffed. "He still wishes to marry me. James is so steadfast, so brave." She batted her eyelids.

Meta held her tongue. She didn't want to disappoint her sister without being in possession of the facts. "You may be right, but what do you care? You refused his suit, remember?"

Lily waved her hand like a fishtail. "In the book I'm going to write, *James and Lily: A Lifetime Together*, our mere misunderstanding belongs in chapter one, I can assure you."

"Fitzy and I are going to pay a call upon the Drexels later this afternoon. Would you like us to take a small detour and stop by Codlington House upon our return? Not to call upon Lady Codlington, but to ask their butler for directions to James's new residence. Then when I get the chance, I'll find his new residence and discover what this is all about."

Lily swung her foot. "You might suggest he resume his addresses to me."

"I will do no such thing."

Lily swung her leg faster. "I don't see why not. Please, Meta. Perhaps just a hint?"

"That is your job."

"The gentleman must open the subject, clearly. The lady could never do such a…forward thing."

She took her sister's hand. "James admitted his

mistake, apologized, and asked for your hand. You must now put yourself in his shoes. Why should he ask again when he knows you will refuse?"

Lily's eyes widened in horror.

"To James, it would mean a third declaration. And gentlemen do not like to expose themselves to being spurned a second time. You hurt his pride with your refusal, so he will be unlikely to seek rejection again."

"But, Meta, he must ask again. I cannot bring up the subject. I'd be too embarrassed, too mortified."

"Now you understand how James must have felt when he offered for your hand a second time."

"Oh, Meta." Her sister covered her face with her hands as her tears began to fall. "I never thought of it that way, from his viewpoint. What have I done? I did not mean my refusal to be permanent, truly. Please help me." The tears continued to roll down her cheeks.

She patted her sister's hand. "I'll discover his new address and pay a call. Maybe the subject will come up in conversation. Perhaps, with your permission, I can tell him that paying a call will be looked upon with favor?"

"Oh." Lily snapped her head up. She ignored the single lock of black hair that escaped its pins and fell to her shoulder.

Meta huffed. "Oh what?"

Her sister's cheeks flushed. "Oh, of course, yes, yes, I am quite sure I will say yes this time."

"Quite sure is not enough, Lily. Besides, he may not ask again."

"Yes, I am *very* sure I will say yes."

An hour later, when Meta and Fitzy were shown into the Drexels' drawing room, they found James sitting by the fire reading business letters. "James, I heard you moved out of your house, but I'm surprised to see you here." Meta approached him.

James bowed, and she curtsied in return.

Mrs. Morris entered and explained that Mr. and Mrs. Drexel would be delighted to receive Fitzy upstairs, so her brother followed the housekeeper out of the room.

Meta admitted disappointment that George was not at home, but she smiled regardless. Now she had a chance to inquire about James's altered circumstance

James explained his mother's unreasonable demands in terms of her approval of his choice of profession and wife. "So you see, with her insisting I practice in Father's court and marry a bride of her choosing, I had to leave. Her interference had become insupportable."

"She must have been very angry."

"Indeed, she cut off my funds." He sighed. "I have a small living, so I won't starve, but it might not be enough to support a wife and children. Only time will tell." He stood and walked over to look out of the giant bay window. "You know, Meta, I used to believe that by this time Lily and I would be wed, and she would be moving her things into Codlington House. My, my, how circumstances have changed. And you know, lately I've surprised myself by finding that I have become used to the estrangement. After severing ties with my mother, I actually feel light-hearted and free. Perhaps this situation will end up for the best for all parties in the end."

"Please, James. Wait until your situation is settled before you make any permanent decisions. Since you are no longer in residence, your mother will miss you and may change her mind. Or perhaps some other event, like a promotion, will improve your circumstances. A year or two maybe? Then at a more convenient time, you can resume your addresses to Lily."

He exhaled a long sigh. "I don't know. I wish I could be certain that all would be well, but I cannot raise my hopes. I must be a realist. My circumstances may never improve."

"But you will ask for Lily's hand again, when they do improve?"

This time he spun to address her directly, his brows knit. "I don't know the answer to your question. I truly wish I did."

"I know Lily will welcome—"

The front door slammed shut, making them both turn. Seconds later George bounded into the room. He must have come from the tunnel construction site, because a great deal of mud marred his coat and trousers.

Mrs. Morris followed him into the room. "Please, sir, hand me your coat and—the state of your trousers! I insist you change this instant, so the mud is not tracked all over the house. Anne swept this room just this morning."

George glanced toward the ceiling and grimaced. "I shall return." He addressed Meta. "Will you be here when I return?"

"Of course. Unless you go into hibernation."

"Ha! Delighted to see you again, Mrs. Russell. Delighted."

She stood by the fire, keeping her gaze on the red coals in a successful effort to hide what must appear to be a ridiculous smile. Heavens, she was glad to see him. She almost danced a jig on the spot. She lacked the wits to carry on the conversation, so she and James remained silent.

When George returned, he stepped forward and took both of her hands.

She blushed and focused on her kid half boots.

He leaned forward to whisper in her ear, "I want to kiss every inch covered by that blush."

Meta rejoiced in his words but found herself thankful that at the old age of twenty-four, she had enough experience and composure not to melt into a pool of trembling female at his feet. She hastily glanced at James. "Thank you for the compliment, Mr. Drexel. I'm pleased to see you too."

A bark of laughter escaped him. "You are very pleased; I can see that." He motioned for his guests to all take a seat. "So what were you discussing before Mrs. Russell greeted me so effusively?"

"I did no such…" *The devil.*

James blithely answered his question. "We discussed the possibility of resuming my addresses to Miss Broadsham."

Next he and George exchanged unusual glances, indicating some secret the two men shared.

She smiled at James. "Which hopefully he will resume in the near future."

George sat back in his chair and crossed his legs.

As a result, his polished black boot rested close to her chair. They were not the boots he normally wore, so perhaps he changed into his best boots to impress her?

"In my opinion," George said, "the game is permanently off and rightly so. Miss Broadsham refused after a fellow apologized. End of the matter."

James furtively glanced at Meta. "Yes, we agreed no further addresses will likely be made on my part."

"We?" Meta examined James's countenance, but his stare remained fixed on George.

She turned to George, but he didn't appear guilty, as he should. Smug was the word that best described his expression, masculine smugness. "Yes, we—James and I—have requirements when we choose a female to become leg-shackled to. The first requirement is that she must *agree*." The smug expression grew into a smug smile. "If I were in James's boots, I'd demand Lily's apology." He leaned toward James. "That's the first thing she must say. After all, you apologized to her. Right?"

"Right." James appeared to have gained an iron spine in the last minute. No doubt it was courage provided by another member of the masculine race. "You know, I do believe that she must ask me to resume my addresses."

"That's the ticket." George pumped his fist in a supportive gesture.

Attempting to dampen her irritation, she counted to three. One.

James responded in like and both men briefly pumped a fist.

Two. Three. "If my sister does apologize and ask

the question you seek, will you resume your addresses? The question is hypothetical, of course."

James met her gaze, a steadfast, mulish expression in his eyes. "If I have assuredness that my suit will be accepted, I might consider it. But to tell the truth, Meta, I might not. Do you have knowledge that she will accept me?"

Meta sighed. She should not reveal confidences and say anything more. "Frankly, I do not understand her, since she refused you after you did the right thing and apologized."

George raised both hands, palms facing them. "Hold on a moment. The man has just been kicked out of his house. Revisit the question again in a month, when cooler heads prevail and everyone has time to think things through."

Meta clicked her tongue at him. Now she felt like the victim of schoolboys who had joined forces to exclude girls they considered "hysterical." Her jaw tensed. George's boots now appeared utterly vulgar. She frowned at him. "It is quite obvious that you have some unwarranted involvement in this matter."

"Possibly," George said. "But you were the one who invited me to stick my nose in this situation, remember? In the same breath, you then spoke of my *vile* field guide. Is that not some excuse for my involvement? Besides, I apologized and did everything I could to forward the match."

She frowned. "And it failed."

"Not my fault, madam."

"Who started all of the trouble by writing the book in the first place?"

Fifteen

STRAINING TO HOLD HIS BREATH, GEORGE FOLLOWED Isambard as both men hurried out of the tunnel. At least five of the miners ran behind them. When the group of men reached the fresh air at the tunnel's entrance, they all violently coughed to clear their throats.

George filled his lungs with sweet, almost clean air. "I never realized the air could become that foul deep inside the tunnel. Today the water smells like you are standing in a privy."

Isambard nodded. "We must revisit the ventilation drawings. With a stench that bad, the men can only work a few hours, at the most, before the shift will have to be changed. Let's examine the plans and devise a solution."

"Hallo," a feminine voice yelled from the top of the pit. "Mr. Drexel."

"Oh yes. Hallo, hallo." More female voices joined the others. "Over here."

George, like most of the workers in the pit, had become immune to the shouts of unruly Londoners above him. Only this time, it was a seemingly large group of women yelling at him. Some even knew his first name. He glanced up to find at least twenty women huddling in a group. They all took turns pointing at him before breaking out in giggles. The women varied in age and station in life, but they all seemed to wave, smile, and nod at him in unison.

"Looks like you have some admirers," Isambard said. "Doing something nights with the ladies you shouldn't?"

"No, of course not," he said. "I cannot imagine what the fuss is about."

"I envy your prowess with the opposite sex, but I suggest you do not encourage them to disturb the site. Their shouts may distract the workers. In that case, progress will slow and Father will not be pleased. The blame will fall on your shoulders and rightly so. If it becomes an issue, your promotion may be at stake."

"Understood, but I have no idea why the ladies have gathered here today in such large numbers." George squinted up to the rim of the pit to discern the ringleader or discover some woman of his acquaintance in the group, but he did not recognize any of the ladies now waving vigorously. "I don't understand it. I have never seen any of these women before." He held his arm high and flicked his hand in a gesture for the ladies to leave immediately. Unfortunately, the attention spurred them on to wave and shout in return.

"Oh! Is that him?"

"It must be."

"He is much better looking than I imagined."

Isambard broke out in whoops of laughter.

George ground his teeth and added more vigor to his gesture. "Away with you. Go away. Nothing to see." This had no effect whatsoever. The ladies continued to wave and giggle. The only recourse he could think of was to hide for the time being. "Let's examine the drawings in the engine room, away from this racket. Hopefully, they will leave once we are gone."

"Oh George Drexxxxel," a lady called out.

"George dearest," another lady shouted, joining the chorus of ladies calling his name.

Isambard pulled out his Meerschaum pipe. "Once *you* are gone. Now they are shouting your full name quite clearly."

George frowned at his friend, and together they ran to the engine house. They spent the next hour examining the plans to improve the ventilation. They devised a temporary solution and set the workmen off to address it. When finished, George opened the door with some hesitation, unsure whether or not the ladies remained, ready to pounce. He peered around the door and discovered that his female chorus had vanished. He sighed and boldly stepped through the doorway, like nothing was amiss.

The next day a similar occurrence happened. Only this time, the number of females shouting his name doubled. Since a half dozen men were working in the small engine house, his only recourse was to seek refuge in the tunnel. But his work soon became difficult, because as much as he tried to focus on improving the new ventilation scheme, part of his mind wondered if the ladies were still lining the top of the pit, waiting for him to emerge.

On the third day, he spotted a larger herd of females before he even reached the site. Their number had swelled to at least a hundred, even though it had rained earlier in the day. Grinding his teeth, he returned home to Blackfriars. He then sent a note to Mr. Brunel indicating he would continue his work later that afternoon.

Once he entered the house, Mrs. Morris approached him, gesticulating widely. "Oh, sir, I am so glad you returned. What *am* I to do with the woman?"

He yanked off his work gloves, oilskins, and wide-brimmed cap, then threw them onto the nearest chair.

Mrs. Morris quickly swept them up in her arms. "When I heard you enter, I asked Cook to restrain the thief. Follow me so you can determine what the baggage wants." She glanced at the bundle in her arms and threw them back on the chair. Then she quickly started down the hall.

George wondered why his father had not taken care of this domestic disturbance. "Where's Father?"

The housekeeper turned on the steps leading down to the kitchen. "He read to your mother all morning, and he just stepped out to stretch his legs and purchase some flowers for her."

By now they had reached the large kitchen area on the basement level of the town house. Cook stood holding a large iron spoon like a lethal weapon over the head of an unknown woman of indeterminate age, well dressed, and seated in the rocking chair by the fire. Clearly Cook had no intention of allowing the lady to rise, much less escape.

"What is this all about then?" George stepped forward and gently took Cook's spoon.

All three women spoke at the same time.

"She—"

"I—"

"Mrs.—"

He held up a hand. "Ladies, please stop. Mrs. Morris, perhaps you can be the first to explain what happened?"

Cook frowned, the stranger tossed her head, while his housekeeper glared at the unknown woman.

"You see, sir," Mrs. Morris started, "Beth went to your father's room to clean out the fireplace and discovered this intruder. Sitting on the bed, free as you like—*the nerve*." Mrs. Morris glared at the woman again. "The housemaid naturally screamed, so I came running."

The unknown lady smiled at him, without a touch of guilt or contrition marring her lovely features.

"My turn to speak," Cook announced with a toss of her head. "I heard a racket upstairs and ran up to see what the fuss was about. Sure enough, I sees this woman sitting on the bed like she owned it. She says she is not a thief, but she has not given an explanation for what she was about. I reckon she's lying, sir. Why else would a lady enter a stranger's house and sit on the bed as free as you please?"

The unknown lady lifted a single brow in defiance.

George placed the spoon on the table, then examined their prisoner. The woman appeared neither old nor young. Her silk dress indicated she was a lady of some means, so he doubted thievery was her intent. "What is your name, why have you broken into my house, and why were you sitting on my father's bed?"

The lady grinned. "Seems I got the wrong room

then. I was aiming for *your* bed." She executed a beguiling smile and coy tilt of the head. "For reasons of modesty, my name I shall keep to myself. Please refer to me as…Mrs. Smith. And to answer your last question, I am here on a wager."

"Pardon?"

"I'm sure she's lying, sir," Cook said, reclaiming the iron spoon from the table and waving it in the air. "Shall I call the constable?"

George strode over, recaptured the big spoon, and pulled out a chair for his cook. "Please sit. Let me handle this…*Mrs. Smith*. Ha." A snicker simmered under his breath. "Are there any valuable items missing from the house, Mrs. Morris?"

"Not that we can tell. The two housemaids searched, but nothing seems amiss. I know for certain she did not enter your mother's room."

"Right, that's a small blessing," he said. "Now, Mrs. Smith, perhaps you would care to explain this wager. Let me guess." He grinned. "You have been put up to this by my friend, Lord Boyce Parker. Confess." The insanity of this charade bore a resemblance to the adolescent jests Boyce made before his recent marriage.

The intruder pulled her shawl tight around her shoulders. "I am not acquainted with Lord Parker."

"Then why—"

"One of my friends received the field guide as a gift," the lady explained. "Naturally, she enjoyed it prodigiously. So the next week at our whist party, she read many of the passages aloud." A rosy hue graced her cheeks. "Oh, I do hope you do not expect me to repeat any of the passages. Certainly, not in front of your servants. It took all of a week for us to determine the real name attached to the initials G—— D——. And since you have been singled out as the…" She glanced at Cook and Mrs. Morris. "Let's just say I drank too much sherry that afternoon. Well, all of us drank too much actually, since the eight of us consumed six bottles." She giggled like an infant.

George decided she was likely disguised even now.

"The long and short of it is," she said, "stronger heads did not prevail and a scheme was hatched. We drew cards and…here I am. Eager to meet *the man himself.*"

Certain his brain spun in his head, George ignored the sense of foreboding overwhelming him. "What man himself?"

This time her smile shone like she had crossed an imaginary finish line. "The gentleman described in the field guide as quote, 'The stallion not in the studbook."

"No need to get vulgar, you hussy," Cook spat out. "I'm going to box your ears right and proper, I am." She leaped forward two steps before he managed to restrain her.

Mrs. Morris took a determined step toward the lady, looking like she planned to assist with the ear boxing.

George gathered the remainder of his wits. "Stud? Field guide?"

Their intruder looked puzzled for a moment. "Oh, I see the confusion. Stud does refer to a horse, but in this case the field guide is using a metaphor. Probably because you are not listed in Debrett's, now are you?"

A white fog of rage started to overwhelm his reason. "What in the devil are you talking about?"

Mrs. Morris studied him. In all likelihood recognizing his transformation into the bear, she took over the interrogation. "I have read the field guide and there is no mention of studs—either horses or men—in Mr. Drexel's book. No mention of any gentlemen, as far as that goes."

Mrs. Smith tittered.

George remembered how much he deplored female tittering. He itched to grab Cook's spoon for himself.

"No, not Mr. Drexel's field guide," the intruder said, holding out a small tome she pulled from her pocket. "This field guide. It was published about a week ago and has become all the crack, you understand. Well, amusing tittle-tattle and the latest *on dits* are always popular."

He swept forward and yanked the book from the lady's hands.

Mrs. Morris glanced at him. "Sir, I don't understand."

On the front cover embossed in gold letters was the title, *The Ladies' Field Guide to London's Rakes*. George closed his eyes and focused on the elegant design of his newest suspension bridge, until the furious war in his brain subsided. After a deep breath, he opened the book to the title page. At the bottom, he found the traitorous author, or should he say, authoresses, indicted in black ink. Black as their hearts, no doubt. The Benevolent Society for the Prevention of Seduction claimed authorship of this ladies' field guide of buffoonery. He grasped at any chance of a simple misunderstanding. "Come on, Mrs. Smith, tell me. How much did Lord Parker pay you to do this?"

"Pardon?"

"Lord Boyce Parker. You know, the gentlemen who funded"—he shook the book in Mrs. Smith's face—"this little farce." He turned to Mrs. Morris. "I cannot believe Parker went all the way to re-cover with fake boards some random book with this title." He flipped the pages to somewhere in the middle. "I'm sure it's some instruction book on boxing, if I know my man." He flipped rapidly through the book, reading only the chapter titles: "Fancy Sports on the Road," "Meeting a Swell," "Overpowering Oratory," and finally, "Larks and Sprees." He stopped reading, and the white fog of rage descended again.

Mrs. Morris took the book from his hands and read a few pages.

"You shameless hussy," she said, turning to Mrs. Smith. "How did you acquire this?"

"My friend, Mrs. Wilkerson." She giggled. "I mean…Mrs. Brown."

Cook sneered. "Of course."

Mrs. Smith wiggled on her seat. "Mrs. Brown bought the book at Hatchards last Tuesday as a gift for me. From what I understand from her, it has become a bestseller."

He questioned fate. He questioned sanity. He questioned his future. Whoever these *benevolent* ladies were—and he had a pretty good idea—they had single-handedly ended any chance of his promotion. Keep the line, Brunel had warned. Now he had become the victim, portrayed as the penultimate rake in a book taking London by storm. His anger grew until he transformed into the upright, snarling bear.

He climbed the stairs to the vestibule two steps at a time, then grabbed his hat and gloves.

Mrs. Morris followed him. "I don't know what you are up to, but I can guess. God save that nice lady from the bear."

"Don't distress yourself. It will be a bloodless mauling only." The sound of his threat gave him a temporary sense of satisfaction.

"That's what I'm afraid of." She nervously wiped her hands on her apron.

"Humph." He grabbed each of his black leather gloves and shoved his hands into them in a single, stabbing movement.

"Remember you have an appointment to dine with Mr. Codlington tonight."

He paused and threw his head back. *Damnation*. The appointment had been forgotten in his raging urge to confront the woman. "Please, send the boy around to cancel the meeting. Have him give James my best, felicitations, et cetera."

"A note would be better."

"No. The boy is capable of remembering a simple directive." He flew through the front door down to the street below in four strides. After pulling down his beaver hat tight on his temples, he inhaled to gather his fortitude and resumed his journey to Swallow Street. Home of just the person to be on the receiving end of the bear's wrath.

George ran, hitting the pavement hard, eager to confront Mrs. Meta Russell. Ever since her involvement in his affairs, and her ceaseless desire to help him, his life experienced spectacular highs and unbelievable lows. With utmost certainty, he knew she—with or without the help of those clever friends of hers—had penned *The Ladies' Field Guide to London's Rakes*. The only question in his mind was the reason behind the publication. Previously, she had assisted him with his career and had even arranged Wellington's visit. So why did she become a turncoat now?

Regardless of her reasons—and he doubted he ever wanted to hear them—the association between them must come to an end, once and for all. No visits of any kind. No joining her brother to pay a call. No recognition when she visited the pit. His normal habit, when paying a call upon the Broadshams, was to change into clothing more suitable for an esquire or a gentleman speaking to ladies. He glanced down to his rough brown oilskins and deplorable cravat knot. Serves the woman right that he appear in her drawing room dressed in attire normally reserved for working in the tunnel.

Halfway to his destination, he observed three lovely ladies approaching him on the pathway. The first lady caught sight of him at a hundred paces and stopped in her tracks. The other women then stopped too. The group conversed for a minute before giggles erupted.

George hated giggles. Women were not high on his list of favorite things at the moment. They ranked right up there with overflowing privies. None of them could be trusted, because they were all inveterate tittle-tattlers, bags of maudlin sentiment, and silly book writers.

"Oh look, that's the very man himself," the first lady said, immediately pulling back her hand when caught pointing at him.

He lengthened his stride, hoping to pass them in seconds.

"Are you certain?" the second lady said.

The first lady furtively nodded.

Ten feet before their paths crossed, he caught a white flash out of the corner of his eye. Upon further examination, it appeared the first lady had dropped her handkerchief on the pavement in front of him. He ground his teeth and swore he had no intention of picking it up. Very likely his chivalry toward the fairer sex may have escaped him permanently. He quickened his step.

A foot away, the second lady dropped her handkerchief right in his path. If he stepped on it, the handkerchief would be ruined, so he had to stop. Glaring downward at the offending cloth, he mumbled a strong swear word under his breath. He inhaled, tipped his hat, and bowed. "Ladies." He then addressed the third one. "Would you care to drop your handkerchief too? It's more efficient if I pick all three up at the same time. Besides, I would hate to leave a member of your party out of my gallantries."

All of the ladies beamed.

The third one shook her head. "I forgot to bring my handkerchief," she said in a disappointed tone.

He feigned a smile. "My loss."

They all continued to smile and repeatedly nodded at each other.

He bent over to pick up the two white linen squares. At the very moment his hand grabbed the first one, a flash of silver and a heavy thump sounded as a silver reticule dropped on the pavement in front of his nose.

Seemingly without a handkerchief, the third lady had thrown in her reticule.

A moment of uneasy silence followed. Finally, he straightened and burst out in laughter.

The three women joined him, and they all laughed together.

After regaining his composure, he shook his head and bent over to pick up the small collection of items on the pavement. He then gracefully handed each piece to the correct owner, followed by a deep bow.

"Thank you, sir."

"Thank you, Miss…"

"Goddess," she said, looking entirely pleased with herself.

"And I'm Miss Widow," her companion added.

Her friend nudged her arm. "Miss Widow Maker, dear."

"Yes, I make widows."

He chuckled and doffed his hat. "Ladies." Once on his way again, he heaved a sigh of relief. Thankfully, he acknowledged his anger did not apply to all women—*just one*.

Before he reached Broadsham House, he spent an additional twenty minutes to formulate what he would say, so his anger had returned to its earlier levels. All he had to do was enter, give the woman a big piece of his mind, and leave. That thought gave him a sense of utter satisfaction.

Two minutes later, he stood in the drawing room as Mrs. Russell greeted him cheerfully. "Well, madam, what do you have to say for yourself?"

The wide-eyed, alluring rabbit expression entered her eyes. "Pardon?"

"You and those...those Learned Ladies friends of yours," he spat out in a near snarl. "Did you set out to ruin me for the fun of it? Or did you plan to put an end to my promotion for some perverse female reason?"

This time she hopped backward, at least one step. "I have no idea of what you are going on about. Please, take a seat and explain yourself."

An oath escaped his lips. He said it in a low voice, but she winced, so she must have caught it. They sat in opposing chairs. He rummaged in his pocket and pulled out Mrs. Smith's copy of the field guide. Then he tossed the tome into her lap. "Tell me with a straight face that you had no hand in this."

She took up the book and opened it. Within seconds of reading a few words, the color drained from her cheeks. "I-I—"

"Let me guess. You and your friends recognized you were up to no good. Your only regret is that I heard about it. Tell me, before I take my leave of you, why? Why did you decide to involve me in a scandal, stop any chance I had at promotion, and ruin my career?"

Her mouth hung open and tears shimmered in the corners of her eyes.

"Try using words, if you please."

She hung her head and focused on the book in her lap.

"I see," he said, his tone sharp. "You can't even look me in the face and give me a decent explanation. Needless to say I regret my association with you, regret trusting you, and regret introducing you to my family. In the future, you will not visit my house under any pretense. You must also warn young Fitzhenry to stay away. At least until the time I can address him without feeling blind rage for his sister."

Her head whipped up. "I did nothing. I did not even know about the Learned Ladies' plans to publish such a book. I confess that I heard about it only a day ago. We are having a regular meeting of the members soon, so I plan to ask them how they could do such a thing. You must believe me."

"I don't." He had to gulp air. "It has been obvious, since the day we met, that you like to muddle in other people's business. You and your messy female emotional flummery."

"Very well, but you cannot let your hatred for me affect Fitzy. Please, I beg you, for his sake."

"Right." He inhaled swiftly. "Tell him to keep to the tunnel site for the time being. Make whatever excuse you deem necessary to keep him from the company of either me or my parents for at least a month." His firm words pleased him and relief flooded through his veins. He stood, snatched the book from her hands, and headed for the front door.

She followed, still wearing a stricken expression. "I have never read the ladies' field guide, so I don't fully understand the problem. Why are you so angry? Are your initials in—"

"Ask those learned friends of yours to explain the passage about the *stud*."

"Pardon?"

"The authoresses, madam, they know. And a brief hint—it does not refer to horses."

"Please stay. Let's discuss this once I have been given a chance to read the book."

"Our acquaintance is over." Before he reached the front door, he turned. "There is something I wish to say, but a gentleman never insults a lady."

Sixteen

WOULD SHE EVER SEE GEORGE AGAIN?

Meta sat in the drawing room, staring at the clock, waiting for her siblings to come down to breakfast. She still struggled with the question that kept her awake all night. Refusing to believe she would never see him again, she couldn't put a finger on the type of relationship she wanted—friend, lover? But a complete separation from his company forever was unthinkable. She could not deny her desire to see him again. Refusing to analyze exactly why she felt this way, she racked her brain trying to discover a way to help him out of the tight spot she had inadvertently caused.

Beads of perspiration formed on her brow and trickled down her cheek. The large morning fire had done its trick and vanquished the evening's chill, but now the room felt like standing in the middle of an iron foundry. She moved to open the window facing the street. The fouls smells and various sounds of London coming alive on a new day entered the room.

"What are you doing?" Lily asked, stepping up to

stand beside her sister. "Is there someone we know strolling down the street?"

"No," Meta said, "the room became unbearably hot."

"Really, it feels fine to me. But then my bedroom was unusually cold last night. I had to add to the fire at three in the morning, or else I would never have gotten to sleep."

"What were you doing awake at three in the morning?"

Lily froze and cleared her throat. "Just thinking about my future. How my life has taken a terrible turn for the worse." She paused, her lips pulled into a tight line. Grabbing a damask sofa pillow, she threw it to the sofa's corner and sat

Meta had no intention of delving into Lily's lost hopes and expectations, at least not for another month or two. Until then, her siblings would have to wait. She planned to do everything in her power to restore her relationship with George—if it could be restored. Today she would take the first step of returning their relationship to the closeness they gained in a small inn on a rainy day. She'd pose her questions about the ladies' field guide during a regular meeting of the Learned Ladies Society. She exhaled a deep sigh, caused by events she could not control.

"Maybe you could speak to James again?" Lily said, the tone of her voice carrying her expectations and her eyes brightening.

Meta met her sister's eye. "No."

"But—"

"I recommend the obvious. *You* go and speak with James. Put your fears behind you and suggest a reconciliation. Yes, he may refuse you. But since you refused him after he reconsidered his hasty decision to call off, you have no right to any expectation that he will agree to resume his addresses. In fact, Lily, I do not want to hear another word from you on the subject again." She fanned her over-warm face with her hand. "For three months, at least, I have done my part to help you. Now it is time for you to do yours."

Lily looked like she had just seen a ghost.

"Come," Meta said, "we don't want to be late for breakfast." As soon as those words escaped her, they heard Tom bound down the staircase like a racehorse in full gallop. One foot slid as he turned the corner into the drawing room. Then under a full run, he started across the room toward the breakfast parlor.

Meta heard a deep rumble coming from upstairs. The second she looked up to the ceiling, she saw the great chandelier pull away from its plaster roundel and fall.

One long arm of the chandelier clipped Tom in the heels as he dove in an effort to escape.

The chandelier crashed to the floor.

The explosion radiated outward in a shower of debris full of plaster, broken glass, and bits of candles.

She hid her face into the crook of her arm until the danger of flying objects passed. Once she glanced up, a cloud of dust still lingered in the air. "I thought the noises in the ceiling had been looked after?"

Fitzy stood in the doorway, helping Tom to his feet. "Clearly not."

Lily burst into tears. "Mother's. Chandelier. She said it would always. Light." She sobbed uncontrollably. "Up. Our. Lives."

Susanna gingerly stepped forward to examine the remnants.

"Don't," Meta shouted. "Come back. Look at the ceiling above you. More plaster may fall. It's too dangerous at the moment to even be in this room."

Susanna hastily glanced up, then walked back to the doorway in a careful, hunched manner.

Lily cried even harder; she covered her eyes. .

Meta had no intention of cajoling her sister out of her fit of tears. Let her have a cry. Actually, despite the loss of a sentimental chandelier, Meta was surprised she had no desire to cry. She examined Tom and asked if everyone was all right.

Tom nodded slowly, his eyes wider than saucers.

Meta bellowed instructions to Fitzy. "I have business that must be attended to this afternoon with the Learned Ladies. I have no time to sort all of this out. You are almost a grown gentleman now, and one day soon you will run your own household. I want you to attend to this matter immediately. You understand me, Fitzy?"

He leaned over to brush dust off his bottle green wool trousers. "I've never been in charge of a household matter before. What do I do?"

"First you make sure everyone in the house is warned of the danger. Then put up signs and arrange furniture, so nobody accidentally goes near the center of the ceiling, or even comes anywhere near those hanging bits of plaster and wood. After that, you will see to the repairs."

"How?"

She brushed plaster off her skirt, then stood with

both fists resting on her hips. "The man of the house figures it out. They would ask other men. I assume you will do the same."

He hesitated for a moment before he straightened his shoulders. "You're right. I'll pop over and ask George then."

"No! No, you will not bother Mr. Drexel. Is that understood?"

He stood unmoving, eyes wide and mouth open.

"You will not speak to him under any circumstances for at least a month. It's a personal matter that does not relate to you. Do you hear me?"

This time her brother nodded. "I don't understand. I thought we all were the best of friends."

"Mr. Drexel and I have recently argued over a matter that is none of your business. For that reason, I request you keep to your job at the tunnel and do not bother him or his family. Understood?"

He huffed. "If he is mad at you, I don't see why I cannot pay a call upon the family. Both Drexels have provided me with support in ways I cannot begin to describe."

"No!" This time the expediency of her tone and earnest stare got her point across.

His mulish expression vanished. "All right," he said, "you don't have to behave like a parent, you know."

"You're right. I am not your parent. Since your parents are unavailable, you will have to gain guidance from wherever you can. I suggest James would be a good gentleman to ask about whom to call to mend a chandelier. He is now living in rooms in Fenton's Hotel."

Lily faced both of them. "Meta, you are being horrible. Come on, Fitzy. You can call upon James today after breakfast. I'll wager you can put the chandelier to rights better than Meta ever could."

Meta wiped her hands and skirt to remove more plaster dust. "Excellent. It's about time the two of you take some of the burden running the household. Now let's not keep Cook waiting. It's time for breakfast."

Two hours later, Meta walked to Lady Sarah's London town house. If there was one thing she believed in, it was efficiency. The best way for her to get her grievances across to her friends would be to stand in front of everyone and point to the metaphorical knife stabbed in her back.

Before she rang the bell, she paused on the doorstep and experienced the guilt of an unkind thought. After all, she firmly believed that you could never fully understand a person's motive for their actions, so granting tolerance and the benefit of the doubt should be her first course of action. Perhaps she should wait until the appropriate moment to ask the ladies why they penned the field guide and why they decided to hide the publication from her. Then she'd do her best to listen carefully before she made a judgment. Still, that knife hurt.

About a dozen ladies mingled in the pretty yellow room when Meta entered. She greeted everyone, but to her dismay, her felicitations sounded perfunctory to her ears. Thankfully, the meeting began soon after her arrival.

Lady Sarah stood first, resplendent in a green silk gown with white bobbin lace sleeves. She opened the meeting. "I officially declare this meeting of the Learned Ladies Society open. Our agenda today will be as follows. First, we shall introduce any guests to our members. Then in open forum, the informal part of this meeting, any member may speak about any subject—even give us the latest *on dit*. Afterwards, we will hear a report by our treasurer on the current state of our funds. This will be followed by a progress report about our current governesses. We will then close the meeting after a discussion of the books we are reading. One person will be chosen to present her views upon a factual book and one will start the discussion on the latest novel. So without further ado, are there any guests present today?" She took her seat at the head of the table.

Clara stood and motioned for a young woman, who could have been mistaken for her twin, to rise. "This is my niece, newly married, Mrs. Underwood. Her husband is a prominent person in the Navy. We share many of the same favorites when it comes to books, so I believe she will be a natural and welcome addition to our group."

Mrs. Underwood stood and everyone gave her a warm welcome.

"Any other guests?" Lady Sarah lifted her brows. "Right then, we now enter open forum. So what are the latest *on dits*, tittle-tattle, or popular jests? Even better, anyone have happy news?"

Lady Sarah's gaze swept the room and fell upon Meta.

Meta ignored the veiled reference that she may have happy news of the matrimonial variety and considered whether or not to air her grievances immediately. However, the meeting had yet to begin, so this was not the appropriate time to address the ladies, especially since any ill feelings might end the meeting prematurely. Perhaps during tea she could informally ask the group about their field guide.

Grizel, her black curls set off today by a white muslin gown covered in an overdress of machine-made orange net, held up her hand.

Lady Sarah gave her a nod.

Grizel grinned. "I heard a jest yesterday. Two gentlemen whispered like they were in a vestry." She blushed, a rare occurrence. "I overheard it by mistake, of course. It is very vulgar, you understand, but quite clever."

"How vulgar?" Clara asked.

"Some might say"—Grizel lowered her voice—"this jest is offensive to modesty and decency—obscene, even."

Mrs. Underwood turned to her aunt Clara. "I've never heard an obscene jest before. This will be my first."

Lady Sarah stood to draw everyone's attention. "Just weeks ago, the majority of us agreed that if we could not present a jest appropriate for ladies, we would eliminate all jests from the open forum part of the meeting, remember?"

"Such a shame. May I ask why?" Mrs. Underwood said.

Daphne, the young lady sitting next to her, explained. "It seemed that the only jests our members knew were vulgar ones. For example, there was a pun about some lady sitting in the gallery of the House of Commons, which everyone deemed only right because she allowed"—she lowered her voice—"members into her House of Commons. Get it—*members?*"

"Oh my," exclaimed Mrs. Underwood, a small grin lingering on the corner of her mouth. "I understand now, any mention of the…gentleman part should be avoided at all times and is considered very indelicate indeed."

The ladies furtively glanced at each other, amusement still shining on several of their faces and snickers mixed with giggles.

Clara raised her hand. "I recently heard some tittle-tattle that will amaze you all. It seems Mrs. Puckle has left her lover of ten years, at last. I saw her yesterday and she didn't seem affected in any way. She even mentioned her new spaniel."

"She gave up a lover for a spaniel?" Bethia asked.

Clara answered. "Spaniels are much better than a lover." She blushed. "I mean in providing good company. Besides, they are so adorable with those soft hairy ears…furry ears."

"Ladies, please stop." Lady Sarah stood. "It always amazes me that the conversation of an intelligent group of women can turn so indelicate at the wink of an eye."

The members grinned and exchanged glances.

"How about a jest with cats? Everyone loves cats, and animal jokes can never be vulgar," Sybella said.

Grizel turned to her. "I know one about a game cock."

They all burst into snickers.

Lady Sarah's voice boomed over the crowd. "The open forum is officially ended. Let us continue on with the reports."

Once they finished the business part of the meeting, the group moved their chairs around another large table for tea.

Meta inhaled deeply, gathered her courage, and stood before them. "Ladies, may I take a minute of your time to ask a question?"

"Of course, Meta dear. You don't have to ask," Lady Sarah said, stirring her tea with a petite spoon.

Meta waited until the polite clanging of spoons hitting fine porcelain came to an end. As she did so, she searched their faces to discover if her friends already knew what she was about to say. A few looked guilty, but she could not really tell. "It has come to my attention that some of you"—she glanced around the table—"have written and published a book titled: *The Ladies' Field Guide to London's Rakes*. Is this true?" She failed to see surprise or even regret written on a single face.

"Yes," Lady Sarah said in a casual manner. "Once we heard how much money Mr. Drexel made publishing his field guide, we all thought it would be a good idea to do the same. I'm sorry you were not present at the meeting when we decided upon this matter. But, as you are fully aware, we could use the extra funds. Now the book has been so successful, we might even be able to rescue every governess we find."

Several ladies nodded in a perfunctory fashion and one clapped.

"Much easier than holding a bazaar, for example," said Sybella, the group's treasurer.

Meta was at a loss for words; her throat seized.

Her disappointment must have shone on her face,

as Clara glanced down to her lap. "Our intent was to protect you. We—I—suggested the book might also save you from the attentions of a scoundrel. I…mean you were observed in his close company, and you surely don't want any hint of scandal attached to your good name."

Meta's irritation overwhelmed her, and a brief silence fell over the room. Her affection for George must have been patently obvious for her friends to attempt such a faulty scheme to save her from him. Close to tears, she remained standing, expecting to run to the door the moment one fell. "If we were seen in close company that evening, it's because it was raining. I had no desire to get wet and become ill."

Many of the ladies appeared unsettled, focused on their teacups, or absentmindedly stirred their tea.

Meta's mind swam in confusion. "I understand your motives were to protect me from him, I guess. I can assure you that is not necessary."

Her friends appeared to relax.

"For personal reasons concerning others, I must insist that all publication of your field guide cease immediately." Her palms became damp, so she nonchalantly brushed them on her skirt.

"But, Meta," Lady Sarah said, "we too have earned a significant amount of money for the accounts, enough for every governess. No more begging husbands or fathers for funds."

Sybella remarked, "Husbands can be particularly troublesome."

All of the married women agreed.

"So true."

"Yes indeed."

"Without a doubt."

Meta turned to Lady Sarah and held out her hands. "I promise to match the expected profits, pound for pound, when you stop the publication. But stop it must. You have hurt Mr. Drexel's reputation unfairly, and now his promotion is in jeopardy."

"We used random initials followed by dashes," Lady Sarah said, her brows knit. "So I don't see how anyone could come to the conclusion it was his name in the book."

Meta gave her friend a resigned smile. "I don't pretend to understand why people attached names to vague initials—for the fun of it, I presume—but I know they do. They consider it a game. Remember Lily's difficulties? Her name was unjustly attached to initials that merely resembled hers."

The women lapsed into uneasy silence, punctuation by a great deal of noisy tea stirring.

"Mr. Drexel," Meta said, in a choking voice, "has worked hard for years to overcome the stain on his reputation from his ill-considered field guide. Today he is considered for promotion, a well-deserved honor for his hard work on the tunnel. Your…well-intentioned field guide may have prematurely ended his career. Civic gentlemen may not seek him out for projects, solely on the basis of rumors derived from your book."

Silence filled the room. The ladies all stared at their laps or out the window.

"I have come into some money recently," Meta said. "So reimbursement is not a hardship, believe me. But further publication *must* be stopped immediately."

Lady Sarah spoke in a low voice. "You must be fond of Mr. Drexel to defend him so."

The word "fond" was sometimes used when one did not wish to mention the word "love."

Was she in love with George?

With the speed of a thunderclap and the heat of a fire's spark, the answer was yes. A sudden clarity assailed her. *Yes, she loved George.*

It began when he had kissed her and she let her hand softly linger on his cheek. Then it grew into a passionate love. Unlike the gentle, friendly love that she felt for her husband, her love for George burned. She now recognized this love as the dream of every female growing up. This love was the subject of novels of romance, the desire for the touch of the children you create together, and the loving tenderness that grows from a life shared. This love would never fade with neglect or time.

"Meta, are you feeling well?" Lady Sarah tilted her head down to catch her eye.

She looked into her friend's eyes and nodded. This was also a love that could never be; George did not need her or want her friendship. Moreover, he was a reputed rake, complete with the unfeeling reputation that came with that title. To him, women were merely a conquest, or names in his book, or a means of celebration. She fought the welling of a tear.

While his barriers against love were ones derived from his personality, her barriers stood even taller— her unquestioned devotion to the needs of her family. This was her duty and her greatest joy. Nothing could make her happier than attending to their wants and desires. So to leave them to reside elsewhere with another spouse was out of the question. She turned around to discreetly wipe away the troublesome lingering tear, then faced her friends again.

Since her love could never be realized—or spoken of—for the future she must deny or hide it. This time another unwanted tear welled so quickly, it fell down her cheek before she could wipe it away.

Silence claimed the room.

"Yes," she said, holding her chin high. "I am fond of the whole Drexel family, but you are mistaken if you think I have matrimonial expectations. Mr. Drexel has gone out of his way to help my brother, Fitzhenry. So you see, he blames me for your field guide and is under the impression I have done him a great disservice for his kindness. That is the main reason for my tears. I regret that terribly, and I am determined to set the situation to rights."

None of the ladies said a word. The only sounds in the room were from spoons banging on teacups and plates.

Lady Sarah spoke first. "Please forgive us, Meta. We never meant Mr. Drexel harm. I suppose we were all blinded by the ease of writing such a book—"

"Yes, we had such fun," Clara stated, biting her lip.

"Frankly," Lady Sarah continued, "we were blinded by the allure of the potential earnings, and we truly believed that we were doing you a favor. Saving you from the clutches of a reputed rake. But I can speak for all of us when I say that now we wish we had not done it."

The majority of the ladies nodded.

"Yes, we all apologize."

"Very sorry."

"Please forgive us."

"So it seems to me," Lady Sarah said, standing to address the group. "We must help our dear Meta in any way possible. Do our best to right any damage to Mr. Drexel's reputation our field guide may have inadvertently caused. Perhaps if we all put our heads together to solve this problem, we can set the situation to rights. Any ideas?"

Seventeen

META OPENED THE FRONT DOOR AND CAREFULLY stepped into the Broadsham town house, her arms full of packages and boxes. Low spirits had claimed her for the last four days, so she decided to lift them with a little shopping. She bought yards of a lovely violet silk that would emphasize Lily's eyes, a fur muff for Susanna, new smart waistcoats for the boys, and an adventure book about travels in Africa for her father. Before the packages could be safely taken from her hands, Fitzy grabbed them and unceremoniously dumped them on the table in the vestibule.

"You must come," he said, tugging on her long glove.

"Is the house on fire? Or can I remove my bonnet, spencer, and gloves?"

He stopped tugging. "If you must." Watching her closely, he motioned for her to follow him the second she had removed her outerwear.

Stepping into the drawing room, she noticed the room had been put to rights and the chandelier restored to its place of honor. All the room needed now was the plasterers to come in and remake another roundel in the Adam style. "Wonderful. I cannot tell you how delighted I am that Mother's chandelier is once again illuminating our lives." She examined it carefully. Something appeared different. "What's that large brass ball hanging in the center?"

He beamed. "After consultation with a gentleman of my acquaintance who had experience with machines, I devised a counterpoise, a brass weight." He pulled a chair directly under the chandelier, stood on it, and lightly pulled the chandelier down to her eye level.

"Can you let go?"

"Of course. It is balanced, so very little force is needed to move it. Now the housemaid will have a much easier time cleaning the crystals." He gently pushed the chandelier upward, all the way into its proper place.

Meta's heart swelled with pride. "Job well done. I am impressed."

He stepped off the chair and tucked his thumbs into this waistcoat, looking ever so much like a young monarch surveying his kingdom.

She smiled, then bit her upper lip. "Can you tell me the name of the gentleman that assisted you?"

"The idea was mine, really. And there is no need to call in the plasterers. I've decided to cast my own roundel, since I need more experience with the medium."

Meta suspected the involvement of one of the Drexels. Perhaps the elder one, since Fitzy spent most of his time with George's father. But for her own sanity and Fitzy's pride, she decided not to pursue the subject further. "This calls for a celebration. I'll instruct Cook to make you whatever dish you choose tomorrow."

"For which meal?"

She laughed. "All of them."

His eyes widened. "I will have to give this great consideration."

"Excellent thought." She sat on the cream silk sofa and rang for tea. "While we wait for tea, I want to tell you about my new plan."

"Ma'am?" the servant said from the doorway.

"Bring us some tea and those cinnamon cakes if the girls have not eaten them all."

"Yes, ma'am." The servant left the room.

"While I was shopping today, I devised a scheme to help Mr. Drexel." Since the Learned Ladies promised to demand that their publisher cease publication of their field guide, Meta needed to remove the ones that remained in circulation. "My plan requires your assistance."

Fitzy stood by the fire, one hand on his hip and looking the part of the master of the house. He wore his newfound confidence proudly, like a new coat.

"So tomorrow, you and I," she said, "and James too, if he is available, will attempt to purchase every copy of *The Ladies' Field Guide to London's Rakes.* This book was penned by some friends of mine and has jeopardized Mr. Drexel's chances of promotion; therefore, we will attempt to remove all of them from circulation."

"That explains why you would not let me call upon the family."

Still overwhelmed by guilt due to her edict not to bother the Drexels, she gave him a feeble smile.

"But removing published books from all of London? It might cost a hundred pounds, maybe even more," Fitzy said. "Do you know how many copies were printed?"

She shook her head. "No, but we will do our best. Money is not an issue. We will start first thing in the morning too. As we may have many shops to cover."

"If you say so. I hope we salvage the relationship. I would dearly love to openly visit the Drexels again."

She bit her tongue. Without doubt, one of the Drexels had helped him with the restoration of the family chandelier, when his own father could not. She saw no advantage to pressing the matter further. "We both want our friendship with the Drexels to continue."

The next morning, at the first appropriate hour to receive visitors, Meta and Fitzy stood in the middle of James's small drawing room. His residence now consisted of just enough rooms for the comfort of his one servant and himself.

When James was apprised of their plan for the day, he sat and rubbed his chin. "What an interesting idea. Of course, I'd be delighted to be of service. If money is no object, every copy available in London's book-sellers can be purchased and removed from circulation. But you do realize there is a flaw in your plan?"

The only flaw Meta considered was the inability to reach those who had subscribed to the purchase. Those books were already in the hands of their owners. "What flaw?"

"There is already tittle-tattle about your relationship with Mr. Drexel. If you are seen buying the books, it might compromise your reputation. So I must ask, do you have an understanding?"

"No, of course not." How did James hear of such a rumor? Was it spread by one of the Learned Ladies, or did it arise from someone else? Regardless, for the sake of her siblings, she needed to remain a respectable widow in the eyes of society.

"While I'm not aware of the source of the gossip," James said, "it would not be helpful or seemly if you purchased the books. So I believe our best recourse would be for me to enter each shop and buy the books alone. Then you and Fitzy can see that they are hidden or returned here for later disposal. What do you think, my dear?"

Why, for the first time in their relationship, had he referred to her as *my dear*? Puzzled, she ignored it. "Thank you, James." His kindness reinforced her belief that Lily has been a fool to refuse him. "We brought a few band boxes and even a portmanteau to hide the books in. So let's get started. May I suggest we head in the direction of Temple of the Muses first? They sell a tremendous number of books, so it is imperative to get the field guide off their shelves as soon as possible."

James agreed, so she and Fitzy chose a box to carry, and the three of them headed out. A light drizzle greeted them, but it soon cleared into a fine day. It was still early and most of London had not yet crowded the streets.

For the first half hour, their plan worked like

clockwork. James entered the establishment and purchased all of the available copies, stating he needed gifts for the members of his club. Once he left the bookseller, he handed the books to either Fitzy or Meta for hiding. Thankfully, the tome was a small one. By the time they left Hatchards, they carried over fifty copies between them.

When they finally reached the Temple of the Muses on Finsbury Square, she and Fitzy hung back, so James would appear to enter the store alone. Within a minute, she saw him hurriedly exit the store.

"Trouble, Meta."

"What sort of trouble?"

"Lackington must have purchased at least a hundred copies for the Temple, and I don't have a hundred friends in my club. If I purchase them all, suspicions will arise that we are trying to remove the book from circulation. So what can we do?"

The three of them stood there, staring at the pavement.

"I've got it. We will all enter and buy all of the books. If asked, we'll say we are missionaries and the books are being purchased to take to India."

"A field guide to London's rakes is appropriate reading material in India?" James sighed. "No, that will never do. They'll know it's all a hum."

"How about we describe ourselves as booksellers from America. And the publishers did not have the number of books we needed at the present time, so we came here to fulfill the order," she said. "If they complain, we will just say they can refill their stocks from the publishers at a later date. We need not reveal that they will no longer be published. Besides, they will sell us—their customers—books. That's what counts to a bookseller."

"Very well," James said. "I have no idea if your plan will work, but we do not have an alternative one, so it's worth a try."

Their ruse worked. After all of the Temple copies were purchased, Fitzy volunteered to carry the heavy load and deposit it at James's rooms. He'd then return with an empty box so they could continue to purchase copies from other booksellers.

By late afternoon, Meta was pleased to realize that no available copies of the books were to be had at central London booksellers. How many copies escaped their efforts because they had been distributed to places like Bristol she had no way to determine. However, their actions today increased her confidence in the eventual restoration of her friendship with George. "I'll ask Lady Sarah if she knows of other cities where the publishers might have shipped books. Perhaps if the journey is not far, Fitzy and I can take the carriage to retrieve those copies too."

James led them into his small drawing room carrying a bandbox full of books. "Well, we have certainly done our job for the day. If you buy up the copies in villages around town, all of London will soon forget that silly little book."

"I do hope so," Meta said, in a more optimistic mood. Still, the removal of the books seemed to be just one of many more steps needed to restore her relationship with George.

James shoved the box of books behind his sofa. "I will wager that by the time of Lady Sarah's ball at the end of the month, this muddle over one ill-advised book will end. Then Mr. Drexel can rightfully take his place at the ball as the person of honor."

"What ball?" Meta wondered if this was another plan the Learned Ladies were attempting to hide from her.

James fetched a white envelope from the sideboard and handed it to her. "It arrived this morning." He paused. "I'm sure there is an invitation waiting for you at home. So you see, by stopping further publication of their book and giving a ball in his honor, your lady friends are doing their best to right the wrong they started with their field guide. You must be pleased."

Meta gave him a smile; her thoughts consumed by the pretty invitation she held in her hands. Had they sent her an invitation too? Perhaps the ladies developed a lingering resentment over her objections to their field guide, or some unfathomable secret reason, causing them to deny her an invitation?

Eighteen

LADY SARAH SLIPPED HER ARM UNDER META'S. "I invited twenty-two of the Season's brightest diamonds to the ball tonight. Are you pleased?"

"I think so." Meta patted her friend's hand and glanced around the ballroom. All of the chandeliers were lit, so the room appeared bathed in light that sparkled off the tall pier looking glasses standing between each of the twelve darkened windows. On the parquet ballroom floor, only three full sets of guests danced the quadrille. As a result, the dancer's noticeable footsteps drew unnecessary attention due to their awkward echo in such a grand room. Of course, the night was early yet, and many revelers liked to arrive fashionably late. If they failed to come, she feared George's attendance might be the reason.

Meta's friends had planned this ball to make amends for the publication of their field guide. Their strategy was to shower their attentions upon George, and in doing so, prove to all of London his desirability and respectability. Meta doubted the success of this endeavor, because the Season had ended several months ago, so society in London had grown thin. Perhaps the ball would be a failure, because no one remained in town to accept Lady Sarah's invitation? Her jaw clinched. "Oh, I hope more people arrive soon."

"Don't fret," Lady Sarah said. The diamonds set in silver hanging around her neck reflected the brilliant candlelight in random flashes of light. "All of the young ladies will be interested in dancing with your Mr. Drexel, I'm sure."

"He's not mine, you know. And whether or not the Season's diamonds will have the courage to stand up in his company is yet to be determined." The thought of George snubbed by the ladies, and the cut observed in such a large company as this one, terrified her. Her palms dampened. A cut direct from anyone might lead to even further damage to his reputation. If that event came to pass, she'd never be able to forgive herself.

"I ended up inviting over three hundred people tonight, so don't be so dashed down. There are enough ladies here that are on our side already, so with their help, it will not appear like society is giving him the cut. On the contrary, if we all do our part, he will be remarked upon as a popular gallant once again."

Meta smiled at her friend. "I hope you're right." All she could do now was wait to see if the scandal of the field guide kept people away or if the invitation for a ball at Stainthorpe House proved irresistible.

"I'm confident our little plan will work. It must." Lady Sarah stood on her toes to survey the room. "I do not see Mr. Drexel yet. Have you seen him?"

"No, not yet. I must confess I'm a little worried

on that score." She addressed Lady Sarah. "What if he changes his mind and fails to come?"

Lady Sarah took Meta's gloved hand and patted it in return. "I must confess that, unlike our other guests, he did not receive a mere paper invitation, but I myself paid a call and invited him personally."

Meta felt the blood drain from her face.

"No, no, please do not distress yourself," Lady Sarah said. "I didn't discuss the ball and our scheme to lessen the scandal of the book. First, I apologized on behalf of the Learned Ladies, and he seemed to take it well. I cannot remember his exact response; however, I do remember it was short, but polite. I then gave him my personal invitation to the ball, because I mentioned his efforts on the tunnel to my father. His lordship is truly interested in Mr. Brunel and the tunnel—in his own way." She stopped and smiled. "Although, my mention of a single, young gentleman in need of my help piqued his interest the most. His first questions about Mr. Drexel were naturally the suitability of the gentleman as a potential suitor. Remember that race he sponsored last year?"

Both women giggled. "Of course," Meta said. "I remember several of us were hiding behind the curtains when your father stepped onto that balcony and challenged London's bachelors to a race. I don't think any event as remarkable as that one will ever be heard in a London square again."

"That was the most ridiculous speech ever made." Lady Sarah nodded. "I don't feel guilty about not falling in love with any of the five winners—not in the least. Really, I don't. However"—she sighed—"it was a shocking waste of funds. Serves him right. Did I ever tell you about that little man who competed in the 'Loyalty to the King and Crown' challenge? What a character he was."

"Is that the gentleman that kissed a sovereign after each step of his journey?"

Lady Sarah stifled an outburst. "Yes, and after he kissed the sovereign, he vowed, 'Your wish is my command, my liege.'"

They both laughed loud enough that their indiscretion needed to be masked by holding their gloved hands over their mouths.

Then Lady Sarah let out a blissful sigh. "Although, there were so many gentlemen with wonderful tales who competed in the 'Service to a Lady' challenge. Their stories forever changed my negative opinion about gentlemen into a positive one."

Meta laughed. "Yes, dear, but didn't most of those tales end up with the winner marrying the lady they performed the service for? Marriage with some other lady, not you. Surely you did not expect your father to bestow a prize on a bachelor who was no longer eligible?"

"Of course not. But it did warm my heart and give me hope, where previously I had none. Hope that one day, I too will find a remarkable gentleman for my husband. Speak of the..." She turned to Meta and winked. "Oh no, here comes Father. Please forgive him; he is rather grumpy at the moment. This is the first ball held in the history of Stainthorpe House in which I have chosen the guests, and none of them are those museum pieces he usually invites."

"Do you mean your father has finally given up his matchmaking?"

"I wouldn't go that far." Lady Sarah grinned. "More like a lull in the battle. He has been complaining about the uncivilized rabble here tonight. So you'd do me a great service if you would listen to his grievances and let him speak his mind. Now please excuse me." Lady Sarah adjusted her gold headband. "There is Mr. Symthes over by the fireplace. I doubt he would ever perform a romantic Service to a Lady, but he is *very* dashing. Don't you agree? Perhaps if I stand near, he'll ask me for a waltz." She laughed. "Fingers crossed."

"Best of luck." Meta glanced at Mr. Symthes. Indeed, he was handsome, but his coloring was too light for her taste. She favored dark gentlemen, like George.

This hasty pronouncement set her aback. She had always admired her husband's reddish blond hair. Especially when the golden strands took on a multicolored hue when the sunlight was just right. When had she begun to greatly admire gentlemen with dark hair?

Lady Sarah managed the timing of her elegant withdrawal from Meta's side without raising her father's suspicion of being avoided.

The earl ambled her way with a slight limp. His expression spoke of something on his mind. "Ah, delighted to see you, Mrs. Russell. Delighted, indeed." His richly embroidered and embellished square coat and satin breeches belonged in the previous century.

"Good evening, your lordship," Meta bowed. "Thank you for the invitation tonight. It appears your daughter's ball has the makings of a great success."

"A success, you say! Have you looked about you,

ma'am?" He randomly waved his hand. "In my day, there was sympathy between dress and manners, but look how society has fallen. Now all decorum is lost in actual rudeness. You must have noticed the mingle-mangle dancing the waltz? Never have I seen a more course and vulgar romp. Everybody spinning like tops and jumping like squirrels."

Meta hid her smile behind her gloved hand. "Well, sir, the minuet is out of fashion."

The earl sighed and wiped his brow with an over-large lace handkerchief. "Ah, the minuet is a refined and dignified exercise, demanding a manly carriage and a firm step. The only dance a fellow need learn. I still remember m' sister practicing with her dance master. A tablecloth tied to her back, so she could learn proper deportment with a train. Ah, happy days, happy days indeed." He glared at the dancers in the middle of a set. "But these smirking quadrillers, nothing more than stuffed dandies whose sex may be readily mistaken." He lowered his voice. "Or shall I say, whose sex is of no consequence. None of these romping privies could ever make a suitable husband for my daughter, mark my words."

"What sort of gentleman do you have in mind to court your daughter?"

A smile broke across his heavily lined face. "I can see the fellow now. A bold, manly carriage, dignified mien, weapon on his belt, and a tricorne hat."

"Despite the differences in clothes and lack of weapon, I believe many of the gentlemen here tonight fit that description."

"Humph. If you say so."

Without meaning to, she pictured George as the earl's perfect suitor. He certainly possessed a bold and manly carriage. Next she imagined him in a uniform, a weapon at his side. Her mouth dried. When had the man she once described as an upside-down pile of coal transformed into an imaginary leader of a great army?

"Tell me, ma'am, is this guest I'm not allowed to speak about here yet?"

Meta surveyed the room but failed to find George. "Not yet, your lordship."

"I understand this fellow messes about under the river. Heard all about this Frenchman, Brunel, at m' club. Astonishing thing, tunneling. After all, the Thames is an open privy—do beg pardon. Don't see how any fellow can get within twenty feet, much less want to tunnel under the thing. I mean men are men, certainly not moles. Don't you agree?"

"I think you will find this Mr. Drexel is a remarkable gentleman. He's an engineer, you know. One of the new breed of gentlemen building what will become a more successful Britain. Bridges are his main area of interest, but the tunnel is a great opportunity for him to obtain influential connections. Gentlemen with the skill to persuade Parliament or local governments to issue public works contracts."

He blew a puff of air. "Men filling the countryside with bridges looking like piles of iron sticks or belching steam engines. It's just not right, not the thing for a gentleman to mess about with, I say. No, it's the land, mother England, that makes all Englishmen who we are."

"You may change your mind after a conversation

with Mr. Drexel. But please, your lordship, try to not mention him in any capacity other than as one of your guests."

"Yes, yes, you sound like m' daughter." With that observation and a bow, he took his leave.

Meta turned to watch the couples on the dance floor. Within the last twenty minutes, the ball had undergone a transformation. Earlier, the ball lingered in that awkward time when not enough people mingled with strangers. Instead, they kept in small groups of their previous acquaintances. Now, however, the boisterous noise of music and conversation shouted between revelers, over a hundred dancing in front of her, indicated the ball should be a success.

Meta's spirits lifted, and she tapped her foot along with the lively music.

Devised with the good intentions of the Learned Ladies Society, this soiree's popularity should make amends to Mr. Drexel over the scandal created by the ladies' field guide. Some little part of Meta found irony in the thought that a man who once penned his own field guide now found himself on the receiving end of the experience. Still, his angry words had left her with sleepless nights and a lack of appetite.

Tonight this would all change. Tonight it would continue to go well or collapse into disaster. If tonight went well, she'd right the wrong she had inadvertently caused, and most important of all, their relationship might be restored to the affection they achieved after their shared afternoon of passion. But if the guests cut George and the ball failed... Her palms dampened and her stomach turned into a lead ball. Refusing to consider any other outcome, she decided to keep busy so as not to dwell on the possible consequences.

Meta headed over to speak with Sybella, standing by the refreshments. As she passed a large gilt looking glass, she checked her dress. Tonight she wore her best silk gown, the expensive one she normally was too frightened to wear for fear of ruining it. The sky blue silk shimmered under an almost transparent white overdress, while small rosettes in straw-colored silk trailed along the bottom of the bodice and hem.

Sybella noticed her approach and waved her closer. "Did you see that? Clara is dancing with that James Codlington again. I understand he doesn't have a feather to fly with now."

"James?"

Her friend wore a guilty blush. "Yes, of course, you are acquainted with him. Do you believe there might be expectations in that quarter?"

Meta observed the two dancing. Much to her surprise, they appeared to share confidences. James laughed at Clara's occasional whispered witticisms.

Lily stood by the punch bowl, watching her former suitor.

Meta could read Lily's expression like a book. Her sister stewed, yet made no move to join the couple. Minutes later, she spied Lily sitting with some friends. It was clear Lily found a safe harbor in her friends' company, yet Meta couldn't help but notice that her sister's gaze rarely left James since their arrival. Lily had created this estrangement, so she was responsible for her own future. Meta had no regrets on that score. She truly wished James happiness in whomever he chose for his future wife.

A whiff of lavender announced the arrival of Grizel. Tonight her black curls had been tamed into a tall coiffure accented with a striped green peasant feather, while a Scottish plaid sash on one shoulder accented her striking emerald gown. "Oh, look, Mr. Drexel has arrived."

The three women spun to find George standing in the doorway the moment his name was called. Tonight he appeared very proper in appropriate black attire and very dashing due to his broad shoulders and confident movements. The very amused twinkle in his darks eyes bespoke of an earlier libation.

Meta held her breath. *Would a member of society give him the cut direct in front of everyone?*

The room hushed for several seconds and the dancers stilled, causing the orchestra to stop playing.

George remained unmoving and merely lifted a sardonic brow.

Meta noticed some of the dowagers whisper and point in his direction.

Lady Sarah, in a gesture that Meta would remember forever, immediately strode over to join him wearing her brightest smile. After a bow and curtsy in return, she led him down the stairs, gave a nod for the orchestra to begin, and provided introductions to her father and two other friends.

Meta vowed to love her friend as long as she lived. She took a deep breath, relaxed a little, and continued to watch him. While he obviously failed to look in her direction or catch her eye, everyone seemed to greet him without reservation. Her heart soared. She turned to resume conversation with her friends, but underneath her layers of silk skirts, she danced a little jig.

Then something amazing happened. Her sister must have derived inspiration from Lady Sarah's forthright move to engage George in conversation, because Lily suddenly stood, strode forward with determination, and joined the party in conversation around James. After what appeared to be a few seconds of awkwardness, the entire group shared a laugh and exchanged smiles.

The dancers were then called for the next set, and once again, the boisterous noise returned to the ballroom.

Meta almost sang with joy when she noticed James and Lily take their position on the floor for the next Scottish reel. Her greatest hopes of the ball's success had now come true.

If the ladies or their mothers had lingering reservations about George, they were removed soon after he engaged in a long conversation with the earl. When finished, any apparent reservation felt by the ladies present appeared to have flown, since many of them gathered around him, silently seeking an invitation to dance.

Meta watched him carefully as he offered his arm to a stunning blonde. As they began to dance, she noticed the other ladies on the floor seemed unable to stop staring at him. Relieved by his popularity, she couldn't help but wonder if he might claim her hand for a dance. Three dances later, as she and Lady Sarah stood to the side discussing the successful ball, she noticed

George head in their direction. She swallowed loudly, causing Lady Sarah to pat her hand in comfort. *Had George forgiven her, enough to ask her for a dance?*

George stood tall before them. Politely and with much gallantry, he asked to partner Lady Sarah in the next waltz.

Her friend agreed, and he bowed in return.

During the entire exchange, he neither glanced at her nor caught her eye. He kept to his word, and soon led Lady Sarah onto the floor when the next set was called.

Two dances later, as she stood against the wall talking with Clara, she caught his gaze. The fierce storm in his dark eyes unsettled her.

A smile briefly flickered across his lips before it turned into a scowl, which then vanished and transformed into exaggerated, feigned gaiety. He strode up to them and bowed. Oozing politeness and deference, he requested the next set from Clara, once again leaving her standing without a partner.

Clara giggled, a blush staining her cheeks. "Oh, I would be so honored, sir."

"I'd be delighted." He bowed again. "I have been in the company of too many widows all evening. It will be a refreshing change to partner a handsome, young lady."

Clara furtively glanced at Meta before they headed in the direction of James and Lily, who waited on the ballroom floor for their second dance.

Meta's cheeks heated. If earlier she possessed some amount of courage, that fortitude had now decidedly fled. Maybe later, before the end of the ball, she might recover from his snub and approach him for a casual, polite greeting only. As she headed toward another friend of hers, she heard several people mention her name in a low whisper. One individual said her name followed by the word "tainted." Could George's cuts have become obvious to everyone in the room, and as a result, the guests considered her to be the one socially tainted? *Or did she imagine it because of her overset nerves?* She shrugged off this ominous feeling and headed toward James to join him for their previously arranged waltz.

For the remainder of the evening, she and George had no further interaction. She sat with the wallflowers watching the dancers and sipping wine. She suffered a moment of panic when George requested a dance from a stunning Diamond of the First Water in a purple velvet gown, and the lady responded by turning her back to him in a motion of indirect refusal.

Meta bit her lower lip, considering if she could mask his cut by running down to pretend the next waltz was hers.

Before she had the chance to take the first step, Lady Sarah returned to his side with Grizel in tow.

After George and her friend took their places on the ballroom floor, she sighed in relief.

Lady Sarah looked in her direction and winked.

She smiled in return and watched in gratification as George seemed never to be without a dance partner. If, by chance, their gazes met again, he immediately turned away. Surprised by his response, she bitterly regretted the loss of their previous shared confidences.

After one o'clock in the morning, as the ball began

to draw to a close, she boldly resolved to seek out his company for a polite greeting, if only to further judge the current state of affairs between them. It took several minutes before she summoned the courage to approach him. Gathering her fortitude, she marched to his side and addressed him. "I hope you had a pleasant evening, sir?"

He narrowed his eyes, his black brows knit. His expression appeared like a thunderstorm rolling in over the rooftops. "This evening is a foolish waste of time and money. As I mentioned to your persuasive friend, while I appreciate the Learned Ladies' efforts upon my behalf—"

She dropped her head and kept her gaze on his gleaming black shoes.

After a long pause, his stiff posture relaxed, and he exhaled audibly. He lowered his voice. "Are you well?"

She nodded.

"I have missed…" He straightened, voice hardening. "This ball cannot possibly make a difference, since the damage has already been done. Madam." He bowed and strode away.

Nineteen

"I'm not lying," George said, standing in the overheated engine room. He stood next to a large set of plans for a new drainage system and watched Isambard light a Meerschaum. Soon the acrid smell of burnt tobacco filled the small brick room.

After two or three puffs on his pipe, Isambard strode to the grimy window and gazed out to the day's spectators gathered around the top of the pit.

George joined him at the window. Outside, the day was a chilly one, the probable reason there were only twenty or so visitors huddled in small groups. "I'm not lying, because I have no reason to do so. I haven't chased females for years. Today I'm more circumspect, one lady for five years, one *very* discreet lady. When young and foolish, I—shall we say—enjoyed myself," George said, smiling from the recollection of pleasant memories. "Women were a game between me and two of my closest friends. I know your history too. All men in their twenties are idiots, admit it."

Isambard laughed and returned to examine the drawings. "Well then, that must account for my recent behavior, since I just turned twenty. You see I have this small boat I'm fond of. You know, a pleasant Sunday outing, willow tree branches hanging over the river to provide a private spot." This memory caused a knowing smile to grace his lips. "But, my friend, you are over a foot taller and two stones heavier than I, so you resemble the tall, dark hero in many of the three-volume novels ladies love to read. My guess is that you are vastly more successful than I could ever dream of. However, if you tell me you are not currently wooing the ladies on the side, I believe you. This whole mess, the postponement of your promotion, is all due to the publication of those field guides. If not for your book, the ladies would never have come up with their idea to publish a similar field guide. So there is some justice involved. Even you must admit that."

"Yes, I started the ball rolling." George continued to stare out the small window. Isambard was right, of course, but the die was cast. While Parker's brother suspended the publication of another edition of his field guide, the books that were already sold would never vanish. The remainder of his life would be spent dealing with them, in one way or another. He ground his teeth. All young gentlemen are idiots, but he was a particularly fine example.

With his chance of promotion delayed or even destroyed, he would do as Isambard suggested in the first place and keep the line. Stay out of trouble for probably years to come before another opportunity for advancement became available. Either that, or earn it by some great accomplishment. He sighed and leaned his forehead against the window's cool glass.

When he glanced at the pit again, he saw Fitzy, drawing pad in hand, heading toward them. The red fire of rage descended from the mere thought of the boy's sister and her friends. So to avoid insulting or frightening the young man, George decided to escape to the barge on the river. The barge held the diving bell and its derrick, air pump, and bags of clay needed to plug leaks. He turned to Isambard. "Didn't you mention a job needed in regard to the clay bags the other day? Did you want a count or was there something else?"

Isambard appeared lost in the drainage plans before his scrutiny. He glanced up. "Pardon? Ah, yes. The barge is moored over the spot where we are currently digging. We just learned a collier has been moored on the spot for a year and may have excavated ballast, so there could be an indentation in the riverbed. I plan to descend in the bell tomorrow and map the area. What I need today is an estimate of the volume of our current clay bags; say if the whole lot was thrown over the side. We may need to plug a hole as great as thirty or twenty feet, so we may need to procure additional bags."

George nodded. "I'd like to avoid the Broadsham boy at the moment." He pulled his lips into a tight line. "At least until I no longer feel like throttling his sister."

Isambard continued to focus on the plans.

"So I will go and make estimates of the volume. Is that all you want?"

The engineer waved his hand. "Yes, I mean no." He looked up. "I'd like your opinion too on the length of the hazel branches stuck through each clay bag. We may have to lengthen them in the future if we want our plug of clay bags to hold together. Oh, and be sure to ask Mr. Duff if the new stronger chain for the bell has been tested more than once."

George nodded and then escaped to the dinghy for the short journey to the barge. The chilly day helped quell the normal stench of the river. For several minutes, he glanced across the Thames to the St. Catherine docks on the north side. All of that part of London appeared alive. Tall ships, their cargo holds filled to bursting, waited for a chance to unload. Upstream, past the Tower, London stood as a hazy outline below a coal soot–tinged sky. The dense, black air made the spire on top of St. Paul's Cathedral difficult to fully distinguish.

He climbed up onto the fifty-foot wooden barge, a vessel of significant length and breadth. On one end loomed the giant diving bell, shaped like an oversized cowbell. In the middle of the barge rose a large derrick to lift and lower the bell into the river. Piled high on the opposite end were at least a hundred saltpeter bags filled with blue clay, hazel rods protruding through each one. The whole lot of bags resembled a pile of bloated hedgehogs.

Mr. Duff, the man in charge of the vessel, wiped his grimy hands on his leather apron and shook his hand. "Pleasure to see you here today, gov. What's it to be then?"

George could feel the dirty slime of the Thames inadvertently transferred to his hand. He gave the man the courtesy of not embarrassing him by wiping his palm. "First off, have you tested the new chain again?"

"No worry there. Yesterday, we hauled it up and down twice. Like clockwork she was."

"Good. Let's hope that is one problem solved. What I really need today is a bag count. I must estimate the possible volume of the plug on the riverbed by taking measurements of the pile. Then calculate the area that might be achieved with the bags we have. Shouldn't take more than an hour, I should think."

"Right then," Mr. Duff said. "I'll leave you to it. Give a shout if you need assistance."

"Will do." George sat close to the pile and began to assemble a long measuring stick. An hour later, he had a pretty good estimate of the area the clay bags could cover if they were all thrown overboard and placed into position. If a small hole, not more than inches, broke through the tunnel's ceiling, the current number of bags stored on the barge and in reserve should be sufficient to stop the water from flooding most of the tunnel. But if the leak was larger, they must have more clay bags on the ready. Once finished with his estimates, he wondered if Fitzy had completed his sketches, so he could return to the tunnel without running into the boy.

A shrill, long whistle broke the silence across the Thames.

George recognized the warning signal of water intrusion into the tunnel. By now men would be frantically pressing straw and plaster up against the water leak, hoping to at least slow it until a more permanent repair. Nonessential personnel would be pouring out of the tunnel. His heartbeat escalated. *Had Fitzy made it to safety?* How could he ever face Meta if the boy came to harm? He almost jumped into the punt to return to shore but stopped in his tracks the moment he saw another engineer on site that day standing on the dock and waving his arms.

George's heartbeat escalated until he could hear it in his ears.

The young man cupped his hands and shouted. "Leak in number twelve, Drexel. *A big one.* Use the bell to see what we got from the top."

Then Isambard came running to the end of the dock. "Man the bell, men. Leak in number twelve coming in fast. Estimate two hundred thirty feet from the water's edge. Hurry!"

George and the three men on the barge leaped into action.

He and Mr. Duff hurriedly tried to estimate the proper distance to drop the bell so it would be over the leak. Meanwhile, the engineer and workmen readied the air pump, leather hoses, and derrick.

As quickly as possible, they maneuvered the barge directly over the estimated site of the leak and threw out several anchors. Mr. Duff and a workman then manned the swing crane to hoist the heavy bell several feet into the air and position it over the water.

Mr. Duff started to remove his coat and hat, but George held his arm. "I'll do it."

"No, gov, that's my job."

George knew the man had two young children. Under no circumstances would he allow a father to risk his life while he was on board. "Pulling rank,

Duff. Let me know if there is anything new about the bell I need to know."

Mr. Duff paused, glanced at the shore, and for whatever reason, he nodded. "You've been down afore; you'll do well. Let's get to work."

George began to strip off his heavy waterproofed clothes. It occurred to him that if he was successful stopping the leak, it might go a long way to the restoration of his esteem in the eyes of the Brunels. If he successfully plugged the hole before any real damage could be done to the great shield, they might quickly forget about "the stallion not in the studbook."

He shed his coat and waistcoat before jumping into the Thames. The cold water stung like a thousand daggers piercing his skin. He clenched his teeth and focused on a positive thought, like a promotion. Thankfully, the river seemed to be at slack water, so he would not have to struggle with a strong current. However, the tide would eventually return. Giving him plenty of motivation to get the job done as quickly as possible.

Surrounded by the clanging of heavy iron chains, the men on the barge started to lower the giant iron bell into the Thames. Once the bell was almost covered with water, George took a deep breath and swam under the bell's edge into the dim interior. He gasped for air, but after hearing the hiss of compressed air from two pumps delivered through a leather hose into the bell, he began to relax.

He sat on a small ledge and watched the water rise up inside of the rusty dome, grateful for the light brush of pumped air upon his cheeks. He waited and watched the water below him darken as the men above lowered the bell to almost thirty feet, hovering just above the Thames riverbed. A sign painted on the inside of the bell stated: "More air, knock once; less air, knock twice; pull up, knock three times."

For several agonizing minutes, he focused on the riverbed, as the bell's position slowly moved. Then he saw the leak. Nothing more than a tiny, dark gash in the middle of a craterlike indentation on the sandy floor. He lowered himself into the water, feet first, to examine the hole.

The small, dark crack of several inches appeared next to a silver streak of water rushing into the tunnel. George tested the depth by shoving his finger into the hole. His finger traveled mere inches before it hit a solid object, possibly the top of the great shield. Not wasting any more time, he started to layer the few iron rods piled in the bell in a lattice pattern over the indentation in the riverbed. The first one disappeared in the swirl of disturbed river bottom. "*Damnation.*" The thought of failure and instant death from being sucked into the hole crossed his mind for a second or two. He closed his stinging eyes and kept heaving the remaining heavy iron rods into place.

When finished, he signaled the men to drop numerous clay bags.

Once several bags were dropped, George swam in and out of the bell to move the bags into position over the leak. After repeatedly holding his breath for a minute or two, he tugged the bags to spread over the iron rods to make a wider plug. After who knows how many minutes later, he pulled himself into the bell, breathing hard. He waited a minute or two before he observed the first signs of success, the lack of any silver streaks of rushing water. Instead, the water around the bags appeared calm, as revealed by the disturbed sediment slowly falling down like snow back onto the riverbed. A dark outline of bags appeared like nestled eggs in the middle of the indentation. He continued to swim out of the bell and drag new bags close to the pile on the floor of the Thames, as fast as his fatigued arms could move them.

When the bags had run out, he signaled with three knocks for the bell to be raised. He had only enough strength to pull himself onto the small seat in the bell's interior and slump to the side. Whether or not he was able to permanently stop the leak, he had no idea. All of the clay bags had been used, so more bags and a man with fresh muscles were needed at this point. His chest painfully constricted and with great difficultly he stifled the urge to panic due to the feeling of no air.

The color of the water below him soon appeared turquoise, indicating the bell had risen to a level where light easily penetrated the water. The bell broke the surface and fresh air burst into the iron dome.

He rolled off the shelf and managed to paddle five feet to hold on to the barge's side. With numb hands and arms, he held on to the barge's wooden railings with all of his remaining strength. He could do no more than that.

Mr. Duff observed his distress, jumped into the water, and swam to his side. In one swift movement, he threw his arm around his waist and heaved him high enough to grab on to the railing. "Up you go, gov."

"The leak?" George managed to spit out with difficulty, his mouth full of foul-tasting Thames water.
Able to hold on with his arm wrapped around the
railing, he lacked the strength to fully heave himself
out of the water.

The workman on deck gripped his arm and pulled,
while Mr. Duff pushed him from below, so George
finally escaped the deathly grip of the cold Thames and
was flung onto the barge. He lay splayed on deck like
a dead flounder.

"Don't you go about worrying about the leak,"
Mr. Duff said, pulling himself out of the chilly water.
"Nothing we can do now but pile on more bags
when the new ones become ready. Thomas is goin'
down next, and maybe after that we'll hear if the leak
'as stopped."

George replied with a nod, the only movement he
had enough strength to execute.

It did not take long before the barge crew loaded
fresh bags from a small boat and prepared to move the
bell into place again.

He remained flat on his back, covered in his oilskins
and coat, listening to the rushed efforts behind him.

Before they dropped the next load of clay bags, they
received word from the shore that the leak had signifi-
cantly slowed—enough so that it could be effectively
managed from within the tunnel.

While the barge was towed back to shore, George
lifted himself enough to lean against a wooden tool-
box. He saw a woman with two young curly-haired
children standing on the very edge of the quay. She
held the smallest child in her arms, resting on her hip

and a thumb in its mouth. The other, a small boy of possibly five years, held on to his mother's skirt in a death-like grip.

Once the barge reached the dock, Mr. Duff hopped off and ran to his family. The four of them seemed to blend together in one big embrace.

George noticed other men's families lingering around the pit as well. The news of a leak must have traveled quickly throughout London—fast enough that entire families came running to the site, concerned for the welfare of their loved ones.

After the Duffs completed their familial embrace, Mr. Duff lifted the youngest into his arms, while his wife held the boy. Both adults exchanged smiles and fleeting kisses.

George sighed; every part of his body ached. Closing his eyes, he heard only the happiness of family reunions happening around him.

Did he save the day, save Fitzy, and earn Mr. Brunel's praise?

If so, the joy from his triumph escaped him. Fatigue or low spirits could account for some of his lack of enthusiasm. However, after watching the Duffs' reunion, he began to fully comprehend the emotional need that drove families to rush from their homes at the sound of an alarm. He had witnessed it many times, but he had not been personally affected or truly empathetic before.

If you asked him a day ago, he would have immediately sought Mr. Brunel's praise. Instead, this very minute, he understood why his father ran to his mother's room when he returned home. Why his father shunned the immediate gratification of the accolades—praise that gave you the pleasure of a pat on the back and a spoken "job well done." Why he sought the highest, most meaningful praise of them all, the proverbial crown of laurel leaves held high above your head—the accolades from the woman you love.

Now he understood his parents. The loneliness banished from his mother's face, replaced by an expression of calm joy when her husband entered the room. Then the moment reached its crescendo by the peace of holding hands with the person you love the most—a single breath of time that defined your life and gave it purpose.

Now his future happiness depended upon finding Meta in order to tell her about the love that coursed through his body and claimed the essence of his soul. Success meant little to him unless he could share it with her. If only she were here now, he'd be a happy man.

So he had fallen in love at last.

He had just enough strength to chuckle weakly. At sixteen, he believed he had fallen in love with the sister of a friend from school. He spent a year planning his life, marriage, and future happiness based on a stolen kiss in a stairwell.

What an idiot.

His sweetheart married another before she even came out. He believed he had been ill-used and the victim of the ultimate betrayal. His anger eventually turned into the certainty that he must have been unworthy of love, too tall and too dark or some other fault he would never be able to rise above.

This sentiment remained with him for years until this moment.

This sweet moment of understanding himself better.

Nothing would ever make him happier than giving himself to one woman forever.

If she would have him?

He shouted a bark of laughter. Now he fully realized why his friend Boyce sang all the time after his marriage and why Ross hated to leave his wife's side for even a day.

He dropped his head back and stared at the cloudy sky. Laying here on hard boards, soaking wet, under the gray heavens, he needed to rush to her immediately and place his weary, spent heart safely in her hands; tell her of his heroic actions; receive her praise and reassurances. He needed this now as much as he had needed air from a fragile leather hose.

At the bare minimum, he should have danced, laughed, or shouted his love to the world. But the memory of his many insults aimed toward Meta returned, the harsh words and bearlike bad temper.

Could she ever forgive him?

He masked his heartache from the thought of her refusal and told himself he did not deserve her forgiveness. He lay on the hard deck, feeling cold, fatigued, and worthless. His accomplishment of little meaning without her to share it.

Without her.

Without her, he was just another piece of rubbish floating on the Thames.

Twenty

GEORGE STABBED THE SHOVEL INTO A PILE OF MUCK. The scraping sound joined a similar noise made by the other men, all echoing throughout the tunnel. The week following the water intrusion, he found comfort in work, the exhausting physical numbness of hard labor mastered. Both the Brunels expressed their surprise when they frequently found him assisting the miners digging out the mud left behind by the leak. George considered his suffering, caused by the nauseating stench of sewage, a form of penitence. He told himself every good engineer must have personal experience doing the dangerous work he asked of others.

Meanwhile, it gave him a chance to assess his newly recognized passion for Meta—and left him wondering if the overwhelming sensations he experienced on the barge were transitory in nature—created by sheer exhaustion—and therefore might fade with time. But he knew better. He wholly recognized his love—romantic love—but he failed to devise a solution for his condition. He knew nothing about her late husband or the extent of her lingering feelings of fidelity or love. Moreover, she likely remained offended by his recent bouts of ill-tempered insults. He would not find it surprising, in the least, if she never forgave him.

What proper lady would?

So if she refused his suit, could he live with his need for her? She had become one of his life's necessities, like food and air. When she rejected him, what would he do? Clearly, he would have to flee England. Live in a land far away, never to be heard of again, lost and forgotten—America, perhaps.

By the end of the week, his distress reached a level he was unable to relieve by himself. Courage failed him—her rejection a possible death sentence.

His only option was to discuss the matter and get another opinion. The choices were a best friend, like Boyce, or one of his new friends, like James, or a man of greater experience, like his father. Not desiring to appear weak or teased in front of his friends, he decided to discuss the matter with his father after dinner. As far as George was concerned, he'd rather have a blacksmith pull his eyeteeth out than discuss such a matter. But he was desperate.

Damnation, he had become a maudlin idiot.

That evening, he entered the parlor first after dinner. The rain came down in translucent sheets on the windows, but a vigorous fire in the hearth countered the onslaught of rain. After two glasses of brandy, he strode to the mantel and grabbed the pile of white cards. As long as he lived, he had no intention of responding to anyone, about either of the two field guides, ever again. He threw the cards into the fire and inhaled the sour smoke of burnt paper.

His father entered the parlor holding a note recently delivered to Mrs. Morris. "Wonderful. It appears young Fitzhenry will pay a call upon us tomorrow. I must say I miss the boy. Sometimes, on rare occasions, he reminds me of you when you were young."

"Pardon?" Struck by the return of Fitzy paying a call, and whether or not his sister approved, he lost the thread of conversation. "Fitzy?"

"Yes. You never really appreciated the emotional impact of your drawings, just the intellectual accomplishment. On the other hand, Fitzhenry expresses a rare aesthetic appreciation for them. Rare too amongst most members of the general public, I have discovered. In the long run, he'll find more happiness being an artist than a draftsman or engineer." He looked at the note again. "This gives me an idea. Mrs. Morris," he called, strolling out of the room.

George ground his teeth. He eyed the brandy and wondered if another glass would put him in his cups. If he became thoroughly disguised, could he effectively communicate his woeful situation with Meta to his father without making a damn fool of himself by blubbering out some nonsense that would never suit?

To hell with it.

There were times when a man needed many, many bumpers of strong brandy, and this was one of them.

His father returned and plopped down on the ivory chair before the fire. "I sent him a note in return. I'm going to ask young Fitzhenry to bring certain supplies tomorrow. I have a plan to engage the lad to create a present for you mother. She will be delighted; I know it."

For the first time, he neither questioned nor complained about his father's attentions to the woman he loved. Instead, it inspired him to consider a future gift for Meta, someday, if he ever got the chance. "I know Mother will appreciate that."

His father cocked his head. "Do you? I'm pleased to hear that."

Right, here goes. "I wonder if I might have some advice?" George congratulated himself on taking the first step. Seeking advice pained him; it might even be fatal.

"Certainly," his father said, a broad grin increasing the wrinkles at the corners of his eyes. "On what subject? Love?"

George choked on his swig of brandy.

His father beamed. "I was being facetious, but from your expression, I must have hit the mark. You know I never expected us to discuss that subject, but I'm pleased, dear boy, pleased indeed. My father and I never discussed females. It was just not the done thing in those days."

"I'd never say a word either if I hadn't made a mull of it."

His father chuckled. "All men make mulls out of romance. I promise you that. It's that lovely Mrs. Russell, isn't it?"

George nodded, then took another gulp of brandy. "I blamed her for my troubles. Justly, in some cases, unjustly in others. I should apologize first, of course. But I'm not sure how to proceed after that. I just cannot go on without making it right between us."

"Have you given her the offer of your hand?" his

father asked, leaning forward. The refection of the fire danced in his dark eyes.

George shook his head and focused on his knee. "No, but now I realize I must offer."

"Regardless of the outcome?"

His stomach seized and it felt like he had eaten a clay bag with hazel sticks protruding from it. Staring into his father's gleaming eyes, he realized there was only one answer. "Yes, regardless of the outcome."

His father burst out of his chair, took two strides, and pulled him to his feet. This was followed by a rare hug. "My son, my son." His voice cracked. "I never thought I'd live to see the day you"—he playfully punched his shoulder—"would fall in love. Understand the emotion too." He threw himself into another tight embrace. "So happy. Wait until I tell Mother."

"Please don't. Nothing may come of it, and I'd be embarrassed. Promise?"

His father paused, then returned to his seat. "Not a word, I promise."

"I just need a little advice." If he was honest with himself, a significant amount of advice. "You see, we are currently not on speaking terms."

"It's unfortunate you are estranged. I'm not going to ask you why, since I doubt it will help. Will it help?"

George shook his head.

"Then the only advice I can give you is from my own personal experience. And that lesson is to not rush into expressing your affections. Take the time to build up the friendship and trust again. I know your first instinct is to rush in and wrestle the situation to rights, tell her you love her, and expect an affirmative reply—but don't. You may irrevocably offend her if you do."

His heart beat erratically. His first instinct to remedy the problem was rejected. "Then how should I proceed?"

His father stroked the gray stubble shadowing his chin. "Do her a service, or make one of her loved ones happy, such as persuading James to resume his addresses to her sister. If those are impossible, just make the time spent in your company a pleasant and enjoyable experience. I know nothing of the relationship or if the result you hope to achieve is even possible, but you understand the idea."

"That's easy enough. I can have lunch with James again. I'd like that."

"Good. Then once she is aware of the service you have rendered her, you express your attentions someplace she feels comfortable. Whether that is at home or a crowded ball, you would likely know the answer better than I do."

George sipped his golden brandy and stared at the smoldering fire.

They sat for several minutes in silence.

"If none of my suggestions are successful," his father said. "Then there is only one recourse."

He turned to stare at his father, brow constricted, unsure of what followed.

"When you are alone and both standing, you must move to hold her. Take it slow, so as not to frighten her, but hold her in an embrace—nothing more.

Remain unmoving until you are both comfortable. If there is no chance of a reconciliation, she will not stay in your arms long."

Would he ever be granted that chance? "Thank you for the advice. I will think about it carefully, before I try anything rash." He set down his brandy and prepared to journey to the tunnel. He had many things to consider, and hard labor had always succeeded in putting his problems into sharp focus.

His father noticed this. "Are you off?"

"Yes, there is a board meeting to discuss the river-bed and the possibility of laying large oilcloths on the bottom of the Thames above the area where we are currently digging."

"Your mother is sleeping, so I'll have to return home soon, but would you like me to join you for the first hour?"

George bit his lower lip. Now he fully comprehended the strength of his father's motivations to stay. "Thank you for the offer, but no, I'll handle it." Of course, he might not be able to handle the situation, but if that came to pass, he decided to be positive and learn from the experience.

"Did you say you will handle…" His father jumped to his feet and rushed over to pat him on the back. "So pleased, Son, so pleased." He sat on his chair. "Since our very likely one and only father and son talk is coming to an end, there is something I wish to say to you while I have the chance. I understand your disappointment, sometimes bitter, although you try to hide it, when I cannot be by your side at the board meetings. I just want you to know that I appreciate, and respect, the fact that you never mentioned your displeasure to Mother. You could have easily complained to her, but you kept from her your fears that without me by your side, you might fail. And for that I thank you."

George paused. Without a doubt, in the past he had bitterly resented his father's absence and felt abandoned at crucial moments of his life. But he would never add to his mother's woes by placing pressure on her to release him. Now after the full realization of his feelings for Meta, he understood the reasons behind his father's actions better. "Yes, I blame my resentment on the foolishness of the young, which for me lasted until thirty. I hope that today, I'm a wiser man."

"Good. You are fully capable of being a success on your own merit."

He chuckled and smiled, pride swelling inside him. "Thank you, Father. For the first time, I believe you."

That evening, George stayed awake most of the night, considering his father's advice. Obviously, his female troubles were a well-trodden path for the male of the species.

Early the next morning, he was truly delighted to see Fitzy bound through the door and greet him without reservation or awkwardness.

"Drexel, I am so happy to see you. Is your father here? Wait till you see what he has planned for a surprise. I cannot wait."

George smiled. "Sit down and tell me about your family, but first explain why you sent a note announcing you'd pay a call. We got so used to you coming and going without a formal invitation, you seem like part of the family. Now the entire household is delighted to learn of your return."

The young man blushed. "Meta said I shouldn't bother you, because the two of you had some sort of falling out." He wrung his hands. "I am sorry about that, Drexel, I truly am. Meta has not included me in her confidences, not really. I know it's some hum about that field guide nonsense. All these hard feelings over a silly book. I don't understand it."

He smiled. "You're right. A silly book, indeed. But if she warned you not to bother us, does she know of your visit today?"

The boy nearly jumped in his chair. "Yes, she urged me to come because of the leak in the tunnel. We all were so worried when we heard the news. She sent me over as soon as she thought you would not be so busy and my visit would be reasonable. Funny thing is, she has not been able to eat since, so I know her concern about the fate of the tunnel must be upsetting her no end."

From the sudden unique sensation within his chest, George came to the conclusion that his heart must be soaring in place. Then wisdom prevailed. Perhaps it was the success of the tunnel after all, and not his welfare, that caused her lack of appetite.

"And as far as that silly book those ladies wrote is concerned," Fitzy said, "well, she and I, with James's help, bought up every copy in London." He laughed. "You should have seen James's face when he ran out of the Temple, arms full of the ladies' field guide. I thought I'd laugh so hard, I'd do myself an injury."

"Your sister and James did what?" He held his breath, while his mind raced.

"Bought up all those field guide books she said insulted you. They're piled high in the schoolroom now. I wonder what she'll do with them. There are so many of them, they'd make a bang-up roaring fire."

His father then stepped into the parlor and greeted Fitzy. "I have a job for you today. Come, follow me."

Fitzy fell in step behind his father as they both disappeared upstairs.

Once at the tunnel, George attended the meeting, then spent several hours on the tunnel's new drainage plans. He accomplished nothing except drawing a square and sharpening a pencil. Instead, he marveled over the news that Meta had bought up copies of the ladies' field guide in a gesture surely meant to save him and make amends. He thought of showering her with presents or words of gratitude, but nothing sounded right.

He laughed aloud. In the past, many people at one time or another had called him a rake. If he was truly a rake, he should know how to please a female in every way, not just in bedroom behaviors and empty words of flattery. No true rake would ever find himself in his current befuddled, anxious condition without an easy solution.

An hour later, Fitzy and his father returned to the parlor. Fitzy had white plaster on his coat and waistcoat. George worried Meta may be angry, so he ordered the boy to the kitchen to be cleaned. "What have the two of you been up to?"

His father and Fitzy exchanged smiles. "I asked Fitzy to make a cast for your mother." A sigh escaped him, then he explained to Fitzy. "I might die before her, you see. If she has a memento beside her during her last years, I know it will give her comfort when I'm gone." The older man's eyes suddenly became a little watery.

George gulped before his throat closed. The subject of his parents' mortality pained him deeply. However, it spurred him to consider the expediency of what he needed to do: how to deliver himself into Meta's good graces, how to restrain himself, and how to offer his hand in marriage at the proper time—the time when her only possible answer was *yes*. The pain centered deep in his chest grew. Right now, he'd give everything he owned, or would own in the future, just for the opportunity to kiss her once.

Twenty-one

PASSING THROUGH THE VESTIBULE OF THE FAMILY'S town house, Meta saw a note on the hallway salver addressed with remarkably large looping penmanship she recognized as George's. Since his admonition about withholding an insult and repeated cuts at Lady Sarah's ball, she had no choice but to believe their relationship was truly at an end. For a reason she could not fathom, she picked up the paper, held it to her nose, and inhaled.

It smelled like paper.

Her heart broke a little. She was not sure what she expected, but she would have recognized if it smelled like George's normal perfume of coal smoke mixed with mud and the well-recognized odor of a man in close proximity. His scent had always set her heartbeat off in a gallop.

But it smelled like paper, washed linen, perhaps a little whiff of iron-laden ink or the lavender-scented drying sand.

She ripped open the note too fast, causing the paper to tear. *Bother.*

In his large handwriting, she read:

Madam, please do me the honor of being my guest at a banquet Friday next. The location will be at the Thames Tunnel. Unless I hear otherwise, my carriage will arrive on your doorstep at five o'clock. If you wish decline, I will understand. Let Fitzy deliver your regrets.

You have my deepest regards,
Geo. Drexel

What a curious invitation, moreover, an equally curious site for a banquet. Did the bear plan to roast the rabbit at the tunnel? Any further thoughts were interrupted by a thumping commotion descending the stairs.

"What ho?" Fitzy said, reaching the bottom and immediately leaning over the letter in her hand until his nose hovered inches away.

She whipped the invitation behind her back. "If you must know, it is private correspondence and none of your business."

"That's a gammon. It's from George; I can tell. Did he mention me? Does he need my assistance?"

She reached out with one hand and tousled his hair. "No, it's an invitation to dine."

"I told you before, don't touch my hair. I've grown up now. I hope you're going to accept his invitation." He tilted his head in a quizzing manner, perhaps suspicious of her ability to restore the relationship between them.

"Should I?"

"What's stopping you?" He pulled an apple out

of his pocket and took a bite with a loud crunch. Juice covered his cheeks, so he wiped them with his sleeve.

She frowned. "Have you forgotten? He blames me for the publication of *The Ladies' Field Guide to London's Rakes.*"

Upon the sudden realization that he flaunted the house rules about eating, he whipped the apple behind his back. "Oh pooh. George has forgotten that, I can tell you. Every time I pay a call he asks about your health. Besides, if he was irrevocably angry with you, why would he invite you to dinner?"

The first words that came to mind were *a dressing-down*. She feared a scene similar to their last encounter. Still, he did send her the dinner invitation. "Perhaps you are right. Are you visiting the Drexels soon?"

"Tomorrow. I'm putting the finishing touches on a plaster cast I'm making for Mr. Drexel and his wife. I must admit it is not my best work. I may have to cast it again."

"Then it will be better the next time, I promise. But before you leave, I will give you a short note accepting his kind offer to dine."

"Yes, yes, capital." He started to run toward the schoolroom.

"Slow down! For heaven's sake. We don't want another chandelier accident."

He slid to a stop and furtively looked up. Then he slowly walked out of the room.

That evening in her bedroom, it took Meta over an hour to write three simple lines. She inquired about the well-being of his family, thanked him for the invitation, and communicated her delight in attending the celebration at the tunnel.

Hours later, she ended the evening by a thorough wardrobe inventory. *What is the appropriate dress for a banquet held at the tunnel?* She had no idea where the tables might be placed. Would it be held outside under a canopy, nearby in rooms at the church, or in the tunnel itself?

Early the next morning, she visited her modiste and ordered a new bronze silk gown, an elegant design with only a few frills on the sleeves and no train. If the banquet was to be held outside the tunnel, a train might be ruined by water and mud. By the end of the day, she had purchased a completely new outfit, the gown and lovely kid shoes instead of silk ones, also to defend against water. Her final purchase was a simple turban of rich claret-colored silk.

For the remainder of that evening, she tried on all of the jewelry in her casket. Standing before a looking glass, she held up a small piece of the bronze silk to determine which of her necklaces would complement her new gown. The bull's-eye Scottish agate drops and necklace won the final choice. Once her garments and jewelry for the banquet had been decided upon, she went to bed. Sleep eluded her until early dawn.

What if the gown turned out to be a failure?

The next morning, she repeated the process again. This time she purchased a blue silk gown, with white embroidered roses along the bodice, and a gold-feathered evening turban. She was satisfied that this alternate choice of dress should meet her expectations, if the first one failed after she tried it on. For the final touch, she chose jewelry for this gown, a parure of the clearest blue aquamarines. She inhaled and relaxed. At least one of these outfits should set off her features well. The question was which one?

On the day of the banquet, she rose early. She needed the extra time for her maid to pin her hair in various styles—all in an effort to determine which one was best at hiding her two strands of gray hair—an unjust occurrence for one just twenty-four.

She spent the remainder of the day in an animated agony. With her mind occupied by the upcoming banquet, none of her directions to the staff made sense, she lacked the discipline to read to her father, and her siblings openly questioned whether she had gone mad.

Forty minutes before George was expected, she sat waiting for his arrival in her drawing room. Fingering the silver chain on her reticule, she gained confidence from knowing that inside the small bag was her last minute addition of her vinaigrette. Not to cover up any stench from the Thames but more as a restorative to divert her nerves from the agitation now overwhelming her. She pulled out and opened the small-latticed silver box. Holding it to her nose, she inhaled deeply. The tingle caused by the vinegar steadied her. The man she loved invited her to a celebration. She inhaled the acid again.

You will survive this evening. Be brave.

Twenty-two

WHEN THE HIRED CARRIAGE PULLED UP IN FRONT OF the Broadshams' home, George thought his heart might fail him on the spot. After all, there had to be a limit to the number of beats per minute for one small organ. He opened the door, tugged on his coat tails, and strode to their front door.

In the muddle of his rapid thoughts, he tried to remember his father's advice. Should he hold her the instant the moment presented itself or wait? The first choice had the appeal of getting the gesture over with, a manly course of action. Then he might relax and enjoy his evening, if not start some event of a more tender nature. But his father had advised him to make his advances slow, with deliberation.

Damnation.

He had never, never felt this nervous about an encounter with any female before. The bear grew inside, so he silently growled and glanced at his flexing fingers. *Take it easy, man, calm yourself. You love this woman, so live up to her expectations of your character.* After a deep breath, he anticipated a successful greeting, so he smiled.

Here goes.

He pulled the bell.

Rather than the expected family retainer, the object of his affections herself greeted him at the door. Resplendent in sky blue silk, his bravado of the previous minute wavered. "Good evening, madam." He executed his deepest, most respectful bow.

Her bright blue eyes appeared unnaturally wide. "Good evening, Mr. Drexel."

Still bent in his bow, he looked up. "Can we return to George?"

"Of course," she said, with a barely detectable rush of exhaled air.

He straightened his shoulders. "I'm pleased to hear that." He withheld his hand for a moment, since he knew it shook. Then he held it out to assist her into the carriage.

After perhaps a second longer than necessary to make a decision, she placed her gloved hand in his.

They exchanged smiles before they entered the town carriage and started their journey to the south side of the Thames.

The coachman started off at a brisk pace.

George was silently grateful for the bumpy ride, since they were able to spend the first awkward minutes clinging on to the handles. He pulled himself up tight, close to his side of the carriage, so as not to bump her against the windows or touch her in any way that might cause offense.

His breathing and heartbeat raced. He doubted he could speak without revealing his distress. Therefore, for the entire journey, they exchanged only the slightest of pleasantries: an inquiry about the health of their respective families and their admiration of the pleasant weather for the banquet. All the while, his brain repeatedly asked a question. Had he ever realized the extent of her beauty before?

He glanced over once or twice and discovered her looking out of the window on her side.

Damnation.

The air in the carriage grew both frosty and heated at the same time. He repressed a desire to punch the roof. He laid back and closed his eyes. Then he cursed his existence, cursed his ineptitude, and cursed his blasted, vulnerable heart.

When she exited the carriage upon arrival, she placed her hand in his and graced him with a simple smile.

He returned the gesture, his heartbeat soaring even higher. Perhaps this purgatory of pleasantries nonsense had come to an end.

Once they arrived at the bottom of the pit, he saw at least two hundred people, many in official regalia, mingling around the tunnel's entrance.

The tunnel's walls and floors had been scrubbed clean. The walls were then covered with giant pieces of crimson velvet. Two long tables, capable of seating at least a hundred guests, stretched down each of the two shafts that made up the tunnel. The tables were covered with fine white cloth and adorned with tableware more at home in a duke's dining room—not surprising perhaps, because he soon noticed three dukes amongst the assembled crowd.

The most remarkable decorations, however, were four giant gas candelabras he learned were provided by the Portable Gas Company. These tall light fixtures were placed on plinths and a few directly on the tables themselves. The sum total of the light brightened the tunnels until it seemed like daylight. Sitting in the tunnel, directly behind the long tables, the Coldstream Guards played *Der Freischütz*.

Once formal introductions were made, the guests took their seats. The dukes and distinguished ladies and gentlemen sat at one table, while in the other tunnel archway, the miners sat at an identical table just a few feet away.

During the excellent dinner, Meta sat next to him and the conversation between them once again became desultory. He seemed inordinately aware of her gloved arm just inches away from his. *Damnation.* If he failed to get reassurances of her affection tonight, he decided to give up entirely. His spirits had spun into a type of volcano about to explode. He had to dismiss them or else lose his sanity altogether.

During the dinner, toasts were made—many, many toasts. After each toast, everyone in attendance consumed a liberal amount of champagne.

He alone drank at least a bottle during the speeches, giving him courage not to flee this torture. Meanwhile, he heartily joined in the toasts to the King (four times four), a blur of several dukes, the navy, the army, and some other fellows. The band played the appropriate song for each, including "Rule Britannia" and "See the Conquering Hero Comes." In the middle of a toast to the miners, and a moment of unbridled enthusiasm, he even took the bottle himself and hovered it over her flute for a fifth glass. "Champagne?"

"Yes."

He began to pour. "I see our conversation is reduced to single words again. How comforting."

"Indeed."

"Enough?"

"Yes."

They caught each other's glance and went through a fit of exchanging smiles and chuckles. From then on, after each toast, their stares locked first, then a smile ensued, and laughter followed.

While he had not been able to hold her, much less touch her yet, his spirits lightened considerably. He might survive this evening, after all.

After the dinner and the toasts, George thought of a plan to have a moment alone. "Please allow me the honor of showing you the giant shield." He pointed deep into the blackness of the tunnel. "It is that hulking iron structure that resembles a ladder at the very end of the tunnel."

She looked at the looming dark structure at least an additional two hundred feet behind them. "Is it safe? I mean it is very far back in the tunnel."

"Yes, don't worry on that score. The tide is low, so there is little pressure on the ceiling at the moment." He whispered in her ear. "I'll keep you safe."

She let out an involuntary sigh. "Yes, I believe you will. It's funny, when I first saw the tunnel, I thought it was wonderful, amazing even. I praised it to the skies. Now I realize those words were spoken in ignorance. Men will likely die digging this tunnel. They always have in great endeavors like this one. I suppose good men's lives are the price we pay for our future."

"Drexel, my boy!" shouted the Duke of Somerset. "Just the man."

"Your Grace," he said with a bow. "May I introduce Mrs. Russell?"

"Ma'am, a delight." The duke nodded, then turned to address him. "Heard from Brunel you were just the man to talk to. I need a bridge. Well, I personally don't need a bridge, but I understand you are the man to build it." The duke glanced back to Meta. "Ahem. Yes, yes, I apologize, ma'am. Not the sort of thing to speak of in front of a lady. Drexel, we will discuss this when I return in a fortnight, dear boy. Have lunch with me at the club." The duke nodded. "Ma'am." Then he strolled back to the brightly lit party, still in boisterous high spirits.

Right now George wanted to sing, a feeling that gave him a better understanding of his friend, Boyce. A man who always believed that sometimes happiness just bubbled up from your toes and overwhelmed a fellow until he broke out in song.

"Congratulations," she said, beaming.

He picked her up, spun her around twice, and put her down immediately after he regained his senses. He remembered his father's advice to be pleasant and take it slow, so he stepped a few feet backward. "It's important to me that you heard that offer."

"If so, I'm pleased and honored, thank you."

Oh, if he could only kiss her now, he'd die a happy man.

He shook his head; he had turned into the idiot again. They started down the tunnel. Once they had gone past the first one hundred feet, he noticed her agitation.

"I see now why some people are afraid to enter," she said, staring at the ceiling and pulling her spencer tight around her shoulders.

"You're not afraid?" He took her cool hand and kept it, since they were deep enough not to be noticed by the guests mingling around the tunnel's entrance.

She squeezed his hand. "No, I'm not afraid."

"That is very bad news. I may have to change your classification to something other than rabbit."

"Friend?"

"Not specific enough. Although I would like to take this opportunity of thanking you for your efforts to buy up all of the copies of the Learned Ladies' version of the field guide. I'm now convinced that it helped further the recovery of my reputation. Perhaps the scandal has lessened enough that the duke proposed such a marvelous offer of considering one of my bridges."

"It was the least I could do, since my efforts led to its publication in the first place."

"And the loss of your sister's engagement was due to my efforts. I apologize for that."

She looked at him in a quizzing fashion. "Perhaps the initial reason James called off. But you behaved like a gentleman and set the situation to rights, so he offered again. No, Lily is the only one responsible for the failure of their relationship. She could not let herself be vulnerable, remaining too proud and too frightened to speak. However, she made significant progress at the ball to overcome her fears. There may be hope for a reconciliation yet."

"I've had a few conversations with James recently,

and I believe it won't be long before we hear some good news. I do believe he will be able to convince her to change her mind."

"I certainly hope so. But if it fails, the loss there is not your fault in the end. Besides, you heard the duke. You impressed Mr. Brunel, so the credit is all yours."

"Thank you." It struck him like lightning that this was the moment his father spoke of. The moment to hold her close. He cleared his throat. "May I give you a hug?"

She batted her eyelids in surprise. "Will it be as dangerous as hugging a bear?"

"Of course, madam, but not lethal, I promise you." He wrapped his arms around her and waited.

Would she flee?

Remaining still, he counted to three: one, two, three. Unmoving, she seemed frozen on the spot too.

She dropped her head to rest on his chest.

"Happy?" he asked, simultaneously agitated and at ease.

He felt her nod on his breast. His breaths quickened upon the thought of his victory in the holding-her-close challenge.

She had not pulled away, but she remained silent. She probably couldn't find the right words either, which seemed a bit odd. Given his extensive knowledge of females, he knew they possessed the ability to talk at all times, except for one time for some ladies— and that sound could never be mistaken for speech.

He stepped back, then cradled her cheeks in his hands.

Her eyes shone; her posture remained relaxed.

He kissed her. Never had a kiss been sweeter to

him. Every manly inch of him melted at the touch of her tender lips and the sight of her peach-tinged cheeks below the soft blue pools of her eyes revealed in the weak gaslight. Inside, he sang in happiness, he cried in frustration, he never wanted to leave her side again.

"Thank you," she said. "I have been waiting for another kiss."

He had two choices: kiss or talk. His body requested a long bout of kissing, while what remained of his reason spoke louder and ruled the day. "We cannot talk here. Let's find some privacy." He moved his hand to gently tilt up her chin. While the darkness dimmed the normal brilliant blue of her eyes, they still sparkled from the reflected gaslights. "Would you like to be alone together, or do you want to stay here at the banquet?"

She nodded and placed her warm hand over his. "Yes, I would like some privacy. I think we have much to discuss. Perhaps this is neither the time nor place, but at least we can start to reach some understanding between us." She pulled his hand off her chin and swung it back and forth. "The question is where do we find privacy at a large banquet with at least a hundred in attendance? How about the inn? Can we leave the banquet without being observed or missed?"

He blushed at her unspoken desire to steal a moment alone together, perhaps like their previous rendezvous. Uncertainty claimed him, if that was her meaning. Thank heavens the tunnel's dim light hid his physical reaction. "Let's head back to the pit. The inn is full tonight because of this event. So in the meantime, I'll try to think of a place close for our chat." Uncertain about the nature of her "understanding," he still maintained a certain hope of final success. When he held her and kissed her, she had not tried to pull away or run. So at the very least, he passed the first crucial bit of advice given to him by his father. But he burned from her suggestion of the inn. He doubted his ability to leave this place a sane man unless he could express his love in every manner available.

"A private chat," she said. "It should not take long before we reach an understanding."

They started walking back to the tunnel's entrance, holding hands. Occasionally it became necessary for them to step apart due to scattered puddles of water, but regardless of their distance, each remained clutching the other's hand tightly. He decided her steadfast grip must be a good sign of eventual success. His breathing quickened.

"How about you show me this diving bell you went down in? I have never seen it before, I guess because it is kept moored in the middle of the river. Tonight I noticed it is tied up to the dock closest to the pit. Do you think there will be enough light for you to show me the bell?" She stopped walking. "Just the outside, you understand. I-I don't think I would ever be brave enough to even stand under it, much less descend into a river that could become a watery grave. I admire you for your bravery. Perhaps we can begin by you telling me about your experiences in the bell."

He straightened, with his heart as light as air, his blood must be pumped around by an organ no stronger than butterfly wings. He yearned to tell her of his successful effort to stop the leak. So he told her everything, his doubts of success, his stinging eyes, and even lying on the deck, too exhausted to move. He withheld Duff's reunion with his family, and the very instant he realized he had fallen in love.

She listened carefully and made a few comments and even several gasps, when he described standing on the bottom of the river as he tried to spread the clay bags to create a broader plug.

By now they had reached the quay and found themselves shrouded in darkness. Only a single lantern lit the gangway to the barge. The diving bell loomed ahead as a dark form blotting out the lights from the docks across the river. They stepped onto the barge and walked over to the bell.

She placed her hand on the bell. "It's so cold, so frightening."

He wanted her to feel something else, not fear. Stepping close, he embraced her fully and turned them, so he leaned on the bell's cold iron. "There is nothing to fear."

She nodded and lifted her head.

In the dim light, he recognized her desires. Did he possess the discipline to postpone easing her wants until they reached their understanding? Perhaps a gentle kiss might smooth the waters and lead to a few simple sentences, like "I love you." Then she would respond, "I love you too." He would propose, and then she would accept—a perfect example of an understanding.

Before any discipline could be summoned, she kissed him full on the mouth.

The bear growled and took her lips in a commanding kiss. He could not get enough of her kisses. In swelling desperation, he kissed her deeper. As he did so, he turned her around, so the bell provided her support. Next he unbuttoned her spencer. With one hand he caressed and teased her breasts through her heavy, silk gown, giving full attention to each one. He became fully erect, fighting the desire to lift her skirts right then and there.

He failed.

A blinding fog of passion overwhelmed them both.

He swiftly unbuttoned his falls, then with more effort managed to unbutton his undergarments. His erection slid free.

She reached down and stroked him.

Suddenly, the air around him resembled alcohol thrown into a fire, an instant fireball.

He lifted her skirts. "Oh, Meta, Meta," he moaned, still repeatedly kissing her. He used his finger to push through the slit in her undergarments to caress her beneath the curls. Then he employed his tactile skills to bring her to the edge of pleasure.

"George, George." She moaned again in the throaty voice of a female lost in the midst of passion.

He thrust into her. Then to his surprise, he lacked the ability to withdraw slowly to extend their pleasure. He transformed into a rutting beast, thrusting again and again.

"Ahhh."

With what remained of his wits, he recognized her teetering on the verge of release.

He gave her a hard thrust. "Marry me?"

She stiffened.

"Marry me?" The sentence came with each push.

"George," she yelled, reaching her moment of bliss.

"Marry me?" He quickened the pace and soon found his release. An extended groan escaped him.

He lacked the strength to stand, so he braced himself by placing his hands on the cold iron bell. He held his ear next to hers as their breathing slowed. "Marry me?"

She cupped his head and bestowed a sweet kiss on his forehead. Minutes passed before she righted her skirt and spencer.

Why no immediate answer to his question?

Had he rushed his fences? Gone against his father's advice? Right, he needed to commit suicide right here and now, but first tell her he was about to perform a charitable act of mercy.

She reached up and stroked his hair tucked behind his ear.

Her touch soothed the bear, but it did not extinguish his agitation. "Marry me. You need not fear you will have to leave your family. I can move in with—"

This time she cupped his cheeks and pulled his head down to tenderly kiss him with her velvet lips. Then in a throaty voice that made him stiffen all over again, she said, "I can never get enough of you or your kisses. Tomorrow when clearer heads prevail, we will discuss our future. Please." She kissed him hard and quick, then looked up at him, a clear message to respond in kind, and he instantly obliged.

He growled under his breath. No woman in his arms had ever undergone such a thorough kissing.

Only one thing remained to convince her of his love. "I love you. Tomorrow then."

She widened her eyes. "Tomorrow."

During the carriage ride back to Swallow Street, they held hands.

After each meaningful exchange of glances, she squeezed his fingers.

He stared at their joined palms. In a flash, his parents' gesture acquired a new meaning for him; he understood them better. Nothing could ever make him happier than holding Meta's hand forever. His thoughts calmed, and he gained confidence that he stood on the brink of the greatest success in his life— Meta's vow to marry him—tomorrow.

Twenty-three

EARLY THE NEXT MORNING, META STOOD IN HER drawing room spinning in circles under her mother's chandelier. A blur of light, crystal, and gilt suited her joyous mood perfectly.

Today George would arrive to discuss their future—together.

A meeting midmorning was later than she preferred, but the first hour allowed for a proper call seemed appropriate. She spread her arms wide and continued to spin as fast as her legs could manage. "Weee." Her spread arms mimicked the elegant brass arms of the chandelier, supporting the brightly lit candles sitting in their cut glass cups draped with crystal drops. Once thoroughly dizzy, she collapsed onto a curved-back chair.

Overwhelmed with the sublime anticipation of George repeating the offer of his hand, she wondered what tender words he'd use; what heartfelt feelings he'd express; what ecstasy she would experience.

"You look funny," Lily said, entering the room, then sitting on the empire sofa across from Meta. "Are you ill?"

"Yes, I am. I'm sick from too much happiness."

Lily rolled her eyes. "Let me see… How would I describe your ridiculous expression in my novel?"

Meta sat straight in the chair and chuckled. "Forgive me, dearest. I did not sleep last night. I enjoyed the banquet so well last evening, I'm still a little giddy."

"I wish I had been there." Lily paused. "Was James there?"

Within two ticks from the clock, Meta's euphoria faded and reality returned. "Yes," she said, hoping Lily would drop the subject.

"Your face says it all. He was there with another woman, wasn't he? No, don't answer. I'll use this moment of betrayal as motivation for my art."

"You'll put what betrayal in a novel?"

"For such a life-changing event, poetry is the best medium, I think." She paused, clearly thinking, then placed her hand over her heart. "My true love breathes life only in my heart's own mind."

"Your heart has a brain?"

Lily huffed. "Meta! It's not edited yet."

Tom bounded down the stairs and ran through the drawing room, taking little notice of its occupants.

"Thomas!" Meta shouted. "You promised no running, remember?"

The boy stopped and hesitantly looked up at the chandelier. "Sorry, I forgot. Won't happen again." With those words barely out of his mount, he started to run out of the room.

"Thomas, no running," Lily said, for the first time joining Meta in the discipline of her siblings.

The boy stopped. Wearing a stunning scowl he

said, "Why are you telling me what to do? That's Meta's job."

Meta took a step toward him. "It's everyone's job, especially when you do not listen."

Tom huffed. "Girls," he said, before running out of the room.

Lily turned to Meta. "You cannot fool me, you know. Please tell me once and for all. James escorted another lady, didn't he?"

While James had spent some of the evening in the company of the sister of one of the tunnel's board of directors, she could truthfully admit her ignorance about the current state of his romantic affairs. "He did not escort a lady; however, several ladies were present at the banquet. Ladies whose husbands, fathers, or brothers sat on the board of directors of the Thames Tunnel Company."

"I knew it." Lily smoothed her white muslin skirt in more of a slapping motion. "You won't tell me everything, of course. But your lack of an answer is still an answer."

"Lily—"

"I know deep within my breast that James and I are estranged forever," she said, placing her hand over her heart once again.

Meta had no intention of encouraging her sister's histrionics. "Nonsense, *my* heart's own mind believes you are mistaken. Instead, she tried to think of a method to stop the frequent hand-over-heart gesture, like the gift of a sharp brooch as a birthday present."

As the clock on the mantel ticked away, Lily sat with her arms crossed, biting her upper lip.

Meta stared into the fire. In the future, Lily must reach out and grab her own happiness. However, since her sister could easily fall into a brooding temperament, Meta decided to put more effort into actively forwarding the couple's reconciliation by holding a number or routs, whist parties, and balls. Hopefully, once they were all settled, she could start entertaining within the next year. "I think you underestimate James. He may come around, after all. Give him time."

Her sister's eyes grew wide. "My suffering will make my art more meaningful. I know it. I will use my troubles to give my heroine more sympathy and greater depth." She stood. "I have an idea. Perhaps I too should write a field guide. I'll give it the title *The Single Lady's Guide to London's Jilts*. Then I can expose James in a roundabout way. I will publish it in secret, of course. The best part—"

"If you do such a tomfool thing, the word that you are the author will eventually get out. Then all of London will condemn you for your spite and poor sportsmanship. You may even be teased or ridiculed at parties. I would think very carefully before I did something so rash. Haven't George's troubles provided you with a lesson on the consequences of such an imprudent decision?"

Lily widened her eyes and dropped her jaw. "Well, I…"

"Please, in the future you will find a man to love and who returns your love, I promise. Only time is needed, a few years at most, when you are ready. My recommendation is to write a tender romance story."

She grinned. "I also recommend you name your hero James." She winked at her sister.

"Very amusing."

Fitzy entered the room carrying a long wooden box. "I am off to call upon the Drexels and will return around luncheon. Cook promised me roast chicken today."

Meta jumped to her feet. The clock on the mantel read nine in the morning, but she could use Fitzy's delivery as an excuse to see George and start their future together sooner. "Wait for me, Fitzy. Give me ten minutes to pin my hair, and then I'll join you. I too wish to pay a call upon the Drexels today." She ran upstairs and implored her maid to redo her hair to hide the two gray hairs and help her change into a more suitable walking gown, her prettiest white muslin with the pink sash.

Half an hour later, the two of them stood before the shiny brass door knocker of the Drexels' town house. Footsteps were heard from inside, and Meta thought she might faint when the door opened.

Mrs. Morris swung the door wide and bade them enter. "Glad to see the two of you this morning and not some emergency from that sewer next to the Thames causing everyone so much grief. Please wait in the parlor, and I'll inform Mr. Drexel of your arrival."

Fitzy spoke first. "Mr. Michael Drexel, please. Tell him our secret project is finished."

Meta bit her lip, then congratulated herself for not immediately shouting out George's name and demanding to see him. "If you would be so kind, Mrs. Morris, we would like to see both Mr. Drexels." Meta might be imagining things, but she distinctly noticed a somewhat knowing gleam in the housekeeper's eyes.

"Yes, ma'am. Right away."

She turned to Fitzy. "What secret project is finished? Is this another bolt?"

He blushed a lovely pink. "I cannot tell you. I promised to keep the secret too, since it's important. I believe it even changed my life. I-I will tell you all about it later. After I give it to Mr. Drexel and his wife."

George was the first member of the family to appear at the top of the stairs. He stood tall, hands on his hips. "So you could not stay away?"

She chuckled. "I guess not. You?"

He effortlessly descended the stairs without holding on to the railing. "I'll never stay away from this moment on. Let's go into the parlor. I'm sure Fitzy here needs to remain in the company of my father for at least twenty minutes."

"Huh?" Fitzy put the box down on the hall table and struggled to open the wooden lid of his precious box.

"You heard me. Your sister and I are not to be disturbed. Understand?"

"Yes," he answered with a sigh. "By Jove." He leaped a foot or two nearer and addressed George. "Does this mean what I think it means?"

"I'll let you know in twenty minutes."

"Yes, yes, well then, I'll go and find your father. He won't mind me going upstairs, I'm sure."

Drexel held one finger up to his lips. "Don't tell Father. Secret?"

Fitzy smiled. "I love secrets. Yes, all right."

George held open the door to the parlor for her as the sound of Fitzy's footsteps headed upstairs. He must have been nervous, because they entered the room, and he made no attempt to hold her.

So she stood there, staring at him.

He cleared his throat. "*Damnation.*" In one stride he crossed at least five feet and pulled her into his arms for a strong embrace. He caught her gaze and dropped his forehead until he touched hers. "Marry me? Please."

Tears of joy welled in her eyes, then a single tear wandered down her cheek.

He took his big thumb and wiped it away. "Is this leak your means of answering *yes*?"

She pulled away. Biting her lower lip, she took several steps backward, until she reached the sofa. Here she stood. A cold hand squeezed her heart. After her husband's accident, when he lay dying, he needed comfort from his wife, needed her to hold his hand, and needed her to tell him that he was truly loved. But she never reached his side in time, and he died alone. She supposed her guilt propelled her to sacrifice her needs for those she loved.

But standing before her now was the handsome man she undeniably loved more than anyone. "You see, I told you we need to discuss things. So many people need me—"

"I need you." He held out his hands, desperation expressed by his movements and on his face.

She glanced at the carpet and remembered when he stood unmoving, challenging her to come to him. An idea came to mind and she straightened; the tables had turned. She'd use the empty space between them to gain the advantage of a clear head: a mind not muddled by strong feelings or overpowered by his physical proximity. "You once invited me to come to you, remember. Now I challenge you to do the same."

He tilted his head; perhaps the bear inside him grew. Then he laughed. "I agree to your outrageous demands, madam. As your noble knight, I deserve a chance to win the fair lady. What dragons must I slay?" He flashed the wicked smile. "However, I must warn you that my restraint can be fragile. I may swoop in, kidnap you like a medieval knight, and never let you go."

"Indeed, I understand my precarious situation." She returned his smile. "For the first step, you must never blame or tease Lily for refusing James. She regrets it, I know, but we all make poor choices in life when we are young."

"I never did." He winked.

She raised her hand to cover her smile. *Be brave; don't let him seduce you into a situation that would never suit. Your family's happiness is at stake.* "Also, once in a while, you may need to listen to Lily's poetry or romantic stories."

He raised his hand and rubbed his chin. "That bad, eh?"

"I'm afraid so."

"I'll survive—maybe."

She swiftly clapped. "Then, sir knight, you may take the first step," she said in a queenly manner.

"Right!" His right foot extended out and about as far as it could, then he took the big step.

She had taken quite a few steps to reach the sofa. By her calculations, he only needed three steps, so she had better combine some of her wishes. Otherwise, this would all end in a bout of passionate kisses. "For the second step, I need you to assist me in the care of my family. In particular, you might have to escort the girls to balls and parties."

"Can I remain in the card room?"

She nodded her head and chuckled. "No, you must partner them in the dance, until you find some nice, unmarried young gentleman for them to wed. Then you may retire your escort services."

He impatiently sighed. "Fair enough. Gather up unlicked cubs for the girls to marry." Then without her invitation, he took another step.

"In a hurry?"

"As a matter of fact, yes. How about you?"

She chuckled. From the exaggerated length of his steps, this request would be her last. "I never realized your steps covered so much ground. So, for my final request, I need you to assist Tom and Fitzy."

"Easy."

"We all teach by example. You must provide the example of the grace and good manners of a gentleman."

"I give you my vow to do my best, but I must warn you. On occasion, I might present an example of what not to do." He reached up to loosen his cravat knot.

She gave him a soft smile. "I do not believe that."

He paused, eyes bright, and gave her a single nod. "Thank you for the compliment." After one quick step, he embraced her, then whispered in her ear. "Meta, dearest, of course I will meet all of these promises. They are important to you, so they are important to me. But all of your requests are for others. What promise can I give you, my love? What do you need?"

No one had ever asked her that question. She stood fixed, staring up into eyes expressing his devotion. Did she herself know the answer? Perhaps she needed to help her family, by setting aside her own dreams of love.

Would she sacrifice her dreams now?

She must either set her life on the shelf to attend her family until they no longer needed her, or acknowledge her desire to spend her life with the man she loved.

The man she loved.

Like a flash of light from a match lit in a dark room, she understood the character of the man she loved better: his offer to reside with her family; his offer to help her siblings; and his offer to listen to an amateur poet. She looked directly into his eyes and felt a tear gather in her own. "I need you."

"I promise to love you forever. Marry me? Please."

"Yes," she managed, stifling the urge to spin around and sing her favorite song. "Yes." She nodded repeatedly. "Yes, yes."

He leaned down, lifted her chin, and took her lips in a slow, achingly tender kiss. "We need to do more of this—much more. As a matter of fact, I wish to be alone with my bride soon—*very soon*." This time his words were followed by kisses of joy and celebration.

"Why would you like to be alone with your bride, sir knight?" She failed to hide the laughter in her tone.

"You know full well, my heavenly hare. I plan to keep you hopping, yes, indeed, hopping."

"And I plan to enjoy that." Another kiss began that turned into a long, delicious moment. For her, this kiss was not about matrimonial celebration, nor tender affection, but simple bodily desire generated from physical closeness to the man she loved.

When they finished kissing, and after perhaps twenty minutes had passed, George led her to the empire sofa. "There are things we must discuss."

"Of course." Should she tell him about her money now? Get the secret out and over with?

"I understand the importance of having your loved ones near." He chuckled. "Admittedly, I did not always realize the importance myself. Therefore, I will move in with you and your family." He leaned over, nibbled on her ear, and dropped his voice. "If you approve?"

Meta knew his parents meant the world to him. His mother's long illness only brought out his protective side, and she knew he would leave it with great difficulty. With her spirits soaring, she placed her hand on his broad thigh. Underneath her hand, she could feel the thick muscle and the warmth of his body. Nothing would please her more than having this man deep within her, caressing her, and loving her. The nibbles were replaced with long and slow kisses around her neck. After a minute, she eased into liquid anticipation.

If she didn't keep her wits about her, she would ravish him right here amongst his models and books. "I don't want you to leave your parents either.

Therefore, let us find a house big enough for our whole family, perhaps closer to the tunnel."

He held her at arm's length to study her face. "You understand we'll have to discuss our funding situation before any decision is made?"

"I'd rather we get it over with, so we can tell everyone about our engagement. You see..."

His brows knit.

Was he cross for bringing up the indelicate subject of money? "It's just—I mean—I'm a wealthy woman."

He pulled back farther. "Then why are you living with your family?" Before she could answer, his brow smoothed, and the grin returned. He slapped his thigh. "The necessity of keeping them close, meeting their needs, and sharing your life?"

She nodded.

"Well, I always figured on marrying a wealthy woman." He winked. "Of course you know what that means?"

She shook her head.

He swiftly moved and lifted her into his arms. "Being plump in the pocket means no possibility that *The Rake's Handbook: Including Field Guide* will ever be published again. If the publisher goes against my wishes, and his brother's wishes, I can now buy up every copy. Thank heavens."

"*We* can buy up every copy. I have personal experience with that. We'll make sure that book is never available again, anywhere, if need be."

They exchanged grins.

"George dearest, spin me around please? I enjoy twirling when I'm happy."

He examined the situation. "Quarters too close, but as you wish, my love." He set her down to lift her under her knees and back, so she was cradled in his arms.

They began to spin.

After four, or five, or six, seven, eight rotations, they both burst into laughter. They heard someone descending the staircase, so George set her feet on solid ground.

Fitzy held the door open, and Michael entered carrying a white plaster cast about a foot long. He carried it to the large desk and set it down. Everyone gathered around to admire the statue.

She could easily make out two hands holding one another, one male and one female. She gasped softly, doubting anyone heard her. "How beautiful."

Fitzy straightened. "I thought you might like it. It's a cast, of course, of Mr. and Mrs. Drexel holding hands. That was our surprise to Mrs. Drexel from Mr. Drexel and me. I could tell she was pleased too. Because when we wanted to take it out of the room to show you, she made her objections known. We had to promise to return it soon."

Michael Drexel wore a winsome smile and nodded. "This memento will mean so much to her when I'm gone."

They all became silent.

George found her hand and squeezed it.

Finally, Fitzy turned to George. "You see, sir, with your permission, I wish to stop drawing and modeling engineering projects. I understand it forwards England's future. Except sometimes the future is something smaller; something more meaningful to people; something as simple as a cast of two people holding hands. Emotion is the real language and the power behind art." He turned. "Right, Meta?"

Tears welled up in her eyes to the extent she could not see, so she gave him a tight smile and nodded.

George stepped forward and enclosed her in a warm, safe embrace.

She let her tears fall on the rough wool of his waistcoat.

"Oh, I didn't mean to make you unhappy," Fitzy said, his brows knit and his palm placed on her back.

"Don't worry, son," George said, giving her a squeeze, then kissing her temple. "These are happy tears. Females tend to do this on significant occasions."

Michael smiled at his son. "And a gentleman should provide comfort by holding them tight."

"Well, I have something to say," George said, lifting his chin above her head to address Fitzy. "Would you do your sister and me the honor of using our hands to make a similar cast?"

She saw Michael grab his son's forearm.

George held her tighter. "I promise our cast too will be cherished forever."

Author's Note

This book is a work of fiction inspired by the lives of Sir Marc and Isambard Brunel and the construction of the Thames Tunnel. Some of the dates and events were changed to suit the story. While the Thames Tunnel was started in 1825, the banquet took place in 1827, six months after the first major water intrusion. In 1828, the Thames Tunnel Company ran out of funds and the tunnel was sealed off. Thanks to the influence of people like the Duke of Wellington, Parliament granted funds and the digging started again in 1835. It was finally opened in 1843.

In 1869, the Thames Tunnel was sold to the railroad company and now the London Underground owns it. In 2002, in order to stop the tunnel from being blasted with a coat of concrete, the tunnel was declared a grade II historical monument and given a careful restoration.

Today fourteen million people travel though the Thames Tunnel every year. The Brunel Museum is on the Rotherhithe side where the public can view some parts of the tunnel and engine house. On rare occasions when the underground trains are stopped, groups of very, very lucky people are guided into the tunnel on foot. Since it is the first tunnel ever constructed under a navigable river, it truly is a remarkable achievement begun in the Georgian era. To me, it will always remain what the newspapers called it upon its completion: "The Eighth Wonder of the World."

The Rake's Handbook
by Sally Orr

— ❧ —

The definitive guide to seduction

The Rake's Handbook was written on a dare, and soon took the *ton* by storm. Now its author, Ross Thornbury, is publicly reviled by the ladies—who are, of course, forbidden to read the handbook—but privately revered by the gentlemen. Unfortunately, Ross's notoriety is working against him and he flees London painfully aware of the shortcomings of his own jaded heart.

Spirited young widow Elinor Colton lives next to Ross's country estate. She's appalled not only by his rakish reputation, but also by his progressive industrial plans. Elinor is sure she is immune to Ross's seductive ways. But he keeps coming around…impressing her with his vision for England's future and stunning her with his smiles.

— ❧ —

"The witty repartee and naughty innuendos set the perfect pitch for the entertaining romance. Sure to enchant readers."
—*RT Book Reviews*, 4 Stars

"A quirky but steamy historical romance. Very entertaining."
—*Tome Tender*

For more Sally Orr, visit:
www.sourcebooks.com

When a Rake Falls

The Rake's Handbook
by Sally Orr

He's racing to win back his reputation

Having hired a balloon to get him to Paris in a daring race, Lord Boyce Parker is simultaneously exhilarated and unnerved by the wonders and dangers of flight, and most of all by the beautiful, stubborn, intelligent lady operating the balloon.

She's curious about the science of love

Eve Mountfloy is in the process of conducting weather experiments when she finds herself spirited away to France by a notorious rake. She's only slightly dismayed—the rake seems to respect her work—but she is frequently distracted by his windblown good looks and buoyant spirits.

What happens when they descend from the clouds?

As risky as aeronautics may be, once their feet touch the ground, Eve and Boyce learn the real danger of a very different type of falling…

Praise for *The Rake's Handbook*:

"A charming romp. The witty repartee and naughty innuendos set the perfect pitch for the entertaining romance."
—*RT Book Reviews*

For more Sally Orr, visit:
www.sourcebooks.com

The Infamous Heir

The Spare Heirs
by Elizabeth Michels

— ❧ —

The Spare Heirs Society Cordially Invites You to Meet Ethan Moore: The Scoundrel

Lady Roselyn Grey's debut has finally arrived, and of course, she has every flounce and flutter planned. She'll wear the perfect gowns and marry the perfect gentleman…that is, if the formerly disinherited brother of the man she intends to marry doesn't ruin everything first.

Ethan Moore is a prizefighting second son and proud founding member of the Spare Heirs Society—and that's all he ever should have been. But in an instant, his brother's noble title is his, the eyes of the ton are upon him, and the lady he's loved for years would rather meet him in the boxing ring than the ballroom.

He's faced worse. With the help of his Spare Heirs brotherhood, Ethan's certain he can get to the bottom of his brother's unexpected demise and win the impossible lady who has haunted his dreams for as long as he can remember…

— ❧ —

Praise for *How to Lose a Lord in 10 Days or Less*:

"[A] richly emotional, wonderfully engaging romance."
—*Booklist Online*

For more Elizabeth Michels, visit:
www.sourcebooks.com

How to Seduce a Scot

Book 1 in the Broadswords and Ballrooms Series

by Christy English

— ∾ —

Determined to find a husband for his unruly sister, Highlander Alexander Waters strides into prim Regency ballrooms searching for a biddable English lord. To his surprise, his presence in the ton causes quite a stir, but in the process opens his eyes to the most beautiful woman he's ever seen.

Debutante Catherine Middleton is also on the prowl for a man to marry—a man with money, specifically. But when Alexander witnesses her preference in throwing knives over having tea, he knows the prim Catherine is as wild as the Highlands themselves…and needs a Highland man who can match her.

— ∾ —

Praise for *Much Ado About Jack*:

"Grace Burrowes and Amanda Quick fans will enjoy the strong ladies in the latest fun read from the ascending English." —*Booklist*

For more Christy English, visit:
www.sourcebooks.com

How to Wed a Warrior

Broadswords and Ballrooms
by Christy English

He's the scourge of the Season

REASONS TO QUIT LONDON:

1. It's not the Highlands

2. It will never be the Highlands

3. It's full of the bloody *English*

When his wild spitfire of a sister makes a scene by drawing a claymore in Hyde Park, Highlander Robert Waters knows something must be done. To forestall the inevitable scandal, he hires widowed Prudence Whittaker to teach his sister how to be a lady—never expecting to find unbridled passion beneath the clever Englishwoman's prim exterior.

Mrs. Whittaker is a fraud. Born Lady Prudence Farthington, daughter of the ruined Earl of Lynwood, she's never even been married. In order to make her way in the world, she has to rely on her wits and a web of lies…lies a sexy Highlander is all too close to unraveling.

He swears he will possess her; she vows he will do nothing of the sort. Yet as passions heat, Prudence comes to realize the illicit pleasure that can be had in going toe-to-toe with a Scot.

For more Christy English, visit:
www.sourcebooks.com

Heir to the Duke

The Duke's Sons
by Jane Ashford

Life is predictable for a duke's first son

As eldest son of the Duke of Langford, Nathaniel Gresham sees his arranged marriage to Lady Violet Devere as just another obligation to fulfill—highly suitable, if unexciting. But as Violet sets out to transform herself from dowdy wallflower to dazzling young duchess-to-be, proper Nathaniel decides to prove he's a match for his new bride's vivacity and daring.

Or so he once thought…

Oppressed by her family all her life, Lady Violet can't wait to enjoy the freedom of being a married woman. But then Violet learns her family's sordid secret, and she's faced with an impossible choice—does she tell Nathaniel and risk losing him, or does she hide it and live a lie?

Praise for *Married to a Perfect Stranger:*

"Marvelous…the perfect blend of interesting, emotionally complex, and open-hearted protagonists."
—*Publishers Weekly* STARRED REVIEW

"A touching, heartwarming story [that] engages readers' emotions." —*RT Book Reviews*, 4 Stars

For more Jane Ashford, visit:
www.sourcebooks.com

About the Author

Sally Orr, PhD, worked for thirty years in molecular biology research. One day a cyber-friend challenged her to write a novel. Since she is a hopeless Anglophile, it's not surprising that her first series is Regency romance. Sally lives with her husband in San Diego, surrounded by too many books and not enough old English cars.